Pra

"Full of unease and stomach-churning dread, *WE USED TO LIVE HERE* creeps up to you like a sly shadow. I wanted to look away. I absolutely could not. Marcus Kliewer is destined to become a titan of the macabre and unsettling. Read this with every single light on."
—**Erin A. Craig, #1** *New York Times* **bestselling author**
of *House of Salt and Sorrows*

"This book is like quicksand: the further you delve into its pages, the more immobilized you become by a spiral of terror. *WE USED TO LIVE HERE* will haunt you even after you have finished it."
—**Agustina Bazterrica, bestselling author**
of *Tender Is the Flesh*

"There is a feeling that a small number of books conjure. It can be distilled to: Oh god, something ain't right here. Their hallmark is a creeping, unaccountable, jangly dread that seeps into their pages until you almost wish you could stop reading—but of course, it's too late. You're in its grip. *WE USED TO LIVE HERE* is one of those rare books."
—**Nick Cutter, national bestselling author of** *The Troop*

"What begins as a Tremblay-ian exercise in ratcheting tension soon peels away to reveal a mind-bendingly fractal horror story that would make even Danielewski sweat. *WE USED TO LIVE HERE* is an expertly paced and structured nightmare, full of surprises; a thrillingly, chillingly participatory anxiety attack of a book."
—**Nat Cassidy, bestselling author of** *Mary* **and** *Nestlings*

WE USED TO LIVE HERE

MARCUS KLIEWER

EMILY BESTLER BOOKS

ATRIA

New York   Amsterdam/Antwerp   London
Toronto   Sydney/Melbourne   New Delhi

EMILY
BESTLER
BOOKS

ATRIA

An Imprint of Simon & Schuster, LLC
1230 Avenue of the Americas
New York, NY 10020

For more than 100 years, Simon & Schuster has championed authors and the stories they create. By respecting the copyright of an author's intellectual property, you enable Simon & Schuster and the author to continue publishing exceptional books for years to come. We thank you for supporting the author's copyright by purchasing an authorized edition of this book.

This book is a work of fiction. Any references to historical events, real people, or real places are used fictitiously. Other names, characters, places, and events are products of the author's imagination, and any resemblance to actual events or places or persons, living or dead, is entirely coincidental.

This Emily Bestler Books/Atria paperback hardcover edition July 2025

EMILY BESTLER BOOKS / ATRIA PAPERBACK and colophon are trademarks of Simon & Schuster, LLC

Simon & Schuster strongly believes in freedom of expression and stands against censorship in all its forms. For more information, visit BooksBelong.com.

For information about special discounts for bulk purchases, please contact Simon & Schuster Special Sales at 1-866-506-1949 or business@simonandschuster.com.

The Simon & Schuster Speakers Bureau can bring authors to your live event. For more information or to book an event, contact the Simon & Schuster Speakers Bureau at 1-866-248-3049 or visit our website at www.simonspeakers.com.

Interior design by Alexis Minieri

Manufactured in the United States of America

1   3   5   7   9   10   8   6   4   2

Library of Congress Control Number: 2024936155

ISBN 978-1-9821-9878-7
ISBN 978-1-9821-9879-4 (pbk)
ISBN 978-1-9821-9880-0 (ebook)

To the readers from the days of No Sleep

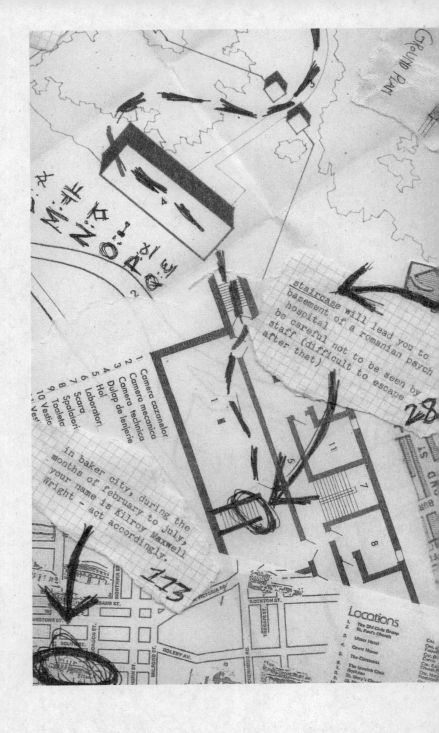

GROUND PLAN

staircase will lead you to
basement of a romanian psych
hospital not to be seen by
be careful
staff (difficult to escape
after that)

28

1   Camera cazanelor
2   Camera mecanica
3   Camera technica
4   Dulap de lenjerie
5   Hol
6   Laboratori
7   Scara
8   Spalatori
9   Toaleta
10 Vestia
    Vesti

in baker city, during the
months of february to july,
your name is Kilroy Maxwell
Wright - act accordingly.

173

Locations
1. The Old Cinic Group
2. St. Paul's Church
3. Ulmer Hotel
4. Court Home
5. The Cinemats
6. The Ipswich Club
7. Ryelston
8. St. Mary's Church

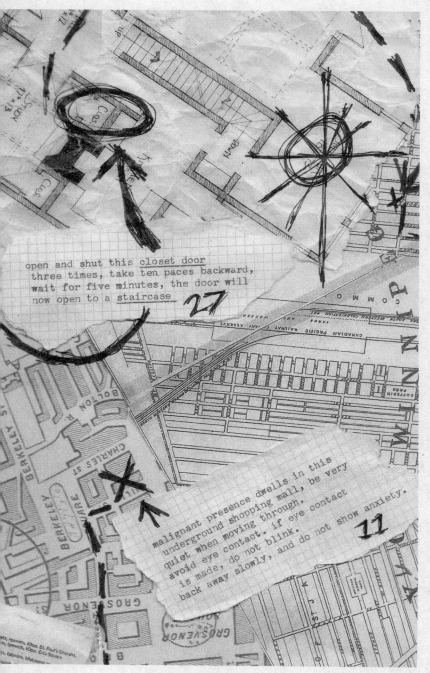

open and shut this closet door
three times, take ten paces backward,
wait for five minutes, the door will
now open to a staircase 27

malignant presence dwells in this
underground shopping mall, be very
quiet when moving through,
avoid eye contact. if eye contact
is made, do not blink.
back away slowly, and do not show anxiety. 11

OLD HOUSE MAP

OUTSIDERS

They'd rung the doorbell unannounced on a chilly Friday night.

The strangers on Eve Palmer's doorstep seemed harmless enough. Yet Eve, ever cautious, peered through the blinds and debated whether to open the door. It was a family of five, middle-class, wrapped in sturdy winter jackets. The parents were in their early forties, Eve guessed. A tall father with broad shoulders and a square jaw. A petite blond mother with cold blue eyes and a silver cross necklace. Between them, three kids lined up by height—one girl, two boys. All in all, they seemed the kind of brood that would cap a Sunday-morning sermon with brunch at Applebee's. Eve was more than a little familiar with this crowd.

Concluding they were no serious threat, she opened the door.

"Hello, miss." The father smiled. "Sorry to bother you so late. I just— I grew up in this house . . ."

"Oh, uh, wow," said Eve.

"We were passing through, wanted to stop by."

Was he expecting her to invite them inside? That was just about the last thing Eve wanted to do. Her girlfriend, Charlie, would be home any minute now—they had a whole evening planned: eating leftover chicken and playing drunken Scrabble. A family of strangers wandering around didn't exactly fit that agenda—

"My dad grew *up* here," the daughter declared with pride. She was clearly the youngest—no more than seven years old. Clutching a bright green pen and a *Blue's Clues* notebook.

"He just told her that," one of the preteen brothers snorted. This one was tall for his age, with cold blue eyes and platinum-blond hair just like his mother.

The father ignored the chatter and continued. "I know this is completely out of the blue—but I was hoping to give the kids a quick tour? Show them where their dad grew up."

Eve hesitated. "Inside the house?"

"Just a quick look around," the father said. "Only if it's not a problem. We'd need maybe ten, fifteen minutes. Tops."

Eve stared past him, considering the request.

The surrounding forest echoed with creaks and groans as a slow mountain breeze swept across the yard and brushed over her face. It was a cold night—the type of chill that sunk into your skin, lay dormant for a while, then started scraping against your bones like chalkboard fingernails. Winter was out there, lurking around in the shadows, but the first snow had yet to fall.

It was then that something, or rather the lack of something, caught Eve's attention. There was no vehicle. Nothing by the old crooked shed at the edge of the woods. Nothing by the alcove where the frosted lawn met the gravel. She looked down the long winding driveway. Nothing. This was more than a little strange, especially considering the cold and the fact that they were in the middle of nowhere. A bizarre image flashed through her mind: the family, hand in hand, wandering out of the darkening trees.

"Where's your car?" Eve asked.

"Hm?"

"Your car?" she repeated. "I don't see it."

"Oh," the father said, "down on the road."

Eve blinked at him, unsure.

"We tried pulling up," he explained. "Too steep, too much ice. So we walked instead."

"Ah, that's quite the trek."

Almost five minutes on foot.

As the father responded, something else caught Eve's eye: a smudge of dirt on his plaid coat. Her focus, especially in moments of stress, was often distracted by irrelevant details. She called it her "broken spidey-sense." A random speck halfway across a room would suddenly draw her attention. A *drip-drip-dripping* faucet would turn louder than somebody speaking right next to her. It was hard for Eve to fully explain. The closest she could get was, "Imagine if several times a day, all at once, every single thing around you became impossible to ignore." Needless to say, she wasn't good at parties.

"Is, that okay?" The father's voice drifted into her thoughts.

She tilted her head. He'd asked a question she hadn't heard.

"It's perfectly understandable," he clarified, "if you'd prefer we not look around. There's no pressure . . ."

Eve let out a strained, one-syllable laugh. "Ah, sorry, I, I'm not sure," she stammered. "My partner and I, we're still in the middle of moving in, and—I just need to call and check?"

"Not a problem," he said.

Of course, a well-adjusted individual would've simply told him no. But self-destructive people-pleasing was another of Eve's plentiful idiosyncrasies. She had a crippling fear of disappointing anyone, even complete strangers— even people she disliked. Over the years she'd found a cheap trick to get around this. Internally called the "Let Me Check with Charlie" card. It had become something of a conflict-avoidant mantra. Eve would never have to say no to anyone if her girlfriend did it for her. At first, Charlie had had no problem shutting people down—in fact, she rather quite enjoyed it. Though, after a while, she started to encourage Eve to stand up for herself a little more. "Voluntary exposure is the best way to overcome fear," Charlie often said. Eve understood this, and was trying, but . . .

"I— I'll be right back." Eve had started to push the door shut when the father said, "Sorry, but is it all right if we wait in the foyer? It's pretty cold out here."

Eve opened her mouth, hesitated again.

"We promise not to burn the place down," he joked.

She tried to smile. "Y-yeah, all good."

"Thank you, seriously. We'll stay right by the door." He motioned his family inside, telling the boys not to touch anything. Eve watched as, one by one, these strangers filed into her home. The distant alarm bells of her subconscious rang out. She vaguely remembered hearing stories. Stories of strangers showing up at houses, claiming they had lived there once, asking to take a quick look around. Then, when the unsuspecting victims had let down their guard: robbery, torture, murder. Though . . . she'd never heard of people doing this while posing as a whole family, kids and all, but—

There's a first time for everything, right?

Something lurking in the deepest, darkest chamber of her mind weighed in. An almost audible voice that had been with her even longer than the broken spidey-sense. She was so familiar with it, the voice of "whatever can go wrong, will go wrong," that she'd even given it a face and a name: Mo. Over a decade ago, a well-meaning counselor had suggested that per-sonifying the terrible voice would disarm it. "Make it something harmless, something familiar," they said. So, Eve imagined her favorite but long-lost childhood toy, Mo.

Mo was a crazy-eyed monkey with cymbals. Not the one most would think of, not the iconic "Jolly Chimp." No, Mo was a cheap imitation of that classic toy. His fur was off-white, not dark brown. And instead of the familiar yellow vest and red-striped pants, Mo wore tacky blue felt overalls and a frayed straw hat peppered with holes. The "Hillbilly Chimp," Eve's father called him.

Where the Jolly Chimp's cymbals were brass metal, Mo's were a cheap and brittle plastic. They made a pathetically dull clicking sound when he was switched on. Like a broken turn signal: *tack-tack—tack-tack—tack.* And when he was bonked on the head, his mouth would open and close, open and close, revealing a set of oversized chompers and bloodred gums. Most people thought of Mo as creepy, but when Eve was a child, he was her favorite toy by far. Maybe it was because a part of her felt sorry for Mo, how everyone called him names. Regardless, childhood Eve couldn't go to sleep without holding him.

And now, all these years later, Mo, the crazy-eyed Hillbilly Chimp, was forever the voice of her paranoia. A paranoia that grew as the family stood cramped in the foyer, huddled around the front door.

Once you let them in, Mo whispered, *they'll never leave.*

"I'll just be a second," said Eve, ignoring Mo's absurd comment. She slipped into the living room, pulled out her phone, and dialed Charlie's number.

Three tones rang and then, "Hello?"

"Hey, Charlie, I—"

"Hello. You've reached Charlie. Leave a message, or don't."

A single tone beeped.

Eve huffed. It wasn't the first time she'd fallen for that dumb trick. Charlie hadn't changed that voicemail since high school, long before they'd met. Anyway, she was likely still in town, picking up booze for tonight. Probably had her phone on silent. Now, Eve would have to shut this family down on her own. She should've just done that from the start. Why did she always drag things out like this? It only made everything way more awkward. Maybe she could lie to the family, tell them Charlie said no, but . . .

Voluntary exposure is the best way to overcome fear. Charlie's voice, a rational counterbalance to Mo's, echoed in her head. *The more you set boundaries on your own, the easier it gets.*

Charlie—or rather, Eve's projection of her—was right. With newfound determination, Eve stepped back into the foyer. But when the father looked up, hopeful, she floundered and pulled out the Charlie Card: "Hey, uh, my girlfriend says not tonight . . ."

To Eve's mild surprise, no one reacted to the word "girlfriend." Not even a blink. She'd half expected the cross-necklace mother to gasp and shield her children's ears, but she didn't so much as shift her weight.

"Sorry," Eve went on. "We just, we still have a lot to—"

"Say no more." The father threw his hands up in a little surrender. "This was an incredibly last-minute stop." Reaching into his coat pocket, he produced a business card. "My email's on there." He handed it over. "If you're open to it, shoot me a message. We can arrange something in advance next time we're in town, but of course, there's no pressure."

Eve studied the card. In a faded green font, it read, "Faust's Photolab." Below that, a logo of a small tree, half of it covered in leaves, the other half spindly branches.

He took a step back. "We should be passing through in another year, maybe two. But again, no pressure."

"Sorry," said Eve. "I just, it's not really the best time. Sorry."

The father shook his head. "No need to apologize. We're the weirdos who showed up out of nowhere." He turned back to his family. "All right, gang, let's head out." Pulling open the door, he motioned them onto the porch.

The mother seemed relieved. And the two boys weren't really paying much attention to begin with. But the daughter—her face was filled with growing sadness—like she'd just been rejected at the gates of Disneyland. As the rest of her family started off, she just stood there, idling in the doorway, staring up at the old house with longing in her big green eyes—

"Jenny," said the mother. After one last glance around, the daughter slinked away to join the rest. Eve stood at the threshold, watching as they trudged off. With every step farther, she felt a growing sense of guilt. Guilt for using the Charlie Card, guilt for dragging things out, guilt for feeling . . . guilty.

"Wait," she called out, almost reflexively.

The father stopped in his tracks and looked back over his shoulder.

Eve cleared her throat. "Fifteen minutes?"

He nodded. "Tops."

DOC_A01_PROPERTY

Description: Real estate listing for 3709 Heritage Lane—transcribed
from the no longer operational www.seeking-home.net

Note: It is believed that [redacted] Bank owned the house at the
time of posting.

Home is our sanctuary. Make this one yours.

A winding driveway pulls you through the peaceful woods. You're not
sure what to expect, but the quiet up here is calming, the crisp
mountain air healing. As you round the last bend, the house slowly
comes into view and . . .

. . . finally, your search is over!

It's everything you hoped for and so much more. Situated on
a private 5-acre lot, 3709 Heritage Lane is a once-in-a-lifetime
opportunity. 4 bedrooms + 2.5 bathrooms with over 2,700 square feet
of timeless Victorian architecture (not including the unfinished
basement). Imagine kicking back on its beautiful wraparound porch,
taking in the gorgeous mountain views. Or reclining in front of the

brick fireplace, cozying up with a loved one. It's a property with the wisdom of old age and the zestful vigor to get with the ever-changing times. And the land itself?

With over 5 acres of Pacific Northwest rainforest to explore, this is mountain living at its finest. Check out the natural pond in the southwest corner, great for ice-skating in the winter, or the waterfall at the north end. Want to go for a longer excursion? Surrounding hiking trails extend all over Kettle Creek Mountain. (With plenty of locations nearby for hunting, fishing, mountain biking and cross-country skiing, this is also a high-value investment for Airbnb hosts and house flippers.)

And rest assured, civilization is closer than you think. This is serene seclusion, without the sacrifice of connection. Only a 30-minute drive to the municipality of Yale and a scenic 1 hr 45 min* jaunt to the city proper. No longer will you have to choose between downtown fun and the serenity of nature. Retreat from the world in your own private year-round getaway, or call it your forever home!

NOTE: As is, the house is ready to be lived in**, but it's also a wonderful opportunity for creative renovation or even a complete teardown. Imagine what you could build from scratch!

*In good traffic/weather

**House inspection pending

- -- .- .. - ..

MEMORY LANE

Eve lingered at the base of the stairs, watching as this family shed their winter jackets. The father slid open the coat closet without looking—a motion that confirmed he'd done it many times before. It was a subtle thing, but one that put Eve a little more at ease. *At least he wasn't lying about growing up here.* The kids, one at a time, handed him their jackets.

Meanwhile, the mother waited by the entrance, eyes scanning over the dirt-stained floors, the water-damaged walls, the piles of clutter. Unimpressed. Eve held her tongue, fighting back the urge to justify the mess, to blurt out something like, "We just moved in," or "You should've seen how bad it looked a month ago." Both of which would have been true.

And in Eve's defense, the cheesy real estate listing had, just a tad, exaggerated the "ready to be lived in" state. On day one, the place was filled with enough old junk to make a hoarder blush. She and Charlie had cleared out most of it, but remnants still remained. And the dust. It had been caked into everything—the walls, the floor, the ceiling. When it came to maintenance, it was obvious the bank had upheld the bare minimum: just enough to keep the place standing, and even that was debatable.

Yet, like all totally not haunted houses in the middle of nowhere, it was listed at a killer deal. It needed work, but that was Eve and Charlie's thing: fix up old houses, flip them for profit. On average, a project would take three to six months, but here, with so much work, they would need at least a year—longer if they did a teardown. Under normal circumstances, they would've figured this all out before buying the place, but again, the deal had simply been too good to pass up. Besides, the land alone would be worth a lot more in a year's time.

Still, with this one, Eve had been more than a little reluctant to take the plunge. They usually did projects on the East Coast, closer to their friends, their families. But 3709 Heritage Lane was way out in the Pacific Northwest, backcountry Oregon. Sure, the scenery was nice, but the isolation, even for an introvert like Eve, was a bit much. Before they'd signed the papers, she brought up her worries with Charlie: "What if something goes wrong up there? Isn't the nearest hospital like two hours away?"

Charlie admitted to sharing similar concerns, but with the last property not doing so well, things were tight. "Not to make you panic, but, financially speaking"—Charlie paused—"we're kind of treading water."

Great. A drowning metaphor. Eve could actually picture the endless void below, the hand of financial doom rising from the bluish-black, wrapping its gnarled fingers around her ankle, dragging her into the depths below, and—

"It's Thomas, by the way." Back in the present, the father held out a hand.

". . . Eve," she replied, still half-lost in rumination. They shook. He had a firm grip, not surprising.

He stepped back, motioned to his wife. "That's Paige."

Paige offered a thin smile. "Nice to meet you."

"You as well," said Eve.

He pointed to his daughter. "That's Jenny, the Inquisitor." Jenny gave a little curtsy bow that Eve couldn't help but return.

Thomas continued. "You can just call the boys Headache One and Headache Two. Or, if you really care, Newton and Kai."

Thomas gestured to the tall blond one. "Kai's the smug bastard."

Paige bristled. "Let's not use that word."

Thomas looked over his shoulder. "'Bastard'?"

Her glare could have just about cut him in half. "Uh-huh."

"What's that mean?" Jenny chimed in, *Blue's Clues* notebook at the ready. She'd already written it down in oversized letters, albeit spelled: "BASSTERD."

"Cross it out." Thomas stifled a chuckle. "That's a bad word. Cross it out."

Jenny furrowed her brow, her nose wrinkling at the same time—an expression she hadn't quite mastered yet. "Why?"

Thomas hunched forward, took the pen from her, and scribbled it out himself. "You'll understand when you're older."

Kai, hands in the pockets of a Portland Winterhawks hoodie, rolled his cold blue eyes. A look that only confirmed his father's jest. Eve couldn't shake how much this one reminded her of a pompous prince. Somehow, Kai looked smug and bored at the same time, like he'd been dragged to the class dork's birthday party. Yes, it was wrong to judge a kid by his face, but . . .

The other boy tapped his foot against the hardwood, a twitchy, nervous movement. With red hair, round glasses, and hazel eyes, he was, in almost every way, the opposite of his brother. Freckled, small, and fidgety, he looked stressed out well beyond his years. Neurotic. It was built into his posture, a forward slouch usually reserved for middle-aged desk jockeys. Standing next to the others, he seemed out of place, like he could've been some random kid they'd picked up on the side of the road. Still, his frazzled "everything's stressing me out" aura made him the most relatable. Go figure.

As Thomas looked around, a slow awkwardness filled the air—one of those silent nothings where no one quite knew what to say or do. It dragged on for three, four, five seconds until he cleared his throat and pointed upward. "There used to be a chandelier right there." Everyone craned their neck. The vaulted ceiling was bare, save for a single brass chain hanging from the center. "My dad installed it himself. It was made completely out of deer antlers." Thomas looked at Eve. "Was it there when you moved in?"

She shook her head, *no*. Technically, this was true. The creepy antler chandelier wasn't *there* when they moved in—it had been in the living room, buried under a pile of clutter. Charlie had sold it on Craigslist a week earlier.

Thomas studied Eve, a look that suggested he knew she was lying, but he didn't really mind. "My father killed every critter on that thing himself," he said with a sigh. "Over two dozen deer."

"Oh wow," said Eve. "Impressive."

Thomas rubbed his jaw. "That's one word for it."

Looking at him now, Eve realized he was a little older than she'd first thought. Under the brighter light, the markings of time were more visible on his face. Lines etched across his skin. Traces of gray hair speckled around his temples. But more than any physical markers, she could sense it behind his eyes. A weary burden of hidden knowledge that only came with age. The kind of eyes that had seen one too many caskets lowered into the dirt.

He started saying something to his family and looked over his shoulder. Now, Eve could see a constellation of pockmarked scars on his left cheek, reflected by the light above. Blotchy and pink. A few more on his neck. So subtle they could have been mistaken for mere blemishes. Eve wasn't an expert, but they might've been healed burns.

Despite all this, or perhaps because of it, he still could've passed for a classic Hollywood movie star. With his broad shoulders and dimpled smile, Eve could picture him playing the leading man, lighting up a cigarette for the femme fatale as she strolled into his office. Cary Grant vibes.

A high-pitched whine caught everyone's attention. It was Eve's dog, sitting at the top of the stairs, peering through the banister, wary.

Jenny pointed up. "That's a dog."

"Yes it is," said Thomas, stifling another chuckle. He turned to Eve. "What's the breed?"

Eve shrugged. "Border collie," she said, "and a bunch of other stuff."

"Great breed," Thomas said. "I had a chocolate Lab growing up."

The daughter chimed in again, almost yelling, "What's the name?"

"The dog?"

"Yup," she replied, turning the word into two syllables with a plosive "puh." She had her notebook and pen ready, like an overeager reporter, prepared to get the latest scoop.

Eve smiled at her. "Shylo."

"How's it spelled?" Again, she was almost shouting.

"Jenny," said Paige, "she's standing right there. You don't need to yell."

"How's it spelled?" she repeated, barely quieter.

"Shylo," Eve replied. "S-H-Y-L-O."

With her green pen, Jenny scribbled that down, nodding. Shylo slunk off and disappeared into the upstairs hallway. Eve said, "She's a little scared of strangers but completely harmless."

"Shylo's shy," said the daughter.

Eve nodded.

The dog, just like Eve, never trusted strangers, and for good reason. About four years prior, Eve had found her curled up behind a highway gas station, abandoned and nearly frozen to death.

A mixed-breed pup with black fur and a splash of white across her chest. Over her left eye was a white, uneven diamond shape. She'd never grown into her big pointy ears—the right one stuck straight up, and the left flopped forward at a funny angle. Her eyes were each a different color: one a pale blue, the other a dark brown. Heterochromia was the technical name for it. Charlie had the same thing. "Witch eyes," she called them. Apparently, some parts of the church deemed mismatched eyes a curse. As Charlie once said: "Don't understand something? Witchcraft."

After Eve had brought the poor dog home, it took weeks to earn her trust. For a long time, Eve was the only person Shylo felt safe around. No one else, not even Charlie, could get near the dog without her shaking in fear. It was like she only had so much trust to give, and she'd given it all to Eve.

But Charlie was determined. She would place a treat on the ground, walk ten steps back, and let Shylo take it. Each time, inch by inch, she reduced the distance. It took months, but eventually Shylo could tolerate Charlie standing three feet away, two feet, one. A few more weeks and Charlie could even scratch Shylo behind the ears. Now, four years later, both Eve and Charlie were the only people in the world the dog trusted.

Thomas drifted toward the staircase. "My father put this in too," he said, running a hand along a varnished oak banister. Jenny shadowed him, taking notes every time he spoke. It was obvious she thought the world of her father, thought he was a superhero. Eve knew the look.

Thomas studied the dust on his fingertips. "So you guys are fixing this place up?"

"Yeah, uh, that's the plan." She didn't have the heart to tell him they were considering a demolition. After all, it was his childhood home. That, and it almost felt immoral to destroy something so historic—but the inspection revealed problems with the foundation, water damage in the support beams, and a litany of other ailments. Sometimes it was easier just to tear it all down, start from scratch.

Thomas said, "That'll be quite the renovation. I might still have some of the old blueprints in storage somewhere—if you're interested."

"Yeah, that, that would be great." She *was* interested, if only because the bank had lost most of the original records. Apparently, there had been a fire down at city hall decades before. Almost everything about the house, from its origin to its chain of ownership, was a mystery. "Clouded title" was the bank's term for it.

"You've got my card," he said, "Just shoot me an email whenever you want; I'll send over the scans."

From his back pocket, Thomas pulled out a white rectangular tin. He flicked it open with a thumb and shook it over his palm. Two, maybe three mints fell out. In one quick motion, he downed them all and slid the box back into his pocket.

Those weren't mints. Mo, Eve's ever-present voice of paranoia, commented. For once, the Hillbilly Chimp might have been right. Eve had only caught a glimpse, a vague impression that was already fading. But whatever Thomas had just swallowed had the pale orange hue of a pharmaceutical. She was fairly certain she even saw pill-splitting indents. Maybe some antianxiety meds. Seroquel? Either way, she wasn't one to judge—she used to take SSRIs herself. That being said, she'd never pretended they were mints.

Jenny, peering up at her father, tugged at his shirt—three short yanks. When he looked down, she held out an open palm and fluttered her big green eyes. Thomas shook his head. "These aren't sweet," he said. "They're spicy, not for kids."

Brushing away Jenny's gripping hand, he took a few steps forward and looked down. "Well, that's a big change." His gaze swept over the hardwood. "Used to be black and white tile, like a diner." He tapped his heel. "The wood's a lot more fitting." Squatting down, he knocked his knuckles against the boards. "Huh. Isn't that something," he mused, half to himself. He motioned his family over. "Check this out." Jenny and the red-haired boy—Newton?—were the only ones who came. Paige and Kai seemed just about ready to leave. Thomas, with two of his kids standing over his shoulder, pointed to the floor. "Right there," he said. "Between the slats you can see the old tile underneath."

Eve narrowed her eyes, leaned in, and, sure enough, if you looked from just the right angle, you could see a sliver of the old floor, long covered. Black and white tiles. Thomas started to get up but stopped short, his eyes landing on something else: white crown molding at the base of the wall. It was carved with intricate designs: abstract flower shapes, and horses. The floral patterns were nice enough, but the horses, when you got up close—the lines were rough, the proportions off. "My mother carved these in," said Thomas, running his hand across. "Took her almost half a year to do the whole house." He looked at Eve as if expecting a response.

"Wow," said Eve, "that's . . . a lot of work, it's . . . really nice, though."

Thomas breathed out of his nose, not buying the compliment. "Don't feel bad if you tear it out." His eyes flitted to something on the underside of the banister railing. "Oh right, I almost forgot about those . . ."

Eve bent down to see. An odd symbol had been carved there. A circle, divided by intersecting lines of varying lengths, all meeting in the middle. It looked cryptic, like some kind of ancient glyph.

"They're my sister's handiwork," Thomas explained. "You'll find more scattered about the place, if you haven't already. She was always hiding little messages everywhere. Quite the imagination on that one—"

It's the mark of a death cult, Mo, the cymbal monkey, chimed in. *This family is part of a demonic death cult and they're coming back here to finish some kind of ritual and—*

Eve ignored the barrage of ridiculous paranoia.

Thomas sighed, his eyes still fixed on the symbol as he spoke to his children. "Your aunt said this one kept bad luck away. Grandpa said it looked like blasphemy." Thomas looked down at Jenny and said, "Here." He held out his hand. Eager, she passed him her notebook and pen. He turned to a blank page and pressed it flat against the underside of the railing. He traced the symbol. All the while, Jenny watched, wide-eyed and mesmerized. When he finished, he handed it back.

"There you go," he said. "Good luck for seven years. That, or you'll turn into a witch."

"Thomas." Paige frowned.

"Right," he said. "Witches are bad."

Paige shot him another disapproving look. A look that reminded Eve of the time her parents discovered she'd been playing with a Ouija board at a sleepover. Couldn't take chances with demons.

"Anyway." Thomas rose to standing. "Mind if we go upstairs?"

◆

As the family wandered down the second-floor hallway, Eve tagged along. Now, she was actually a little curious to hear Thomas's anecdotes. Shylo followed too, but at a safe distance. Stranger danger.

"This room used to have green wallpaper," said Thomas, pointing into a blue-walled guest room. "Mom worked on all her paintings here—"

"Grandmum," Paige corrected him.

Thomas stared at her for a lingering moment, then turned away. "Your *grandmum* used to work on her paintings here."

Jenny said, "Grandmum was a painter?"

Thomas tilted his head. "I wouldn't say she was a *painter* painter. But she painted, as a hobby."

"What's that?"

"A hobby?"

"Yup."

"It's something you do for fun, like how I play guitar."

Again, Jenny wrote this down.

As he moved to the next room, everyone followed. He pushed open a heavy oak door to reveal a long, rectangular study. Empty bookshelves lined either side. At the far end was a small stained glass window. With vibrant colors, it depicted a gnarled apple tree. Dark green leaves, bloodred apples. It overlooked the forest behind the house, a claustrophobic view—the pines lurking so close it felt like they were peering inside, spying on you.

"This was your grandpa's study," said Thomas. "He'd spend hours at a time working here."

"Working on a hobby?" asked Jenny.

Thomas shook his head and looked down at her. "Grandpa didn't like hobbies."

That simple statement conjured a vivid picture in Eve's head. A wiry man with gray hair, a pointed beard, and tired eyes that never slept. A man who took no pleasure in life and made sure others followed suit. The nemesis of fun.

Just then, something caught the corner of her eye. The two boys—they were standing off down the hallway, facing each other, eyes locked in some kind of staring contest. Without warning, Kai slapped Newton across the face—a percussive SMACK. The impact left behind a bright red mark on his pale cheek. *Guess he lost.*

"Boys," Paige snapped. They both stood at attention. She motioned them over. "You stay with the family." They slinked back into the group.

Out of sight from his parents, Newton rubbed his red cheek. Kai looked down at him, gave a smarmy grin, and messed up his red hair. Newton did nothing to defend himself; he just stood there, looking more defeated by the second. Poor kid.

"That window." Thomas pointed at the stained glass. "I . . . I don't remember it being in this room." He scratched his temple. "I thought it was at the front of the house." After a silent moment, he added, "Funny . . . how memories can change like that." With his family in tow, he turned away and continued down the hall. He lurched to a sudden stop, looked over his shoulder, and raised an eyebrow. He stared at the yellow wallpaper, puzzled. "What happened to the dumbwaiter?" He glanced at Eve.

"Hm?"

"There used to be a dumbwaiter here," he said, resting his palm flat against the wall. "Went all the way to the basement." He started to slide his hand down.

"Oh," Eve replied, "who knows?"

His fingers caught on something. Something beneath the wallpaper. Squinting, he leaned in closer—it was an oval bump. A handle?

"Huh," he mused. "Looks like somebody covered it up."

Eve detected the slightest hint of discomfort in his voice. A quivering timbre from deep within his gut, so subtle it might've been imagined.

Jenny, still standing at Thomas's side, chimed in with another "What's that?"

He stepped back and looked down at her. "A dumbwaiter?"

"Yup."

"It's like a miniature elevator," he explained. "We used it for laundry, tools, food. If somebody got sick you could send a meal up without getting too close."

"Why?"

"If you got too close," said Thomas, "you might get sick too."

Jenny noted that down. "Why's it called a dumbwaiter?"

Thomas shrugged. "Beats me."

Eve, half to herself, said, "Because it's a waiter that doesn't talk . . ."

Everyone looked at her.

A little self-conscious, she elaborated. "It delivers food like a waiter, and—"

"It's stupid?" Kai interjected.

Eve shook her head. "Dumb used to mean mute. Unable to speak. It's a silent waiter." This was something she'd learned from Charlie. Her partner was a walking encyclopedia of obscure facts.

"Huh," said Thomas. "That's . . . interesting."

Jenny finished writing, then turned to Eve. "Thanks, Emma," she said.

Thomas quirked an eyebrow. "Her name is Eve, no?"

Eve nodded. "Yeah, it's okay." If he hadn't said anything, she would've just gone with it, accepted "Emma" as her new name for the duration of the family's tour.

"Anyway." Thomas continued down the hall until he stood face-to-face with a white cord hanging low from the ceiling. A pull-string for the attic's trapdoor staircase. He blew on it, a swift puff, like putting out a birthday cake candle. It swung back and forth like a metronome. "This leads to an attic," he said, "but you've seen one attic, you've seen them all."

In the two months they'd lived here, Eve hadn't been up there herself yet, not even a quick peek. She wasn't exactly a fan of dark places, musty rank, and cobwebs.

Thomas pushed around the corner and slowed to another stop. There was one last nook here. It went for about five feet, then ended with a plain white door. He studied it like it was a melancholic painting. Hesitant, he stepped forward and reached for the handle. "This used to be your aunt Alison's room." His hand clasped the doorknob, lingered, then slipped away.

Sensing a private moment, Eve cleared her throat, "Anyway," she said, "feel free to keep showing yourselves around." At this point, she'd decided they probably weren't going to rob the place. "I'll be downstairs if you need anything," she added.

Thomas smiled at her—grateful.

◆

Eve returned to an earlier task: prying out rusty nails from above the living room fireplace. The nails used to hold picture frames, judging by the discolored rectangles on the wall. But they had been mounted off-center, all a little too far to the right. She had just about finished the task when, behind her, Shylo whined. Eve looked back. The dog was standing in the middle of the room, rigid, ears pricked, staring at a closed door. The basement door.

"Shylo . . . ?"

No reaction.

More so than attics, Eve was no fan of basements. She'd only been down there once, and even then, she just reached the bottom of the stairs and took a quick look around. It was pretty much what she'd expected, a cramped collection of unfinished hallways, nooks, and low ceilings. Relatively common in older houses like this one.

When she was a child, thanks to an overactive imagination, she half believed something evil dwelled in each and every cellar. She used to have nightmares about it. The nameless terror. Always lurking just out of sight, silent and faceless and so horrific it couldn't even be described. No matter what basement, what house, it was always that same feeling. As if this unspeakable terror could divide and multiply itself throughout all the basements of the world.

Fortunately, over time, that childhood anxiety had faded away, like a brightly colored toy discarded in a sun-bleached desert. Yet, like all childhood monsters, it was only replaced by the mundane, and arguably worse, terrors of adulthood: credit card debt, car accidents, funerals. Things that sometimes made Eve think back to imaginary ghouls with rosy nostalgia.

And despite all the years gone by, her lingering aversion to basements remained—along with one specific remnant of childish fear: walking up basement stairs. To this day, every time she walked up and out of a basement, she remembered the nameless thing, stowed away in the depths of half-forgotten memories. She had this nagging conviction it was following her, an unshakable chill that grew with each upward step. She could almost feel it, hear it—rushing from the darkness below, breathing at her heels, giddy with evil intent.

Part of her still had to fight the urge to scramble, to run away from that imaginary nothing. Of course, 99.8 percent of the time, she could ascend basement stairs at a slow and measured pace like any reasonable adult should. But, every time she stepped out of the shadows, she couldn't resist the compulsion to peer back down, only to confirm what she already knew—nothing was there.

The dog kept whining . . . the orange glow of the fire dancing over her black fur.

"Shylo?" Eve tried once more.

But Shylo didn't look back; she kept her eyes fixed on the basement door. Eve set the hammer aside and strode over. Kneeling down, she scratched the dog behind the ears. Shylo was trembling, a jittery vibration beneath Eve's hand.

She leaned in closer. "What's wrong, girl?"

Shylo's gaze drifted upward, as if tracking a slow-rising object—nothing was there, just the basement door. "Shylo?" Eve repeated, still to no reaction. The dog froze, eyes locked on empty space.

Uneasy, Eve got to her feet, marched over, and pulled out a ring of keys. Without thinking, she locked the door and . . .

She finally saw it. A black dot climbing the frame. She squinted. It was only a common house ant. Eve sighed with embarrassed relief—Shylo, believe it or not, wasn't a fan of bugs. The ant slipped between the crack of the door, and the dog's tense posture relaxed. Eve shook her head. "Shylo," she said, "don't scare me like that."

The dog, with her mismatched eyes, looked up and blinked, uncomprehending. Eve couldn't help but smile. She reached down, scratched Shylo behind the ear again, and returned to work.

Just as she pulled out the last nail, the family filed into the room. Thomas motioned at the fireplace. "Looks just like I remember it," he said. "We had one going every night during the winter." Turning away, he stepped up to the basement door and placed a hand on the frame. "Your grandparents would measure our heights here." He slid his palm over its smooth white surface. "All painted over now, though." He tried the handle—locked. Looking toward Eve, he said, "Do you mind if we tour the basement?"

She hesitated. They had definitely overstayed the fifteen-minute promise. "Oh, uh, there's a lot of tools lying around down there," she exaggerated. "It's a little dangerous—"

Jenny chimed in. "Danger doesn't scare me."

Eve forced a smile. She put the hammer down on the coffee table. "The lights aren't working yet either," she said. "Something's up with the circuit breaker and—"

"That's why I brought *this*." Jenny clicked her green pen twice. It cast a white circle of LED glow onto the floor. She swept it around, like a manic warlock wielding a wand. "It's bright enough to be seen from *Pluto*—"

"Jenny." Thomas set a hand on her tiny shoulder. "She'd rather we didn't go in the basement, okay?"

Downcast, Jenny gave a single nod, clicked off her pen, and tucked it away.

Thomas's eyes flicked to a nearby clock. "All right, gang," he said, "let's get outta here—for real this time."

Jenny tugged on his shirt. "But there's still, there's still more house to explore."

Thomas shook his head. "We've long overstayed our time limit, kiddo." He motioned his family toward the foyer. But as they filed out, he lingered behind, hands in his pockets, eyes still on the basement door.

Eve padded into the nearby kitchen, and started washing dishes that didn't need washing. Thomas looked at her. "Thanks for letting us take a look around," he said. "It really meant a lot to my family."

Aside from Jenny, it didn't look like it meant anything to anyone, but Eve kept that to herself. Without looking at him, she grabbed a steel wool scourer and started scrubbing a spotless pan. "All good," she said.

Thomas meandered closer, taking one last look around. "Must be nice, huh?"

Eve looked up. "Hm?"

He stopped at the threshold between the kitchen and living room. "Moving into a new place, fixing it up, settling in."

"Ah, yep." Eve sent him a brittle smile. Again, she and Charlie weren't even close to settling down, but once more, she kept that to herself. Now, she just wanted to be alone. "Anyway, it was really nice to meet you all," she said, a gentle signal she was done talking.

Yet Thomas hovered in the edge of her vision. Fidgety, as if building up the courage to ask her something. *Please don't.* He glanced toward the foyer, making sure his family was out of earshot. He turned back and lowered his voice. "I know you've just moved in, but"—he paused for a moment, reluctant, embarrassed—"have you ever noticed anything—"

A commotion interrupted him. One of the boys was shouting, "STOP IT."

Thomas marched off toward the foyer. Eve followed.

At the front door, the two boys were fighting while Paige tried to break them up. Without skipping a beat, Thomas strode over and ripped them apart.

"Newton started it," Kai, the taller one, whined.

"Of course he did . . ." Thomas fell silent, head on a swivel. "Where's Jenny?" he asked.

Everyone looked around—the young girl was nowhere to be seen.

"She, she was just here," Paige stammered.

"JENNY," he called out, his voice booming with authoritative resonance. No response. Only the *tick, tick, tick* of a nearby clock.

"Jenny," Paige tried as well. No luck.

Rubbing his temples, Thomas turned back to Eve. "Our youngest," he sighed. "She likes to hide."

"Hide?"

"Spontaneous hide-and-seek," he explained. "We thought she'd grown out of it, but—"

"Jennifer," Paige shouted in the background.

He went on. "We should be able to find her easily enough . . . I'm really sorry about this."

"It— it's okay," Eve said.

Thomas pivoted away, barely suppressing the anger in his voice. "Jenny, come on out."

As the family started searching around, Eve wandered up to the window by the door. Snow had begun to fall, the first of the year. Normally, the sight would have filled Eve with a wistful comfort, but tonight it only made her uneasy. Where was Charlie? Were the roads safe? She checked the time: 8:57 p.m. Only twenty minutes behind schedule. Still, Eve reached for her phone when—

Off in the distant woods, a light snapped on. Eve paused, narrowed her eyes. It was a glowing point of pale blue, far away in the looming black—it seemed to be drifting toward her. A flashlight? Who would be out there at this hour, especially in the cold?

Jenny?

No, it was too far, but . . . Eve stepped closer to the window. As her vision adjusted, the blurry image became more defined. The light was stationary; the movement had only been an illusion, created by the falling snow. A porch light? A parked car? Was there a road out there? The precise distance was hard to judge through all the trees. Without warning, the light snapped off, and the darkness returned.

Above her, another commotion. Muffled voices.

Eve rushed upstairs. The family was standing in the middle of the hallway, huddled in a tight circle, looking at something. Eve stepped closer and peered over Paige's shoulder. The wallpaper that had once covered the dumbwaiter was now torn back, a hanging flap. A square metal door was ajar, revealing a gaping throat of pipes and beams and reddish-pink insulation. There was no cart in sight.

Thomas leaned in, called out, "Jenny?" No response—only his voice echoing back. With an exasperated huff, he turned to the group. "Looks like she found a way into the basement after all."

DOC_A12_K9

Description: Transcript of a classified ad in the Free section of the *Yale Courier*. Date unknown.

◆

FREE CHOCOLATE LAB

We are looking to rehome Buckley, our purebred Labrador Retriever. Two years old. Food provided for up to one month. We can no longer keep him due to an incident with our son. Details can be shared upon request.

He will come with a kennel, toys, a bed, and liver treats. Buckley is up to date on shots and is in good health as per a vet check last November.

We're seeking a loving home with an experienced owner who can accommodate a reactive dog. If you're interested, please call me at [number redacted].

-- .- -.

HIDE-AND-SEEK

Flashlights in hand, Thomas and Eve descended the basement stairs. He led the way, Eve in tow, while the rest of his family waited above. At first, Paige had proposed they all search for Jenny as a group. But Thomas vetoed this: "The more dramatic our response," he said, "the longer she stays hidden."

As they navigated down the creaky steps, Eve steadied herself on the brick wall, its texture coarse against her palm, like sandpaper. At the bottom, they entered a narrow hallway that branched off in two directions. They scanned their flashlights around. There was an unusual heaviness to the dark down here, as if it were soaking up the light, hoarding it away for some unknown purpose.

And the air was dense. Humid. Every breath filled with a stagnant must you could actually taste. Metallic, like a mouthful of pennies. Sour, like bark mulch after a rainstorm. The dampness had sunk into the beams above, lending them a slick, glistening sheen. Something that would lead to structural integrity issues, if it hadn't already. All the more reason to tear this place down.

Thomas looked both ways. He studied the shadows with apprehension, almost like there might be something dangerous out there. Something only he could see. Shaking this off, he strode up to a nearby support beam. He rapped his knuckles against it, using that classic "call and response" secret knock pattern:

Duh—duh-duh-duh—duh . . .

He left out the last two knocks, awaiting an answer. But there was only silence. Empty and dull. He looked around more, his eyes landing in a murky corner. There sat the dumbwaiter, veiled in darkness, its door cracked ajar, the cart empty.

Thomas frowned. "We should be quiet, split up. This is all like a game to Jenny. If she hears you, she'll run or double down." His voice was strained with the exhaustion of having done this one too many times.

"The basement's bigger than you'd think," he said. "Goes beyond the edge of the upstairs footprint. Lots of nooks, crannies, places to hunker down." He sighed. "If you see Jenny on the move, just run after her, grab her. Seriously. We'll be here all night otherwise."

Eve blinked, unsure if she'd heard him right. "Just, grab her?"

"I know, I know." His tired face acknowledged the absurdity. "It's all part of her game. You could call me over, but by the time I get there—she's fast, good at hiding."

"Okay . . ."

Thomas looked past Eve. "You go that way." He glanced back. "I'll go this way."

Before she could respond, he disappeared around the leftward corner. Alone, Eve lingered there, ruminating. This was supposed to be a relaxing Friday night. Now, she was standing in a dingy basement hunting down a kid she didn't even know. And of course, Charlie's absence echoed in the depths of her mind. As soon as Eve got back upstairs, she'd give her a call.

Resigned, she pushed rightward down the narrow corridor. Rounding a corner, she entered a room the size of a two-car garage. It smelled like a garage too—a watery mix of cardboard and mystery chemicals. Lovely. Rickety shelves lined the space, four rows in all. They were crammed with boxes, each one filled with rusty knickknacks. She plodded forward, her footsteps creaking on plywood. Someone had just slapped the boards on top of the hard-packed dirt and called it a day. Huh. As she wound her way through the aisles, her light cast distorted shadows through the shelves. Sweeping and shifting. She checked each corner, every possible hiding spot. No Jenny in sight. She was just about ready to move on when, behind her—

Something clattered to the ground, a shrill, snapping sound that made her whip-turn toward it. About ten feet away, a tin can rolled in a lazy half circle. Around it was a scattered mess of nails and screws, some still spinning in place. *Great*, thought Eve, *now this kid's gonna step on a nail, get tetanus, and we're gonna get sued.*

In a huff, she crossed over and crouched. She put down the flashlight and swept the nails back into the can, careful not to get pricked. Then, an unpleasant question finally arose:

How did the can fall over?

There was no kid in sight, so it couldn't have been that . . . Mo, the paranoid monkey on her shoulder, was about to take the wheel, when: plywood.

Of course. Her weight must have shifted the boards, unbalanced the shelf, and caused the can to fall. Occam's razor. That was a term Charlie had taught her: the simplest explanation was usually correct. Eve smiled, feeling proud in an embarrassed sort of way.

As she finished cleaning up the nails, her flashlight slowly rolled away. *Uneven floors, great.* She kicked out her foot, blocked its path, and . . . something in the circle of light caught her eyes. One row over, tracing along the floor, was a thin trail of tiny black dots. She grabbed the flashlight and skulked over. More ants.

They were spilling out from a crack in the plywood. All going the same direction, they marched down the aisle and slipped out of sight. *Is this normal ant behavior?* Eve wondered. Vague memories of a nature documentary played in her mind—David Attenborough pontificating on what normal ant behavior ought to be. Curious, she padded forward into yet another narrow hallway. This one had green doors on either side, ran for about twenty feet, then forked left and right. Way too many hiding places down here.

On the verge of another anxiety spell, she stopped herself, drew in a deep breath, and exhaled. She took in her surroundings. Details she could see, feel, hear, smell, and taste. The low hum of a nearby air vent, its cold draft against her left shoulder. *Stay present*, she reminded herself. The concrete walls, dull and gray. This was another technique she'd picked up from that counselor: grounding.

In times of stress, take mental notes of your environment, your senses. Stay focused on the present moment.

She noted the smell of must, the lingering taste of a peppermint tea she'd drunk earlier that evening.

A little calmer, she shone her light down. The trail of ants moved like an oil slick across the dusty floor, curving around the far corner. Eve could almost hear their tiny feet tapping against the plywood. She felt a compulsive need to know where they were going, why they were all moving in the same direction.

Pressing onward, she veered around the corner and came upon a door, bone white. The ants slipped under it, filing into a thin line of dark. She turned the knob, stepped inside. This room fit the house's theme of having no unifying theme. Here, the brick walls were painted a fleshy pink, and the floors were a familiar black and white tile. The ants moved in a straight line to the far left corner and disappeared beneath an old wardrobe that was painted sky blue, cracked and peeling. It had shuttered doors and slats through which a sneaky child could peer. The perfect hiding spot.

Right on cue, her light caught the glint of blinking eyes, gazing out from the shutters. Bingo. Jenny was cornered now. Forgetting the ants, Eve tiptoed over, wrapped her hand around the knob, swung it open, and—

Empty.

No kid in sight. There was just a painting, leaning up against the back panel, facing away. A three-by-two-foot frame, coated with flaking silver. That explained the glint of eyes.

But weren't those eyes blinking? Mo proffered.

Must've been an illusion, created when she moved the light. Occam's razor. She tilted the frame back. The painting was obscured by a thick layer of dust. She crouched down and used her sleeve to wipe it clean.

It was an oil painting—a tree line lit by dreary sunlight. The colors were cold, pale greens, light grays, and bluish-browns. In the foreground, a chocolate Lab faced the woods. Its tail was straight, ears pricked up, sensing some unseen threat. On the ground to its left was a red gas lantern casting an orange glow into the woods, revealing nothing but branches, trees, and shadows.

Whatever the creator's intent, the image certainly evoked a sense of dread. It wasn't the sort of thing Eve would hang up anytime soon, but the artist, whoever they were, undoubtedly had skill. If this was the work of Thomas's mother, he was selling her short. It was the kind of painting that almost made Eve want to go back to art school. Almost. Careful, reverent, she set it back and closed the door.

She aimed her light down at the ant trail. The last of them were receding beneath the wardrobe. On her knees, she put her head to the ground and peered under. They led straight to the corner, amassing over a crack between the tiles. Now, they moved with delirious urgency, writhing and crawling over one another as they forced their way through.

Uneasy, she returned to standing and looked back toward the exit. Next to the door was a wooden pegboard. The outlines of tools were faded into its brown veneer—a drill, a handsaw, a hammer. Not thinking much of it, she strode out of the room, stepped around the corner, and halted in her tracks.

Someone was standing down the narrow hall. Back turned. Looming. It was Thomas. His posture was pin-straight, his arms hanging limp. His flashlight, white-knuckle-gripped in his left hand, was pointed straight down at the floor, casting a tight circle of harsh light half over his shoe, half over the concrete.

"Thomas?"

No response. He just stood there, unmoving. Somehow, he looked stiller than the hallway itself . . . *was he even breathing?*

"T-Thomas?"

Nothing.

Tense, Eve glanced over her shoulder. He was blocking the only way out. She cleared her throat and tried one more. "Thomas . . . ?" Still no response. He just kept standing there like a storefront mannequin, frozen in time. If he was trying to scare her, it was working. Should she bolt past him?

She took another step closer. Another. She was less than an arm's length away when he suddenly spun around. "Jesus." He set a hand to his chest, startled. "You snuck up on me there." He paused, clocking her wary expression. "You okay? You look . . . spooked."

"I, uh." Eve was lost for words. "I tried calling your name like three times."

He smiled apologetically. "Yeah, my hearing isn't what it used to be. You're sure you're okay, though?"

"I . . ." Eve fell silent and considered prodding further, but: "I— I'm just not a fan of basements."

"You and me both."

Eve rubbed her arms, fidgety. "Any luck?" she asked.

His mouth pressed into a straight line. "Sort of."

Thomas led Eve to the opposite side of the basement. He crouched in a corner and aimed his light down a gap so narrow even a child would've had to turn sideways just to fit. The glow shone through beams, insulation, and pipes, landing in a small open space. It was likely a remnant of the original layout, a vestigial organ created by the many additions over the years.

"She's hiding in there," Thomas sighed. "Just out of view."

"Well," Eve said, "shouldn't we call her out?"

He tilted his head, pretending to consider the suggestion. "I've seen this pattern before," he said. "Jenny finds a spot, sets up camp, and she won't surrender unless we give her space."

"Okay, but— I'm just, I'm not sure it's safe back there . . ." Again, visions of potential lawsuits swirled.

"It's safe," Thomas said. "My sister and I used to hide out there all the time; it's just a concrete nook, no bigger than a walk-in closet."

"I— I could go in and get her?" It would be an extremely tight fit, but she could do it. Maybe.

"I appreciate that, but it's not a good idea. Even if you managed to squeeze through—good luck getting her out without some kicking and screaming. Jenny's a biter."

She studied him. *Didn't he say to grab her earlier?* Also, the kid didn't strike Eve as the type to kick and scream, but . . . she wasn't about to argue with a parent on their own child's behavior.

Thomas crossed his arms and tapped his foot, thinking. After a few seconds of this, he leaned in close. "Like I said, right now, our best course of action is to go back upstairs, give her space, wait until she's ready to come out." He checked the time on his watch. "When she gives up on that spot, she'll come right up. Always does."

Eve thought about this for a moment. "What's to stop her from just finding another hiding spot?"

Thomas gave a polite but terse smile. "She won't. When Jenny gives up here, she'll come straight upstairs." He said this as if it were an immutable law of the universe, on par with gravity. Turning back to the narrow passage, he threw his voice into the inky dark. "Jenny, we're going back up."

There was a damp dullness in the silence, as if the shadows had swallowed his words before they even made it halfway. "Jenny?" Thomas repeated, suppressing the slightest hint of worry.

Still no response.

A tendon in his neck twitched. He tugged at his collar, nervous. Then he clucked his tongue as if to say, "Right." Slowly, he raised his arm. And with a flick of his wrist, he knocked that pattern onto a nearby pipe:

Duh—duh-duh-duh—duh . . .

A long stretch of silence crept by, and then, from somewhere beyond the end of the passage, two faint knocks echoed in response. Knuckles against concrete.

"There she is," said Thomas, rising to his feet. "Let's head back up." He walked off, but Eve lingered behind, staring into the claustrophobic opening, the unwelcoming void. *Shouldn't he be a little more concerned?*

"Eve?"

She turned to meet his gaze.

He was standing a few yards away, flashlight raised. "You coming?"

"Yeah . . ." She took one last glance into the dark passage, then trudged after him.

As they wound their way out of the cellar, she couldn't shake how off everything felt. Sure, she was no parenting expert, but didn't this type of behavior warrant a firmer response? At the very least, some kind of ultimatum: "If you don't come out in the next three minutes, we're going to take away your Pokémon cards"—or whatever it was the kids played with these days.

Tepidly, Eve brought up her concerns, but again, Thomas insisted that giving Jenny space was now the only route to go. Eve relented. Honestly, she was just glad to get out of the basement.

They rounded onto the rickety stairs. And as they ascended, for the first time in a while, Eve didn't feel the juvenile sensation that something was following her, didn't feel the urge to run. Though, as they stepped out of the basement and into the living room, she couldn't help but look over her shoulder, down the narrow staircase, only to confirm what she already knew—nothing was there.

DOC_B12_SHOW

Description: Advert from the *Yale Courier*.

◆

HEAVY METAL INVADES YALE

Local favorite metal group "Ring of Eyes" will be rocking Maguire's Pub this Sunday. Fifty cents at the door. Expect classic covers from AC/DC, Black Sabbath, Judas Priest, and even some brand-new originals!

   Ages 21+ only

   Music starts at 7PM!

.-- .. - ....

COMMUNION

Up in the living room, the rest of Thomas's family was stationed around the fireplace, oddly silent. An orange glow was set against their faces—shadows casting long, jittery fingers in every direction, weblike. Paige sat on the edge of a wooden chair, arms in her lap, eyes closed. For a moment, it almost looked as though she was meditating and, judging by her frown, not enjoying it. The two boys sat at her feet, legs crossed. They tossed flecks of wood into the fire, each one combusting with a hollow crack.

Thomas cleared his throat. "It's a waiting game now."

Paige blinked at him, unimpressed. "You're giving up already?"

"We found her tucked in a nook," he said. "I give it ten, maybe twenty minutes before she caves."

"A nook?" She wrinkled her brow as if she hadn't heard him right.

Thomas nodded. "It's safe but . . . out of reach."

Paige's jaw tensed. "So, we're just going to let her hide down there, all by herself, in the pitch black?"

He shrugged. "She's got her flashlight pen."

Not the answer Paige wanted.

Thomas paused, choosing his next words carefully. "You know how this works. The more we chase her, the longer she hides."

Paige let out a weary sigh. "She could get hurt, Thomas. If this was happening at our place, that would be one thing, but at a stranger's house?"

Thomas shook his head. "I know, I know—"

Eve withdrew from the room, not wanting to stick around for the fireworks but . . . despite herself, she listened in, safely out of sight with her back to the wall. Morbid curiosity. She could see them reflected in a nearby window.

Paige rose to her feet, paced away from her sons. "Jenny hasn't done this in years."

Thomas trailed after her, speaking in hushed tones. "She's a smart kid," he said. "She can take care of herself."

That did nothing to comfort Paige. "It's the move," she said. "Ever since we left home, it's like she's not the same kid anymore."

Thomas stepped closer, reached out, and put a hand on her shoulder. A gesture that was likely meant to be consoling but came off as patronizing. "Paige," he said, "I'd be more worried if she *wasn't* acting different. Once we're all settled down, things will go back to normal."

Shrugging off his hand, Paige faced a window. She stared into the cold night, the blasts of wind kicking up flurries of snow into swirling blurs. "Minnesota." The word flicked off her tongue like she considered it an obscenity. "You know winters there get to forty below, right?"

Thomas mumbled an answer that Eve couldn't quite make out. Whatever he said, it actually made Paige smile, but from where Eve was, she couldn't tell if it was a happy smile or a bitter one. Paige huffed, crossed her arms. That settled it—a bitter one. She glanced toward her boys as if to make sure they weren't listening in. They were debating who was faster, Superman or the Flash.

Paige turned back, lowered her voice. "My brother told me a story from his EMT days out there. Some old woman, her station wagon broke down on the interstate during a blizzard. When Jay and his team finally arrived, her hands were frozen to the steering wheel. Thirty minutes, Thomas. That's all it took for the cold to kill her." Paige breathed out her nose. "Some say it's a pleasant way to go, freezing to death, but Jay said the look on this woman's face suggested otherwise. They had to pry her hands off the wheel—just to get her body out." She paused, letting the image sink in. "That's what happens in Minnesota," she added. "Old women freeze to death in their station wagons."

Thomas considered this for a moment, then said, "I'm not happy about the move either. But we don't have much of a choice, and besides—"

"If you say 'Change is opportunity in disguise,' I'm going to scream."

Thomas hesitated, mouth half-open. "That's not what I—"

In the window's reflection, Thomas's eyes suddenly flicked to Eve, catching her listening in. Mortified, she slipped away, retreated into the foyer, and slumped down on the steps. Back in the living room, out of view, Paige and Thomas continued their quarrel. Eve fought the urge to listen in again.

Instead, she sat there, chin resting on her hands—all of the evening's strange occurrences rattling around in her head, like pebbles in a tin can. Sure, no single thing was big enough to warrant extreme concern, but everything together—everything adding up, and—

Where was Charlie?

Eve checked the foyer clock. She was almost an hour late now—

Truck broke down, the Hillbilly Chimp chimed in, nonchalant. Eve could almost see him, sitting on a rickety fence, tuning a broken banjo. *Her hands are probably frozen to the steering wheel by now.*

Eve tried to push the thought away, but—she looked out the window; the snow was falling faster now. Those mountain roads weren't exactly safe at the best of times, and—had Charlie put on the winter tires yet? What if—

You're never going to see her again.

She pulled out her phone and . . . the screen was cracked. A jagged line that started in the bottom right corner and veered up to the left. When had that happened? The crack distorted Eve's lock screen image—a portrait of Charlie and Shylo, the dog licking a smiling Charlie's chin. She tapped into the home screen. One missed call, one voicemail. Both from Charlie, both recent. She was about to listen when . . .

Right on cue, the front door swung open and Charlie stepped inside, a pack of beer in one hand, a bottle of wine in the other. "I'm late," she said, shaking off snow. "Roads are shit. Getting shittier."

Relief, warm and soothing, washed over Eve like a tidal wave. In one quick motion, she shot to her feet, surged across the foyer, and wrapped her arms around Charlie so tightly it made her wheeze. "Uhh." Charlie hesitated, more than a little confused by the sudden outpouring of affection. After all, it was the kind of embrace normally reserved for an airport arrival gate. Charlie set down the booze and hugged her back. "Nice to see you too . . . ?"

Eve held on a few moments longer, then let go.

"Everything okay?" Charlie pulled open the coat closet, tilting her head at the unfamiliar jackets. Eve started to explain, when Thomas stepped around the corner. Charlie blinked at him, even more confused than before.

"This is Thomas," Eve said. "He grew up here, was just showing his family around, and—"

"And now our daughter is playing spontaneous hide-and-seek in the basement," he sighed, holding out a hand to Charlie. They shook.

"Name's Charlie," she said. "Charlie Bastion." She hung up her coat. "Spontaneous hide-and-seek, huh? My younger brother used to do that all the time. You sure she's safe down there?"

"She's found a little nook out of reach," Thomas said, embarrassed. "She'll give up any minute now. Then we'll be out of your hair. Really sorry about all this."

"Right . . ." said Charlie. Her eyes flicked to Eve, then back to him. "That your moving truck down on the street?"

He nodded. "Didn't block your way up, did it?"

"No."

So it's confirmed, thought Eve. *The family didn't walk out of the forest, hand in hand.*

"Anyway," Thomas said, "we've long overstayed our welcome." He gestured to Eve. "Your partner has the patience of a saint, and I know you didn't even want us here in the first place, completely understandable—"

"I didn't want you here?" Charlie interrupted.

They both looked at Eve. Blood rushed into her face. "Yeah, on the phone earlier," Eve lied. "I called you to check if they could look around?"

Charlie finally realized what was going on. Eve had used the Let Me Check with Charlie Card. "Ahh, yup." She forced a smile. Charlie didn't like lying, especially when it came to something as mundane as avoiding social discomfort. *Just be direct*, she'd always say. *Don't like someone? Tell them to fuck off.* Easier said than done, Eve had often thought but never voiced.

Charlie gave Eve a silent *You okay?* stare. Eve replied with a tepid nod. *Sure . . .*

Charlie shut the closet, looked at Thomas. "So, is it like you remember?"

"The house?"

Charlie nodded.

Thomas shrugged. "Been a lot of changes—things added, things taken away. But it's still the same as it always was, more or less. Honestly, if you ask me, most of the additions are a big improvement." He paused for a moment, glancing up to where his father's chandelier used to hang. He looked back at Charlie. "Eve mentioned you guys were planning to fix the place up?"

"Maybe." Charlie looked around the foyer as if appraising it for the first time. "That or tear it down, start from scratch, we haven't decided yet—believe it or not."

Eve almost flinched at this. It was classic Charlie, nonchalantly telling a man you might tear down his childhood home.

Eve side-eyed Thomas, searching for his reaction, but he seemed unfazed. He just stood there, hands on his hips, smiling that movie-star smile. "Well, if you knock it down," he said, "please send me a video. My inner child would love to see it."

Charlie actually chuckled at that. *Seriously?* thought Eve. *Is she already warming to him?* Although maybe it wasn't *that* shocking. After all, Charlie hadn't seen the weird shit Eve had seen. That, and Charlie often assumed the best in people. She was hospitable and trusting, but not out of obligation or naivety—rather, she gave people the benefit of the doubt, and if anyone was dumb enough to break her trust, watch out. In this, and many other regards, she was Eve's polar opposite.

"Anyway," said Thomas, "don't let us spoil your dinner. We'll stay out of your way until Jenny surrenders."

"I mean." Charlie looked to Eve, then back to Thomas. "You might as well join us."

Eve's jaw tensed.

Thomas hesitated. "You sure? I think we'll be okay; we had a big lunch."

Charlie shrugged. "It's your call, but we have more than enough leftovers."

Thomas glanced at Eve, as if checking for her approval. "Only if it's not a problem," he said.

Charlie, not noticing his glance, answered, "Wouldn't be offering if it was."

Thomas started to reply, but Eve wasn't listening anymore. Her eyes were locked to an irrelevant fleck of snow stuck in Charlie's jet-black, pixie-cut hair. The fleck was melting, edges turning to mush as it trailed down the back of Charlie's ear. Eve suddenly wanted to grab her by the arm, yank her aside, and tell her to kick this family out right now, kid in the basement or no. How could her partner not sense how uncomfortable she was? Sure, Charlie wasn't always the best at picking up on emotions, but Eve clearly wasn't thrilled about having this family here and—

"Would you mind if we had a moment?" Eve interjected.

They both turned to her, mid-conversation, smiling. "Hm?" Thomas asked.

"Just, just need a moment alone with my partner," Eve repeated.

"Oh, of course." Thomas withdrew into the living room.

Charlie waited until he was out of earshot. "Jeepers." She smirked. "I leave for one hour and the whole Brady Bunch moves in?"

Eve didn't laugh. She stared down at the floor, chewing on her lip, searching for words.

"Hey," said Charlie, "what's up?"

Eve huffed. Part of her wanted to blather out everything that had happened: the ant trail, the strange basement encounter with Thomas. Yet the more she dwelled on those things, the more insignificant they seemed. And deeper than that, she was simply afraid to say her thoughts aloud, as if doing so might make them tangible, almost physical creatures. Little goblins that would scream and cry and embarrass her like unruly brats at a Denny's. So instead, she kept them locked up in the same room as Mo. Mo and his army of thought goblins. That absurd image summed up her entire mental landscape: repressed, chaotic shame. Regardless, she was probably just blowing things out of proportion, looking for reasons to panic like she always did, but—

"Eve?" Charlie said. "You can talk to me . . ."

Eve, in hushed tones, decided to let loose the most reasonable of the thought goblins. "I just—doesn't it seem odd they're not more concerned about their daughter?"

Charlie nodded. "He said she's hiding out of reach, right?"

"Yeah . . ."

"If she's anything like my little brother was, they'll have to just wait it out, seriously. My parents tried everything with that guy, even offered him candy. No dice. God, it was fucking annoying—"

"I'm sorry, but I don't buy it." Eve rubbed her arms as if a cold chill had swept through the room. "Most parents I know lose their mind if a kid goes missing for more than a minute. I mean—"

"Look." Charlie set a hand on Eve's shoulder. "If she's not out by the end of dinner, I'll raise hell. Okay?"

"Okay . . ."

Charlie frowned, studying Eve's face. "Did something else happen while I was gone?"

A flashback jolted through Eve's head, a chemical imprint so vivid she could almost see it: Thomas, with pin-straight posture, looming in that basement hallway. Back turned. Arms limp. Flashlight pointed straight at the ground. The way he didn't respond to his name.

"Eve?" Charlie prodded. "Do you want me to boot them out right now? Just say the word and—"

Eve swatted away the offer. "You being late made me worry, that's all. Mountain roads. The weather."

"I'm here, okay?" Charlie tucked a strand of hair behind Eve's ear, took her by the hands, and kissed her gently on the forehead. Nothing calmed Eve like that did.

Outside, the wind picked up, making the house shift and creak like some old machine, stirred awake from ancient slumber. No storm was in the forecast, but if this kept up . . . Eve worried the roads might close, trapping these strangers here even longer.

"One way in. One way out," Mr. Dayton, the Realtor, had said as they first crossed the Kettle Creek Bridge four months earlier. "Roads used to close at least once a winter on account of the weather," he'd added in his Southern drawl. "Been a couple decades since that happened, though."

Mo yawned. *Sounds like it's overdue.*

◆

While the weather raged outside, Paige helped Eve and Charlie prep dinner. Not that there was much to prep. Leftover chicken, instant mashed potatoes, microwaved veggies. Moving into a new home kind of food.

Meanwhile, Thomas was back down in the basement, trying to coax their daughter out. Paige had told him to say that they were all having a big fancy meal without her, and if she came up in the next fifteen minutes, they *might* have enough left to share. Thomas didn't have faith in this plan. Again, he insisted that giving Jenny space was the only way to go: "She'll hear us eating without her, and that'll be enough." But Paige persisted, and Paige won. Eve suspected she often did.

Eve still didn't know what to make of her. Of the two parents, it was clear Paige was the stricter—a role she seemed to both embrace and resent. And judging by her silver cross necklace, she was more devout too. But there were contradictions in Paige's actions, her body language. She had a timid, almost docile demeanor that would slip away when she had to break up a fight between the kids or make a sly comment toward her husband. Eve sensed a great deal of suppressed anger simmering beneath Paige's surface. A *tick-tick-ticking* time bomb.

Newton shuffled into the kitchen, pushing up his round glasses with a thumb. "Mom," he said, "I think I have an idea to prevent this in the future."

"Prevent what?" Paige glanced at her son and went back to cutting up vegetables.

"Jenny sneaking away," Newton clarified.

"Interesting." Paige said this with a sense of finality as if to signal the conversation was already over.

But Newton didn't pick up on the cue. "Maybe we could get her a harness?" he said.

Eve looked at Charlie. Was he trying to make a joke? He wasn't. This was a sincere pitch.

Newton went on. "Like, one of those child harnesses for kids that run away." He scratched his temple. "I think you can buy them online, I dunno. Just an idea."

"Thanks, Newton," said Paige. "We'll, uh, look into it."

Kai strode up behind his brother and rolled his eyes. "Like a dog harness?"

"No." Newton frowned. "Not like—"

Kai cut him off. "Probably not the best idea, Newt." It looked like Kai wanted to say something more, something meaner, but he glanced at his mother and remained quiet. Newton slouched into the living room, his brother following.

Minutes later, the food was ready, the table was set, yet Thomas was still in the basement. Apart from him and Jenny, everyone was seated around the table. Silent. Deep down, Eve was beginning to worry that, one by one, this family might start vanishing into the cellar. This time, she couldn't even blame Mo for the intrusive thought.

Uncomfortable tension hung over the table. Eve could almost hear it, a low, buzzing thrum. The inevitable feeling of precarity that came with having complete strangers sitting around your home. It was an oddly intimate thing, sharing a meal with people she barely knew, and it was especially odd considering this family was one kid and one parent short. All she could do was hope the conversation would remain neutral. Hope that Charlie wouldn't stir the pot for fun. She remembered her father's three golden rules for a conflict-free meal: No politics. No more than two drinks. And no politics.

"So," Charlie broke the silence. "When did you live here?" Reaching across the table, she grabbed a corkscrew.

"Oh, I didn't." Paige shook her head. "This was Thomas's childhood home." She tucked a strand of golden hair behind her ear.

"Right." Charlie twisted the corkscrew into a bottle of red.

"If I'm being honest," said Paige, "I didn't even want to visit." There was more than a hint of shade in the comment. *This was all my husband's dumb idea, don't blame me for it.* She put her hands in her lap, stared down at her food, and didn't touch it. Her boys did the same.

Eve, realizing they were waiting for Thomas, followed their lead. A childhood reflex back from the grave. But Charlie, oblivious, uncaring, or both, started to chow down. "Pretty far off the highway," she said.

"It certainly is," Paige said.

Charlie took a sip of wine. "Where you headed?"

"East."

East? Charlie and Eve shared another brief look. It sounded like an answer an old cowboy might give, gazing out over a sun-dappled horizon.

"Where from?" Charlie inquired.

". . . Portland."

Right then, Eve noticed the faint remnant of a penny-sized tattoo on Paige's neck, just below her left ear. It was a simple black circle, a thin line, but it was blurred, mostly faded. Laser removed, she assumed. Some distant, unthinking part of her mind connected it to the cryptic symbol on the banister. But logic prevailed again, stifling the notion. Circles, after all, weren't exactly a rare shape. Paige glanced up, catching her stare. Eve averted her gaze, pretended she was looking at something else, but—

"I got it in college," said Paige. "Before I met Thomas." She was looking at Eve, but it sounded more like she was talking to her boys, justifying her past.

Charlie tilted her head, not following.

"The tattoo," Paige clarified, pointing at her neck.

Charlie squinted, struggling to make out the faded image. "A circle," she said. "Laser removal?"

Paige nodded.

"Painful?"

Paige nodded again.

Charlie held up her left hand. Turned it to show, on her index knuckle, an inverted black triangle tattoo. "My seventeen-year-old self thought this was a great idea."

Paige smiled tersely, not thrilled to have something in common with Charlie.

Kai, poking at his food, asked, "Why'd you get it?"

Charlie shrugged. "Just wanted a tattoo."

Newton squinted through his round glasses and asked, "Do you regret it?"

Charlie considered the question. "Regret's a part of life," she said.

Kai snorted. "Yeah, I'd regret a choice like that too."

Before Charlie could respond, Paige cut in, "Kai, if you don't have anything nice to say—"

"Yeah, yeah, okay." He waved a dismissive hand.

Paige bristled. "Watch your attitude."

Kai rolled his eyes. "I'm sorry, okay?"

"Don't apologize to me." Paige gestured at Charlie.

He faced her. "I'm sorry if your feelings got hurt."

Charlie glanced at Eve, a vaguely amused "this little shit" smirk on her face. She turned back to Kai. "I'll recover."

Eve, desperate to avoid any more escalation, changed the subject. "So, uh, how did you and Thomas meet?"

Paige opened her mouth to answer when—

Thomas entered the room. Eve was almost startled by his sudden appearance. He stepped up to the table, pulled out a chair, and sat down next to his wife. She looked at him, awaiting the verdict on Jenny.

He shrugged. *No luck. I told you so.*

Paige shut her eyes, held something back.

"Stubborn kid, huh?" Charlie took another sip of wine.

"Didn't get it from me," he joked.

Paige actually sort of smiled at that, but Thomas picked up his fork, plunged it into a piece of chicken, and—

"Thomas." Her smile evaporated.

"Oh, right." He looked at Eve. "Is it okay if we say a quick prayer before dinner?"

"Uh, I," Eve floundered.

"It's your house," he added. "Wouldn't want to impose."

Charlie seemed about to step in when—

"That's okay," Eve relented. Raised in a religious household, she never really had a problem with prayer. However, it had been nearly a decade since she'd said grace before a meal. *A whole decade?* Despite all the years gone by, the remnants of religion had clung to her like a strange aftertaste. Technically, Eve had stopped believing at seventeen years old, but her faith limped on well into her twenties, like staying in an obviously doomed marriage because, hey, maybe things will turn around eventually.

Now, in her early thirties, faith was demoted to passing conversations and bad dreams. All these years later, and she was still having nightmares about Judgment Day. Go figure.

One in particular always came up. She'd find herself standing in line at the gates of heaven. It always looked different—sometimes, just like the paintings, majestic clouds, pearly gates. Other times a hole-in-the-wall pub, downtown streets, neon lights. Either way, Jesus was there, minding the entrance. Usually rocking a tie-dyed T-shirt and cargo pants. When it was Eve's turn to be let in, he'd look at her, confused. "I'm sorry, who are you?"

"Eve, Eve Palmer . . ." she would say.

He'd glance at a list, reply, "Hm, nobody here by that name," then look back up. "Are you sure you're in the right place?" Before she could answer, the ground would always open up, and she would plummet into the depths of hell, her body shredding into endless bloody ribbons until she jolted awake in a cold sweat. No residual trauma here.

Thomas clasped his hands together and closed his eyes. His whole family followed suit. He cleared his throat, let a moment of thoughtful silence pass, and then, "Good food. Good meat. Good God, let's eat." The boys chuckled. Thomas opened his eyes, grabbed his fork, and—

"Thomas," Paige hissed.

"Right," he said. "Amen." He cracked another smile that was not returned. Instead, Paige clasped her hands together and, without saying a word, ordered the two boys to do the same. They obeyed. But Thomas hesitated, his hand still wrapped around his fork, which was stuck in a wedge of chicken. After a tense moment, he relented. Now they all bowed their heads again, eyes closed, hands clasped.

"Heavenly Father," Paige began. "Thank you for watching over us as we travel across your country. Thank you for providing all our needs and leading us into a new life. Thank you to our gracious hosts, who have welcomed us into their home. Thank you for . . ."

. . . As she went on, Eve looked around. The two boys' heads were dutifully bowed, eyes shut, but Thomas, his eyes were open. Open and staring blankly at the meal before him. Between this, the curse words, and the mocking prayer, Eve suspected he might not be religious at all.

Part of her felt sorry for him. She wondered if he'd always been faithless or if he was an ex-Christian. For Eve, losing her faith way back in high school was hard enough. A world-shattering rug pull. She couldn't imagine how hard it would have been to lose it even older. Especially being married to someone like Paige.

"Forever and ever. Amen." Paige opened her eyes, unclasped her hands, and surveyed her surroundings as if waking from a peaceful dream.

"Amen," said the boys.

"Amen," Eve mumbled, another childhood reflex revived. Charlie shot her a sly look, then turned to Thomas. "You want a drink?" She held up the bottle.

His eyes went to Paige, then back to the wine. He shook his head. "We, uh, we don't drink."

"Wise choice," said Charlie, setting the bottle down.

Paige, in silent agreement, took a sip of water, the ice cubes clinking in her glass. She lifted her fork and began to eat, taking dry, puckering bites as if testing the food for poison.

Everyone ate in silence for a few moments, until Charlie said, "So you guys are moving?"

"Mm-hm," said Thomas, mouth full of food. "Minnesota."

"That's a long way," said Charlie.

Thomas nodded. "I was offered a professorship in Duluth."

"Oh?" Charlie said. "I have some family out there. What school?"

"Denman," Thomas said.

"Huh, not familiar." Charlie took another bite. "I'm sure it's a great university, though."

"It's a community college," Paige interjected, a hint of resentment in her voice. "Not a university."

Thomas clicked his tongue and went back to eating.

"What're you teaching?" asked Charlie.

"Photography, composition and darkroom development."

Charlie's eyes brightened a little. "What do you shoot on?"

"Nikon F2. You into photography?"

"I used to dabble."

"Used to?"

Charlie gave a little shrug. "Don't have the time anymore."

"Well, when you did, was it film or digital?"

"Film, always. Digital doesn't hit the same."

Thomas nodded in agreement. "There's just something about knowing it was shot on film," he said. "Wish more people felt that way. I used to run a photo lab back home. Digital pretty much wiped us out and . . ." He trailed off, regret forming in the creases of his face. "Anyway." He tapped his knuckles twice against the table. "Onward, upward." Clearing his throat, he changed the topic. "How do you two like it up here in the boonies?"

Charlie weighed the question. "The quiet is nice, but . . . takes some getting used to."

Thomas nodded again. "It's one of the few things I miss about this place. Meet any of the neighbors yet?"

Charlie shook her head. "Not yet—"

Right then Charlie's phone pinged, a techno jingle of Beethoven's Fifth. She pulled it out and frowned. "You guys got winter tires?"

"Hm?"

She held up the screen; on it was a warning:

✦ ALERT: STORM FORECASTED FOR TONIGHT ✦

✦ WINTER TIRES RECOMMENDED ✦

"We'll be fine," Thomas said.

Charlie tucked her phone away. "There's some tire chains up in the attic."

"We'll be fine," he insisted. "I lived in Maine for five years."

More silence trudged by until, out of nowhere, Paige turned to Eve and said, "Are you married?"

"What, us?"

Paige nodded.

Charlie almost scoffed. "Nope."

Paige nodded again, as if to say, *I expected as much.* "Are you religious?" she asked, still looking at Eve.

"Me?" Eve said. "No, not really. I mean, I used to be."

Paige settled back in her chair. "I only ask because I noticed a Bible in the living room."

"Oh . . . that was a gift from my parents."

It was a leather-bound burgundy King James Bible. Eve's full legal name was inscribed on the spine in gold lettering:

Evelyn Patricia Palmer

She barely remembered unpacking it, let alone placing it in the living room. But she was going to eventually; after all, her parents were coming to visit in a couple of months. They'd long accepted their only child was no longer religious, but hey, at least she kept a Bible around in case of emergencies.

Now, Paige interrogated her much the same way her parents used to: "Do you still go to church?"

Eve looked at Charlie, tempted to seek her help. Normally, Charlie would have jumped in by now, but a few weeks ago, Eve insisted she could fend for herself. She didn't always need a heroine to swoop in and save the day. Charlie held back.

Eve shifted her weight. "No, not anymore."

Paige blinked, disapproving.

"Well," Eve backtracked, "sometimes on Christmas."

Charlie side-eyed her. *Are you seeking approval?*

Smiling tightly, Paige jabbed a fork into a piece of chicken and began cutting at it with a steak knife. "What about them?"

". . . Who?"

"Your parents. Do they still go to church?"

"They do."

"What denomination?"

"Uh, Protestant . . . ?"

Paige's eyes flickered to Charlie, then back to Eve. "And they're aware?"

Eve cleared her throat. "Of what?"

Paige glanced at her sons as if the following words might be too much for their innocent ears. "Aware of you and your partner's"—Paige's mind shuffled, almost audibly, through a wheel of phrases until it landed on—"lifestyle choices."

Eve let out a short laugh that echoed around the room, nervous, brittle. Again, Charlie seemed just about ready to jump in, but still, she held back. Paige remained silent, waiting for an answer. Kai, the "smug bastard," looked rather entertained by it all. Newton just stared straight ahead, silent, disassociating. And Thomas? He looked more uncomfortable than the rest of the room combined, his mouth open, looking like he wanted to say something but couldn't find the words.

Eve turned back to Paige. "My parents know . . ."

"And they accept it?"

Eve was about to respond but—

Charlie, chewing on a mouthful of mashed potatoes, interrupted. "What about yours?" she asked, staring straight at Paige.

Paige looked at her. "Excuse me?"

"Your parents," Charlie said. "They know about your lifestyle choices?"

Paige furrowed her brow. "I don't understand what you're getting at."

Charlie remained silent, reveling in the awkwardness. Unlike Eve, she actually enjoyed this kind of conflict, sometimes even sought it out. Right now, Charlie had her kid gloves on. If Paige kept pressing, things would get ugly.

"Look," Paige relented. "I'm sorry if you misunderstood, but it's not exactly—"

"Paige." Thomas finally intervened. "That's enough."

She looked at him, then stared at Charlie.

Dead silence.

Charlie held her gaze, didn't break eye contact, didn't say a word. There was a spark of fire in Charlie's eyes, a spark that made Eve a little scared. A look that dared Paige to keep on talking. Seconds dragged by like minutes until, at last, Paige looked away and returned to eating, acting like nothing had happened.

Sweet relief washed over Eve. Charlie settled back into her chair, disappointed. She'd wanted a fight, and if Eve hadn't been there, she would've gone at it until Paige started crying.

"I was only curious," Paige added, somewhat talking to herself. "I didn't mean to offend anyone."

"It's . . . okay," said Eve, reflexively switching into caretaker mode. Somehow, she felt responsible for the whole ordeal—her default reaction to most conflict. Even when the event was completely out of her control, even when the other party was blatantly overstepping her bounds, she always found a way to blame herself. Always felt this nagging sense of guilt for everything, as if her very existence was a violation of some stone-etched decree.

Right then, a blistering gust of wind hit the windows. The house lights flickered, and a quick succession of tiny blackouts rippled around the room like dominoes. Outside, a groaning creak preceded a thunderous boom.

"Holy smokes," said Thomas, all too happy to change the topic. "That sounded like a tree." He looked over his shoulder, out the window. "Hopefully the power holds up." He turned back. "Went down all the time when I was a kid." He gave a nervous laugh and looked at Eve. "You guys have a backup generator, right?"

Eve nodded. "Yeah . . ."

Before Thomas could respond, a familiar little voice cut in, "SORRY." Everyone turned to see, standing in the middle of the kitchen, clothes stained with basement dust, Jenny.

Thomas sprang to his feet, hurried over, held her by the shoulders. And barely two seconds into his scolding, she burst into sobbing, kept saying, "Sorry, sorry, sorry—"

Paige spoke over her. "Words without changed behavior mean nothing—"

"Sorry, sorry, sorry—"

"Jenny," she snapped.

Her daughter fell silent, face streaked with tears. She looked up and, one last time, whispered a meek "Sorry."

"Don't ever do that again," Thomas said. "You could have gotten hurt."

Jenny nodded, her head bobbing up and down. Eve caught a glimpse of her hands, red marks on her palms, probably from pulling on the dumbwaiter rope.

"We should get going," Paige said, "before the roads get any worse."

Thomas murmured agreement. "Let's help them clean up first—"

"It's fine," Eve practically blurted out. "We can handle it."

"You're sure?" He looked at Charlie.

"We're good," Charlie affirmed.

Jenny, face still red from crying, chimed in, "I lost my pen."

Everyone looked at her.

"In the basement," she added. "I dropped it somewhere."

Paige sighed. "We are *not* sending down another search party."

Jenny looked like she was about to burst into tears all over again.

Eve jumped in. "Tomorrow, I can take a look around for it. Mail it out to you guys if I find it." At this point, she was just saying whatever she could to get them out the door.

"That— that won't be needed," said Thomas.

Jenny made a loud sniffing sound.

"We'll get you a new one," Thomas added.

Jenny nodded, despondent.

◆

At last, Eve watched as the family huddled back into the foyer, pulling on their winter coats, preparing to leave. But she wouldn't let herself feel any relief until they were all outside, far out of view.

"Thanks again," said Thomas, helping Jenny put her coat on. He looked at Eve and said, "So much for fifteen minutes tops, huh?"

She didn't even fake a smile.

"Okay." He swept his eyes around, doing one last head count, talking to himself. "All your favorites are here. Faust family is ready to go." He opened the door and motioned them outside. As the last of them filed out, he turned back to Eve, gave a little wave, and said, "Have a good one."

"Thanks," Eve replied, giving him her first real smile of the night.

And then, praise the Lord above, the door clicked shut. Eve rushed over, locked it, and braced her back against it. A bit of an overreaction, sure. Regardless, she and Charlie were alone at last. She peered out the blinds and watched the family descend the porch, cross the yard, trudge onto the gravel laneway, and disappear from sight. Halle-fucking-lujah.

But as she lingered by the window, she couldn't shake the sense something was off. The same feeling she used to get during morning commutes—a nagging suspicion that something important had been left behind. Keys? Wallet? Then it hit her. It was what Thomas had said, right before he was about to leave the first time:

"Have you ever noticed anything . . ."

. . . strange? Was that the word he didn't get a chance to say? More than the question itself, his look of suppressed embarrassment stood out. Eve had assumed he was about to tell her a ghost story or something paranormal. The fact he was reluctant, if not ashamed to do so, made it all the more compelling.

Throughout her life, she'd heard many stories about encounters with ghosts and the unexplained. She half believed some, disbelieved most—but before Thomas, there was one thing they all had in common. One thing that made her doubt: the people who told them were always far too eager to share. There was always a twinkle in the would-be storyteller's eye, a visible spark—a look that said, "Well, do I have a tale for you."

Whatever their motivation, they were simply way too keen to have any sort of credibility. Even the ones who started their stories with "I don't believe in ghosts or anything like that, but . . ." Deep down, Eve sensed they all wanted it to be true. Desperately wanted to tell anyone who would listen.

Like this ridiculous story her uncle Benji had told more than a dozen times. And every time he shared it, he had that twinkle in his eye, that spark of excitement as he talked about the "yellow-eyed, humanoid, winged monstrosity." He said he'd been out hiking in the La Sal Mountains of Utah. The sun was setting. Golden light. Long shadows. In the distance, he saw the shape of something, crouched in the branches. "There was a menace to its posture," he would say, "predatory like."

As he stepped closer, his foot snapped a twig and the thing's head swung toward him—yellow eyes wide open. "We both froze," Uncle Benji said, reenacting the scene as he slowly reached toward his coat pocket. "I didn't have my gun on me, so I went for my camera. Figured if I'm gonna die, folks may as well know what got me. And then, just as I pulled it out, the creature shrieked like a Ringwraith, leapt from the trees, swooped over my head, and—WHOOSH—disappeared into the darkness. Vanished. Into thin air. Literally just . . . gone."

At this point in his story, depending on how many beers deep he was, Uncle Benji would sometimes stretch his arms out and imitate the screeching sound. A shrill wail. "It had arms and hands!" he would say, holding up his own as if the audience might not be familiar with the concept.

As a child, and even into her early teens, Eve believed with all her heart that Uncle Benji had seen a demon, Mothman, or something in between. And, in her defense, his story had come with "proof." A blurry photo he'd snapped with his disposable camera. A photo he carried in his wallet, and, at the climax of his story, just before people had a chance to raise their doubts, he would pull it out like an ace in the hole.

To a young Eve, the image was quite frightening. A blurry, four-by-six glossy of something, admittedly humanoid in shape, with blinding yellow eyes, soaring through the trees. Not exactly proof of anything, but when it came to spooky stories, this shred of "evidence" certainly put Uncle Benji above the rest.

But then, he made the mistake of telling the story in front of Charlie Bastion. At the crescendo, right on cue, he pulled out the photo and held it up for all to see. Charlie, barely looking up from her meal, said, "That's a great horned owl."

Uncle Benji, not used to being challenged, flipped the photo back, blinked, and squinted. "I've seen a heckuva lot of owls; that ain't one."

Charlie went on. "You were down in Utah?"

"Uh-huh."

"Yeah, they're pretty common there."

His face grew redder. He turned the photo back to her, thrust his arm across the table. "But its body is long and slender, humanoid."

Charlie narrowed her eyes. "Overexposed," she said. "The camera stretches out moving objects." With a pinky finger, she pointed to the corner of the image. "See there. The trees. Stretched out."

Uncle Benji flipped it over, studied it. His eyes darted back and forth like he was reading an unexpected court summons. "But the—"

"Screeching?" she interrupted. "Owls screech, especially when they feel threatened. They're loud," she went on. "Sounds like bloody murder." She pulled out her phone with one hand and brought up a YouTube video. Sure enough, the owl made a shrill, screeching sound, just like the one Uncle Benji had often imitated.

He deflated. His drunken face filled with a slow realization as he sank back into his chair, peering down at the photo on his lap. He looked like a little kid who'd just learned the truth about old Saint Nick. Eve felt bad for him, but Charlie, as usual, didn't care.

After that dinner, Eve had pulled her aside and, uncharacteristically, called her out. "You didn't have to do that in front of everybody."

Charlie blinked at her, not following. "Do what?"

"Humiliate Uncle Benji," she clarified.

Charlie scoffed. "He did a pretty good job of that himself."

"Charlie . . ."

"Eve. He's a grown man who thinks a blurry photo is proof of demons. I did him a solid."

"Yeah, but . . ."

"But what?"

"Never mind." Eve dropped it.

And that was the last time Uncle Benji shared his story of the yellow-eyed monster.

All that to say, Thomas, unlike Uncle Benji, had not seemed eager to share whatever he was holding back. In Eve's estimation that lent him a certain credibility. Now she'd have to forever wonder what kind of ghost story that guy was stowing away. She reckoned it was a meager sacrifice on the altar of peace and solitude.

But when she rounded the corner, Charlie was standing in the living room, phone in hand, face filled with bad news. Eve's heart sank; she already knew what had happened. Still, Charlie held up the screen:

✦ DUE TO SEVERE WEATHER CONDITIONS ✦
✦ THE KETTLE CREEK BRIDGE HAS BEEN CLOSED ✦

Mo yawned again. *Called it.*

DOC_B07_PROCEDURE

Description: From Wikipedia entry on laser tattoo removal.

◆

Laser tattoo removal is a painful process that often takes one
to two years, and even then, the results are not guaranteed.
Multiple sessions, commonly spaced eight to ten weeks apart,
are always required. Even after years of treatment, a faint
imprint is often visible, and some scarring remains.

–   . . . .   .

REFUGE

Charlie told the family they'd be sleeping in the upstairs study, using sofa cushions for bedding. Really, she was just telling them to *leave us the fuck alone*. Thomas took the hint. "We'll stay out of your way," he said, his face filled with *I am so sorry about this*. At the very least, they were all grateful, apologetic. Even Kai.

Eve supposed she could handle one night of strangers under the roof. Besides, the weather was set to clear by sunrise. Still, she deserved some kind of medal, or maybe a story in the local paper: "Heroic Pagans Shelter Religious Fanatics from Winter Storm." Either way, this family would be gone first thing in the morning—

You sure about that?

Eve slapped an imaginary piece of duct tape onto Mo's mouth, shoved him into a closet, and barricaded the door.

◆

With the family retired upstairs, Eve and Charlie were, once again, "alone" at last. They shared a blanket on the living room couch, Shylo curled up at their feet. Fireplace warmth filled the room, keeping the cold at bay, warding off shadows. Its soft crackling peppered the silence, hypnotic, soothing.

Charlie had leaned forward to grab a bottle of wine off the coffee table when her eyes caught the hammer and bent nails from before. She looked at Eve.

"I took out the nails," Eve explained.

"From above the fireplace?"

"Yeah."

"What?" Charlie leaned back. "That's where I was going to hang our crucifix."

Eve smiled. "Stop."

"So . . ." Charlie twisted a corkscrew into the bottle. "Whatdya think of our new roomies?"

"Uh." Eve hesitated. "I— something feels off."

"No shit." Charlie popped the cork. "Paige is a real saint."

Eve shook her head. "No, well . . . yes, but there's something else." She fell silent, her mind again running through all the strange events. The ill-timed storm. The trail of ants. The way Thomas had stood in the cellar. The . . . weird vibes?

"Something else?" Charlie nudged.

Eve sighed, reluctant to say more, but: "I, I just feel like something's wrong."

"I need specifics."

"Okay, fine," Eve relented. "When you were gone Thomas and I went down to the basement to search for Jenny. We split up, looked around a little. Eventually, I rounded this corner and came across him just . . . standing there, blocking the only way out. Back turned. I tried calling his name like three times until he finally snapped out of it. He blamed it on bad hearing but . . ."

Charlie blinked at her, waiting for more. But that was it. She cleared her throat. "He was standing with his back turned, and he didn't hear you?"

"I know, I know, but . . . it was the way he was standing. Like, arms straight to his sides, flashlight pointed at the ground. As if . . ." Eve paused. "As if he was frozen solid." She tensed up her body to show.

"Uh-huh," said Charlie. There was more than a hint of skepticism in her tone. Skepticism that Eve had to admit was warranted. After all, when it came to blowing things out of proportion, Eve had a long and storied track record.

Like the "Redwoods Incident": This time when, during a camping trip, she'd been absolutely convinced a murderous bear was lurking outside their tent. In a panic, she'd shaken awake a half-drunk, sleep-deprived Charlie and urged her to investigate. Turned out the "bear" was just two bushes swaying in a breeze. An optical illusion. And that was only one example of many. In short, Eve was the type to blame a bump in the night on the Zodiac Killer. Vigilant to a fault.

Still, Eve crossed her arms, not finished yet. "Also, just before they were about to leave the first time, Thomas, he started asking me if we'd ever *seen* anything. Then he got interrupted . . ."

Palpably underwhelmed, Charlie filled her wine glass. "And . . . you think he had a ghost story?"

"I don't know, maybe. He just, whatever it was, it didn't seem like he wanted to tell me. Like he was embarrassed."

"So . . . he looked embarrassed to tell you a ghost story?"

Eve threw up her hands. "I know it sounds stupid out loud, but . . ." She trailed off, grumpy.

"Hey." Charlie set a hand on her shoulder. "It's okay."

"What do you think?" Eve asked.

"About the family?"

"Yeah."

Charlie took a small sip of wine and handed it to Eve—then she grabbed herself a beer off the table, cracked it open. "I mean, Paige aside, they seem pretty unremarkable. Or at the very least, I doubt they're gonna murder us in our sleep."

Eve didn't laugh. She was too busy thinking, searching for an answer to a question she didn't know. She stared into the fire, as if the solution might be hidden in the embers, conjured up in red, flickering letters. But of course, there was only fire, smoke, and ash. "I just, I never should have invited them in," she thought aloud.

Charlie scoffed. "You think they're vampires?"

"No." Eve paused, tilting her head. "Maybe . . . ?"

Charlie smirked and took a swig of beer.

"Would've been a quick night if I answered the door . . ."

"Hello miss." Eve pretended to be Thomas. *"Can we come in?"*

"Nope."

"Roll credits." Eve snorted.

Just then, a shiny glint caught her eye—an oval locket, connected to a thin brass chain around Charlie's neck. How hadn't she noticed it before?

"What's that?" asked Eve.

"It's a necklace."

"Ha."

Charlie held it up and flicked it open. Inside was a photograph. A blurry picture of Eve, hiding her face behind one hand, shooing away the camera with the other. Eve remembered the exact moment it had been taken. When they first started dating, Eve had been notoriously camera-shy. Still was. Charlie often joked that there were "less than zero photos" of her in existence. And, believe it or not, it was almost true. Aside from driver's licenses and the blurry backgrounds of parties and family get-togethers, Eve had somehow managed to avoid most cameras since her early twenties.

But one day, about six months into their relationship, they went for a hike up Bawlry Mountain. At the top, Charlie, wielding a 35mm Pentax, snuck up from behind. But Eve, seeing her at the last second, turned away, holding up a hand and hiding her face. Close call.

Charlie clicked the locket shut. "The only known photo of Eve Palmer . . ."

"When did you get it?"

"Today, in town." She shrugged. "Kinda cheesy, huh?"

"No, I think it's sweet," said Eve. Charlie was never the sentimental type, but Eve was always a big sap, so the surprise, cheesy or not, was a welcome one. Their eyes locked for a long moment. Charlie set a hand on the side of Eve's face, leaned in closer, and then—

Shylo whimpered. The dog stood at the far end of the room, tail straight, nose pointed toward the foyer.

"Shylo?"

The dog let out a low growl, punctuated by another short whine. She slunk away and cowered behind the couch. From the foyer, a gentle knock echoed. *Is somebody at the door?*

Charlie got up and marched over, Eve in tow. They rounded the corner. The front door was wide open, swaying in the breeze, bumping against the wall. Rhythmic. *Knock, knock, knock . . .* Snow was drifting in, collecting on the hardwood, an oblong square. In a huff, Charlie went over and started to shut the door before stopping halfway. She narrowed her eyes, peering out into the wintry black. "The hell?" She motioned Eve over.

Kneeling in the middle of the yard, obscured by shadow, Thomas. Hunched over, shaking. Charlie called out, "Thomas?" But her voice was drowned by the wind. She stepped onto the porch. A motion light snapped on, casting a harsh wedge of fluorescent glow across the yard—over Thomas. He was dressed in nightclothes, a baggy shirt and sweatpants. Snow clung to his hair, pooled on his shoulders, his skin. *How long has he been out here?*

"Thomas?!" Charlie tried once more.

Again, he didn't respond, didn't even look at them. *Is he even awake?*

Wasting no more time, Charlie pulled on her winter boots and jacket and stomped out toward him. Eve followed suit. As they approached, she could see his face was red, streaked with tears. His hands were clenched over his mouth, as if trying to keep unspeakable horrors from writhing out. And his eyes, bloodshot, wide, were filled with terror. The kind of dread that spread like fire. Contagion. He began to whimper, the words slipping between his fingers, frantic: "No, I'm sorry, I'm so sorry. I didn't mean to, I—"

His voice was childlike, high-pitched with fear—

"I didn't know, I didn't mean to—"

"THOMAS," Charlie bellowed.

His head swung toward them. His hands fell to his sides, dangling like the limbs of a marionette. Then, in an instant, he snapped out of it. His terrified expression transformed to bewildered confusion. "Wh-where am—how did I?" He looked around, breath short. "Where's my—"

"Thomas, you were sleepwalking," said Charlie, assuming the most rational explanation.

He blinked at her, still catching his breath, still disoriented. "Where—"

"Let's get you out of the cold—"

"Where's Alison?" he said, half to himself. "She was just . . ." He looked back, out toward the dark trees, and fell silent. His breathing began to quicken. It looked like he was about to have a panic attack. That, or he was already in the middle of one. Charlie moved over and gently grabbed his shoulders, looked him in the eyes. "Just breathe in," she said. "Breathe out, okay? You're okay. You were only sleepwalking. Just a nightmare. Breathe in."

He drew in a deep breath.

"Breathe out."

He exhaled.

"Breathe in," Charlie repeated. "Breathe out." She'd done the same thing with Eve many times, pulling her back from the brink of countless panic attacks.

After a few more breaths, Thomas calmed. "I— I'm sorry." He glanced around, a vague sense of relief filling his eyes: his family hadn't witnessed the scene. He looked up at Charlie. "I'm so sorry."

"It's okay. You're good." She helped him to his feet and threw her jacket over his shoulders. "Let's get you inside." As Charlie led him to the house, Eve stayed behind. Her eyes scanned the trees, the columns of dark between the snow-stained trunks. It was a sight that made her feel watched. Made her feel like something might be waiting out there. Something worse than death.

"Eve?" Charlie called out.

Eve looked over her shoulder.

Thomas and Charlie were shuffling onto the porch, outlined by the glare of the motion light. Charlie tilted her head. "You coming?"

DOC_A21_SLEEP

Description: Excerpt from *Parasomnia & the Collective Unconscious*, an unpublished manuscript by Tanya F. Bauer.

◆

Sleep Paralysis:

Often confused with night terrors, this is a phenomenon that generally occurs at the REM sleep stage. During an episode, a subject feels fully awake but is unable to speak or move. Under normal circumstances, our brains temporarily disconnect motor neurons during REM sleep to prevent us from physically acting out our dreams. In sleep paralysis, however, this disconnection continues even when a person is fully conscious, resulting in an inability to move. It is often accompanied by vivid and disturbing hallucinations, leading to a sense of dread, imminent death, and/or a malignant presence in the room.

NOTE: There are themes in these hallucinations that have persisted across history, culture, and language. Imagery dates back thousands of years. Most common: shadowy figures, black cats, and a man in a wide-brimmed hat.

And the bizarreness of these hallucinations cannot be under-
stated. One subject reported waking every night to see a cardboard
cutout of her deceased father standing in the corner of her room.
An old woman would be hunched behind the cutout, hiding, stifling
laughter. Each time the patient took a breath, the old woman moved
the cardboard cutout a little closer. This would continue until the
old woman stood right at the patient's bedside, at which point the
patient would wake, screaming.

Upon further testing, this patient showed mild signs of hypoxic
brain damage from lack of oxygen. More tests revealed she was suffering from severe sleep apnea (repeated interruptions of breathing
during sleep). Once the patient was treated for sleep apnea, the
sleep paralysis episodes became less frequent.

. . .   - . - .   . -   . - .

OLD HOUSE

Back inside, Thomas was slumped in the armchair by the fire, a blanket draped over his shoulders. He was still getting his bearings. Warming from the cold. His gaze swept the walls, landed in the far corner, and held there. Memories clouded his eyes—melancholic, bittersweet. He looked at Eve and Charlie. They were sitting on the couch across from him, concerned. His eyes dropped to the beer in Charlie's hand.

"You want one?" she asked, reading his mind.

"That . . ." He hesitated. "That would be great."

Charlie pushed herself off the couch and headed for the kitchen. As she slipped out of view, Thomas turned to Eve. He looked embarrassed—ashamed, even. "Sorry I frightened you back there," he said.

"No." Eve shook her head. "It's okay, I was just—worried." An understatement, but it seemed to make him feel better.

He rubbed his jaw with the back of his hand. "Haven't done that since I was a kid . . ."

"Sleepwalking?"

He nodded. "Used to have night terrors too." He settled back into his chair, the glow of the fire spilling out over his face. "Parents told me it was caused by demons, so that didn't really help either."

Charlie strode back in and handed him an open beer.

"Thank you." He smiled. "Might help me sleep." He took a swig.

Sitting next to Eve, Charlie said, "Caused by demons?" She'd only caught the tail end of the conversation.

"Night terrors," he said. "Sleepwalking. My parents said it was Satan, trying to drag me down into the fires of hell." He chuckled bitterly.

Charlie frowned. "Jesus . . ."

"That's right," said Thomas. "They told me if I 'called on the name of the Lord,' the 'devil' would flee."

"Did you?"

Thomas said, "Call on the Lord's name?"

Charlie nodded.

"Every single time."

"Did it work?" Charlie asked, already knowing the answer.

Thomas's eyes flicked to hers, fire reflected in the corners. "Once or twice." He looked away, scratched his nose. "Funny thing is, in high school, when I finally learned what actually caused my sleep disorders, misfiring neurons . . . It all just . . ." He did a flourishing gesture, like a magician making a coin disappear. "It all just went away." He tilted his bottle toward the foyer. "Like I said, that was the first episode I've had in decades. Familiar environment triggering old habits, I guess."

Charlie nodded in silent agreement. Occam's razor. He'd taken the explanation right out of her head.

More silence filled the room, another of those soundless nothings in which no one knew what to say. Thomas stared down at the floor and took a sip of beer. "Sleepwalking in the snow," he mused, half to himself. "When I was a kid"—he pointed up—"they found me on the roof once, swinging a broom around. Still don't know how I got up there, but thank God they found me before . . . you know." He drank some more. "Maybe I used the broom to fly up there."

Eve laughed politely.

Thomas fidgeted, twisted his wedding band. "Oh and, I'd, uh, I'd appreciate it if you didn't tell my family about any of that, out there." He looked toward the foyer. "I don't want to worry them . . ."

"Of course," Charlie said.

Thomas turned from the fire. "Anyway," he said. "I'll see myself back to bed." After a few more glugs of beer, he got up, started to leave, and—

"Wait," said Eve, almost blurting it out. Both Thomas and Charlie looked at her, puzzled.

Eve went on, morbid curiosity taking the wheel. "Earlier, you asked me if I ever noticed anything . . ."

"Oh." He nodded. "If you'd ever noticed anything weird around the house? It's nothing." He waved a hand, his face flushed. "It's nothing." He started to leave again, but—

"Wait," Charlie said. "Now I'm curious."

With a sigh, he turned back. "It's just—odd things happened here when I was a kid, that's all."

"What kind of things?" Despite her skepticism, Charlie was actually a fan of paranormal stories. Not because she believed in them. No, it was because of what they said about the storyteller. They "revealed truths about human nature and misperception."

Thomas shrugged. "I mean . . . I don't think it's haunted." He hesitated. Again, Eve felt his reluctance. She was about to tell him it was okay, he didn't have to share, but then he said, "Have you?"

"Have we what?" Charlie asked.

"Noticed anything strange about the place? I mean, aside from the usual quirks . . ."

Eve and Charlie shared a look. "No," Charlie answered.

Disappointment flashed across Thomas's face. As if their common experience might've validated whatever the hell he had been through. Of course, even before tonight, Eve did have moments here, fleeting sensations of impending doom, being watched, followed. But that was par for the course wherever she went. "Normal" anxiety stuff.

Thomas glanced over his shoulder, once again confirming they were alone. He trudged back and sat down.

After a long silence, he began. "I was around eight years old when this happened. We'd been living here for the better half of a decade, no incidents. Not even a bump in the night. But . . . we had this coatrack in the foyer, painted white. One of those old Victorian ones with the hooked arms." He held up his hands, making a crooked U shape to show. "One day, my sister, Alison, about fourteen at the time, started asking where it came from, she'd never seen it before. We told her it had always been there, and she agreed, but she was certain it had been a light gray, not white. When everyone—me, our parents—assured her it was always white, she let it go. The whole little incident was written off as a case of the gets."

"The gets?" Charlie inquired.

"Forgetfulness," he clarified. "Misidentification. After all, light gray and white are quite similar. We even laughed about it later that day, but . . ." He tapped a finger on the armrest, a twitchy, off-kilter movement. "The next morning, Alison claimed a painting had appeared on her wall. At first, she was just annoyed. She'd assumed one of us had put it there while she slept. A bad joke. But no one took credit. Like the coatrack, this painting had always been there. Hell, our own mother had painted it years before."

He rubbed a thumb into the back of his hand, leaving behind white marks that filled with red as the blood returned. "With alarming speed," he went on, "things got worse, much worse. She insisted the wallpaper was changing, the floors, furniture—even the layout of the house. Old rooms vanished; new ones appeared. And all the while, she was the only one who could see it." He paused. "Of course, our parents should have taken her to a psychiatrist, a doctor, gotten her real help . . ." Thomas inhaled, let out another sigh. "Alison believed something in the house, or the house itself, was toying with her. Altering her reality, bit by bit. And our parents, they did nothing to dissuade her of that belief. In fact, they all but encouraged it. Said it was the work of the devil. After all, if Lucifer was responsible for my sleep disorders, why not this?"

He set his jaw. "Just like with me, they told her to pray, to invoke Jesus's name. When that didn't work, they accused her of doubting the Lord, allowing the devil into our home. In their eyes, it was her fault. Then, they caught her carving those symbols, like the one from under the banister."

Charlie raised an eyebrow. Thomas, remembering she hadn't been there earlier, added, "You'll find them around the house." With his index finger, he drew an invisible circle in the air, then added the intersecting lines. "Furious, my father asked her what they were, why she was carving them, but she wouldn't answer. She literally wouldn't say a word about it. So, he assumed it was paganism, or something worse, and they punished her. Wouldn't let her leave the house, not even for church, and that's when . . ." He trailed off yet again, gravely silent. "Her core memories began to change. People she'd known all her life became strangers, and strangers became . . . familiar."

Familiar.

The word plunged into the depths of Eve's mind, breached the gray matter and, like a parasitic worm, burrowed a home there.

Thomas shifted his weight, uncomfortable. "Almost overnight," he said, "Alison believed that our parents had been altered. According to her, even their names, their personalities, their pasts were different. Eventually, she thought everyone around her was an imposter, that the real versions of us had somehow been replaced. So . . . she tested us, asked us questions about the past, desperate to know if we were actually *her* family or, well, you get the idea. She begged us to believe her, to save her, but— I . . ." He cleared his throat.

"Sometimes I feel responsible for what happened. I know I was only eight. I just, I feel like I could've done more—could've gotten her real help . . ." He rubbed his forehead with the back of his thumb. "I— I guess I thought coming here might bring me some sort of closure, but . . ." He tugged at his sleeve and turned to the fire. Its pallid glow cast black shadows across his solemn features. "And . . . if I'm being honest, every now and then, over the years, I've wondered if there *was* something else going on. If maybe Alison was right. Maybe something truly incomprehensible happened here . . ." He looked around. "But coming back . . . It's just an old house." He looked to Charlie and Eve, his eyes apologizing for the dark story.

They remained quiet, half expecting him to say something more, but that was it—loose ends and all. Eve and Charlie glanced at each other, now feeling more than a little guilty for nudging him to share. But, in their defense, they hadn't expected a story about a tragic descent into madness. Still, Eve fought back the urge to interrogate further; she wanted to know more. Know what happened, where his sister ended up.

Charlie said, "It wasn't your fault. You were just a kid."

Thomas nodded, appreciating the words but not accepting them. His eyes wandered to the empty spot above the fireplace mantel. He stared at the blank wall for a somber moment, then looked away. His face twitched, a barely perceptible movement beneath his right eye. "Anyway, I should get some sleep." He pushed himself to stand. "Thank you both, for . . . calming me down. Letting me vent."

". . . Of course," said Charlie.

Grateful, he drifted out of the room, into the foyer, and back upstairs. Charlie waited until his footsteps receded into quiet.

"Jesus Christ," she said.

A growing knot was forming in Eve's chest. "Why would he come back here?" she mused aloud.

Charlie shrugged. "People cope in different ways."

"I guess." After another short silence: "What do you think happened with his sister?"

"Definitely some kind of psychosis," Charlie said. Of course, the possibility of anything supernatural hadn't even broached her stratosphere. Not even for a second.

"Where do you think she ended up?" Eve asked.

"With parents like that? Nowhere good."

Eve settled back into her seat, her eyes fixed on the fire once more. Charlie stretched out her arms and rose to stand. "Anyway, we should pack it in too."

Eve, still lost in rumination, nodded.

When they retired upstairs, Shylo was already waiting for them, curled up on the foot of the bed. Both Charlie and the dog dozed off within minutes. But Eve, with Thomas's story running through her mind, couldn't sleep. All the strangeness of the night was still rattling around in her head. Everything replaying over and over. But slowly, despite her racing thoughts, Eve's eyes began to close, everything fading into murk until, finally, she fell into a much-needed slumber.

RUN

You have to hide . . .

She scrambles through the dark. Pushing through branches, weaving around trees. Behind her, voices call out, shouting, searching. They speak words she recognizes but doesn't understand. Sweeps of light cut through the woods, frantic. If they find her, they will drag her back to some terrible labyrinth. She trips, tumbling through dirt, branches, thorns. She crashes into a stony basin and clambers to her feet. Keep moving. Keep running. They are almost upon her, light throwing shadows, contorted, flickering. She picks up speed, breaks into a clearing, and lurches to a stop at the edge of a cliff. Hundreds of feet below, shallow water, jagged rocks. She looks back. The pursuers are near, fighting through the thicket. There is nowhere else to go.

She jumps.

The ground rushes up, eager to meet her. In one quick and terrible snap—everything turns to nothing.

A pitch-black void.

Once they're in, they never leave . . .

The phrase repeats in her head, flitting with the singsong rhythm of a deranged limerick.

Once they're in, they never leave . . .

A pale blue light forms in the distance.

Once they're in, they never—

SHUT-EYE

It was still dark out when Eve jolted awake, heart pounding. She'd been having a nightmare, but of what, she couldn't remember. Only the vague aftertaste of dread remained. She sat up and looked around. Both Charlie and Shylo were still asleep. She slid her feet off the bed and rubbed her temples. Her head throbbed—low, aching pulses like a distant war drum. Was she hungover? From two glasses of wine?

Either way, she needed water.

Out in the hallway, the door to the study was ajar. As Eve passed, she glanced inside. The family was sleeping, scattered across cushions and foam mattresses. Moonlight spilled in through the stained glass window, lending their skin a pallid hue of green and red. She descended the stairs.

Down in the kitchen, Eve stood over the sink, sipping tap water from a dirty wine glass. The strangeness of last night was fading, and so was the storm outside. By sunrise, this family would be gone. The whole ordeal would become nothing more than a weird campfire story: the family with the sleep-walking father and the hide-and-seek daughter.

Ready to return upstairs, Eve set down the glass, glided into the living room and . . . the basement door was cracked open. The rather innocuous sight triggered a flood of questions: Wasn't it closed before? Had Jenny snuck back down there to look for her pen? To hide? Please, God, not again . . .

In a huff, Eve marched over and threw open the door. She gazed into the uninviting dark. A dim wedge of moonlight stretched downward, the blurry shadow of a swaying tree layered over the coarse brick. She called out, "Jenny . . . ?" Her voice tumbled down. No response. She was about to call out again when she remembered the two-part pattern. The one Thomas had used before. It was a long shot, but . . . she reached up and rapped her knuckles against the frame.

Duh—duh-duh-duh—duh

Lingering silence followed. No answer. With a shrug, she turned away and had slipped into the foyer when, behind her, around the corner, down at the bottom of the basement stairs, two hollow knocks echoed. Knuckles against dry wood.

Jenny.

Eve bolted back and slid around the corner. Almost falling, she caught her balance on the doorframe and peered down. "Jenny?" Squinting, she forced her eyes to adjust, but the shadows were stubborn. She was about to leave, go get a flashlight, when . . . at the bottom of the stairs, a small silhouette. Motionless. Child-sized. Shrouded by the shifting darkness. Jenny.

Eve crouched, making herself smaller. The same way one did when trying to coax the attention of an unfamiliar cat. "Hey, Jenny," she said, almost whispering. "Do you think now would be a good time to come back upstairs?"

Jenny remained silent, unmoving.

Eve cleared her throat, changed strategy. "If you come back up, I bet your dad will tell you more secrets about the house . . ."

Jenny's head tilted, but otherwise, she remained motionless. Now, all Eve could see was the slightest glint of moonlight in the child's eyes—two white flecks in a distant sea of black. There was something off about her stare. Almost like Jenny was trying to tell Eve something without saying a word. A long silence dragged by as Eve's eyes slowly adjusted and . . .

Jenny wasn't blinking. Ten, maybe twenty seconds had passed, and she hadn't blinked. Not once.

Suddenly, as if in reaction to Eve's realization, the figure rose up to standing. It wasn't child-sized after all—it had only been hunched down. It rose to its full height—over six feet tall. Slender. Gaunt.

Eve, in one quick motion, jumped to her feet and slammed the door shut. She scrambled upstairs in a cold sweat.

As she raced down the hall, she glanced into the study. The whole family was still there. Still asleep.

She burst into the main bedroom and shook Charlie awake.

"W-what?" Charlie mumbled.

"There's someone in the basement."

Charlie blinked. "The kid?"

"No, an adult."

Charlie rubbed her eyes and pushed up to sit. "One of the parents?"

"No . . ."

"In the basement?"

Eve nodded. "On the stairs."

Charlie frowned. *Is this another mistaking a bush for a black bear incident?* she seemed to be thinking. "Was it dark . . . ?"

"Yeah."

"And you're sure it wasn't a trick of the light?"

Eve scoffed. "I know what I saw . . ."

"Okay . . ." Charlie said, still unsure. Even Shylo looked skeptical, curled up at the foot of the bed, one eyebrow raised. "I'm spent," said Charlie, "and still a little drunk. Can we figure this out when the sun's up?"

"Charlie, there's a stranger in the basement."

"I know. I believe you, but not enough to look around half-drunk in the pitch dark. Let's do it in the *morning* morning. That's only like"—Charlie looked at an alarm clock: 3:27 a.m.—"a few hours away."

"I— Charlie, I'm serious, there was—"

"Eve. I'll look when the sun is up, okay?"

Eve took a deep breath and let it out. Despite herself, she relented. "Okay . . ." Maybe Charlie was right? In her mind, Eve replayed the image of that figure rising to its feet. The brick walls, the shifting tree branch shadows. Now, she was less certain of what she'd actually seen, and . . . no. There was no way that was a trick of the light.

She opened her mouth, ready to try one more time, but her partner had already fallen back asleep. Charlie had this uncanny ability to doze off in seconds. Didn't matter the time or the circumstance. Earthshaking construction next door? No sweat. Plane full of crying babies? Who cared. Girlfriend freaking out about a shadow person on the basement stairs? Good fucking night.

Eve looked over her shoulder and peered into the hallway. She listened. Listened for the click of the basement door, the creak of floorboard footsteps. Anything. But there was only silence. Eve huffed, marched across the room, pushed the door shut, and locked it. Just in case.

She sat up in bed after that, arms crossed, eyes glued to the door, vigilant. Whatever she'd seen, it hadn't been a trick of the light. This wasn't another Redwoods Incident.

Right?

As the minutes crawled by, her eyelids started to grow heavy . . .

DOC_C04_FIRE1

Description: Blurb from *Rhode Island Daily Paper*, date unknown.

◆

There was a fire at the Kent County Memorial Hospital around
9:00 a.m. today. Its origin has been traced to a shattered gas
lantern found in the basement. The building was safely evac-
uated and no lives were lost. At this time, police and fire
have provided no further details.

DOC_C05_FIRE2

Description: Radio broadcast transcript from KCVN 90.5, date unknown.

◆

Good morning, folks. Authorities are still investigating the cause
of a fire at Yale City Town Hall early this morning. As of now,
foul play is not suspected, but the fire chief tells us he's un-
willing to rule anything out. We'll be sure to keep you posted as
more info comes in. For this and everything else, keep your dials
tuned to KCVN!

.... .‾ ...

WAKE

A thin ray of sunlight crept up the walls, across the bed, and beamed into Eve's left eye. Turning away, she reached for Charlie, only for her arms to wrap around empty space. Charlie was gone, her side of the bed cold. Shylo, however, was still curled up at the foot of the mattress. Asleep. The dog whimpered, her legs twitching. A nightmare? Eve leaned forward and scratched her behind the ears. Her whining stopped, but she did not wake.

Reclining back against the headboard, Eve crossed her arms. The storm had now subsided to a whispering breeze. Ebbing swells. Aside from that, it was quiet. Had the family left already? She could only hope.

With a languid stretch, she yawned and climbed out of bed. A sense of tenuous calm fell over her. Once more, all the strange events of the day before seemed distant, like foggy remnants of a nightmare. The figure on the stairs? Perhaps it was nothing more than a play of shadows or even a sleep-deprived fever dream . . .

It was the devil, Mo whispered.

Whatever it was, Eve shoved it down into a container of repressed anxieties. A mental cabinet that stowed away all her worst paranoias. Though it was more like an overstuffed bunker these days—an underground safe with a steel-bolted hatch, bulging at the seams with cartoonish exaggeration. Sometimes the rivets would burst and every single one of her deepest, darkest fears would spew out and rain down all over her psyche. Then Eve would have to go around and clean up the shrapnel bit by bit, stuff it all back inside, screw down the hatch and pray to God she didn't leave anything behind. Inhale. Exhale.

Still dressed in sweatpants and a baggy T-shirt, Eve meandered into the hallway. The smell of eggs, bacon, and coffee wafted up from below—Charlie's favorite breakfast. Eve smiled.

Downstairs, she shuffled into the kitchen and, in an instant, her smile vanished. Paige and Jenny were at the table. Paige was reading aloud from the red leather Bible while her daughter listened, or pretended to. The two boys, Kai and Newton, were nowhere to be seen. Thomas and, more importantly, Charlie were also absent.

"Morning, Eve."

She leaned to see Thomas standing at the stove, cracking eggs into a cast-iron pan. "How do you like your eggs?" he asked.

"Where's Charlie?"

"She, uh . . ." He adjusted the burner heat, jostled the pan. "She just left for town, said something about—"

"Mom." Newton poked his head around the corner, his round glasses making his big eyes look even bigger. "Kai's opening a box."

Paige blinked at him. "A box?"

"I dunno." His eyes flicked to Eve, then back to his mom. "Like a moving box? I told him we don't touch things that we don't, uh, that don't belong to us, and he told me to . . . *f-word* off."

Paige, partly annoyed, partly embarrassed, looked at Eve. "I'll take care of it." She said this with a conviction that left no doubt she would. Careful, she set down the Bible and strode out of the room, telling Newton to keep an eye on his sister.

Eve, stress levels rising, turned back to Thomas. He was humming an off-tune rendition of Black Sabbath's "Iron Man" riff, oblivious to Eve's growing irritation. She cleared her throat. "Who said you could use our kitchen?"

"Oh." He suddenly looked embarrassed. "Sorry, I should've told you: Charlie was kind enough to offer it. I hope it's not a problem; it's just a bit of a trek to the nearest diner and—"

"Why did she leave?"

"Charlie?" He flipped an egg. "She said she had an urgent meeting? Thought she would've let you know . . ."

Eve furrowed her brow. It wasn't like Charlie to leave without checking in first. Especially considering the odd family being here.

"Oh, right." Thomas pointed at her with the spatula. "And she told me to tell you the basement is all clear. Not sure what she meant . . ."

Eve figured it was a reference to the lurker on the stairs, but again, why hadn't Charlie just told her that in person?

Thomas, finally sensing Eve's concern, said, "Are you all right?"

Eve didn't reply. She was too distracted by the fact that Charlie had just up and left. The fact this family had made themselves right at home. On top of that, all the strange occurrences from the day before were bubbling back up like a bad lunch. A knot formed in her chest. Her breath shortened. She checked the time: a quarter past nine. Jenny had been found, the storm had settled, the bridge was open, this family should be long gone.

"Eve?" Thomas prodded. "Is everything—"

"Why are you still here?"

Thomas opened his mouth, but nothing came out. He was caught off guard by the question, offended even. As if he'd assumed they were besties by now. He scratched his nose. "We— We're leaving right after breakfast. Is something wrong?"

Grumbling to herself, Eve retreated into the foyer. Despite having no evidence of outright malice, she didn't trust this family, not one bit. And again, why had Charlie left without saying a word? Eve had to call her, make sure everything was all right. When she reached into her pocket, her fingers grasped air, lint. No phone. She racked her brain, trying to remember the last time she'd used it. The night before. Broken screen. Foyer staircase . . . She looked around. It wasn't there. Must've left it in the bedroom.

Back upstairs, she checked every nook and cranny, the dressers, beneath the bed, even under the mattress. Nada. She stomped downstairs. In the living room, she searched around the coffee table, under the couch, between the cushions, but still, nothing.

"Lose something?" Thomas called out from the kitchen. The whole family was sitting around the table now, eating.

Eve stood up. "I need to borrow a phone."

Thomas shook his head. "We, uh, we don't have phones."

She blinked at him, unbelieving.

He went on. "Modern-day family, no phones, in the middle of a cross-country move." He shook his head, as if surprised by it himself. "I know how absurd it sounds. Believe me."

"Uh-huh . . ." Eve said, more than a little skeptical.

He elaborated. "We just started a digital fast, through our church. The whole congregation handed in their phones to the pastor. At the end of the month, he FedExes them back. No cell phones, no screens, not until then." His eyes flicked to Paige: *It was her idea.*

"Right," said Eve, still not buying it. "What if there's an emergency?"

"That is an excellent question." Again, Thomas glanced at his wife, deflecting the blame to her. "In that case," he said, "we're allowed to borrow a phone, but—"

Paige interrupted. "If there's an emergency, then it's part of God's plan."

"Of course," said Eve. "The power of prayer." She was feeling a little more snarky than usual. Maybe it was the lack of sleep. Maybe it was the fact this family had used up the last of her favorite coffee beans. Probably both.

Paige started to say something more, but Eve marched off, ready to continue the search. Perhaps her phone was in the cellar? What if it slipped out of her pocket? With newfound resolve, she swung open the basement door, and . . .

The dark stairwell greeted her, marred by uninviting shadows. An instant flashback of the figure on the stairs played in her mind. She slammed the door shut. Fuck that. Back in the foyer, she slid open the coat closet. Charlie's winter jacket was gone, as were her boots. Eve peered out the window. Charlie's parking spot, the alcove at the edge of the woods, was empty. No truck in sight. So far, everything matched Thomas's version of events, but—

She's probably locked up in the basement. Mo stirred awake. Eve could almost see his crazy eyes, snapping open, like a vampire in a coffin, bloodthirsty at the chance to raise paranoia. *You'll be next.*

Imaginary Charlie, the voice of reason, countered, *Or maybe—just maybe—I actually had to go into town for something urgent and didn't want to wake you?*

Eve supposed Charlie's counter was more likely, but . . .

She wandered back into the living room. The family, unaware of her presence, was still eating, laughing about something Jenny had just said. The scene was oddly normal—wholesome, even. Had she let anxiety get the better of her again? She took a deep breath, let it out, and told herself everything was fine. *Everything is okay.* She grounded herself. *White door. Brown floorboards. Leather couch.* Her heart rate slowed. Breathing tapered. She calmed. But then, something caught the outskirts of her vision. She turned. Across the living room, above the fireplace, hanging from a crooked nail: Charlie's locket.

For a second, Eve didn't trust her own perception. She narrowed her eyes and drifted closer, as if drawn by some unseen force. Sure enough, it was Charlie's locket, hanging limply from one of the nails Eve had removed last night. Somehow, there was a sinister mockery in the sight. A marker that something terrible might have happened to Charlie, and this was the only thing left of her . . .

Wary, she reached up for its brass chain, only to pull back at the last second, as if it might transmit a deadly shock. Shaking off the incoherent thought, she lifted the necklace and stepped back. She turned it over in her palm, studying it. She flicked it open. Inside, as expected, was the blurry portrait of her shooing away the camera, hiding her face. *The only known photo of Eve Palmer.* She clicked it shut and tucked it into her pocket.

She looked back to the kitchen. Had someone from the family done this? Stolen Charlie's locket and mounted it up on the wall? Not only that, but put back one of the nails she'd removed? She supposed it was possible, but . . . why? Was Charlie responsible? Some kind of weird joke? A reference to their conversation the night before—no, that didn't make sense either. Or . . .

Her gaze flickered to the basement door—a small shiver ran down her neck. "I'm going for a walk," she said aloud. The words escaped without her brain's approval, like some part of her, deep and primordial, was forcing her to get the fuck out of there. Get away from this family, that basement.

Thomas, chewing on a mouthful of eggs, looked at her. "What's that?"

She started toward the foyer. "I'm going for a walk. Borrowing a neighbor's phone."

"Oh?" Thomas wiped his mouth with a napkin. "We'll, uh, we'll show ourselves out when we're done here. Thanks again for—"

"Sure." Eve slipped out of view.

Get to a neighbor's house. Call Charlie.

DOC_B13_CYMBALS

Description: Copy/paste of a conversation on rare-toy -forums.net. <u>Typos and other errors have not been corrected.</u>

◆

<u>POST #A312tlceko3hte2rhe6evgi8</u>

USER: Iris_197

➤ Im looking for this weird toy my cousin used to own. Its a monkey with cymbals, pretty similar to that one from Toy Story 3. Except he's got white fur, clear plastic cymbals, blue felt overalls, and a straw hat. Ive searched literally everywhere—cant find ANYTHING. I think the company was called "Rileys fantastic toys" or something . . .

➤ Please help this is driving me CRAZY!!!

➤ EDIT: Changed symbol spelling to "cymbal"

REPLY 1:

USER: True_Collector-1

➤ You're not the first person to ask about the "Straw Hat Monkey." I don't know if you're all just 4chan trolls, delusional, or both. Either way, such a toy does not exist, and neither does "Riley's Fantastic Toys." It's a juvenile internet hoax.

➤ Also, FYI, questions like this should be posted in the "what is this toy?" subforum.

➤ EDIT: And the "monkey from Toy Story 3" is correctly referred to as Daishin C.K's Jolly Chimp. I understand you're not an expert, but you could at least do the bare minimum of research before posting.

➤ EDIT: Also, please use apostrophes.

REPLY 2:

USER: Wurtler115

➤ WTF. I've been looking for this exact same thing! I asked my siblings about it and they said it never existed!! Creepy. It's like a Mandela effect or something.

REPLY 3:

USER: Only_says_Monkee-13

➤ Monkee.
```
                    c(..)o
                /___(-)____\
                    /\
                  _/(_)\_
```

REPLY 4:

USER: Navidson_27

➤   Mandela effect?

REPLY 5:

USER: Tripster_115

➤   Explanation copy/pasted from Wikipedia: *The Mandela effect
    was coined to illustrate an occurrence in which a large num-
    ber of people believe that an event has occurred, when in
    fact it has not, e.g., many people mistakenly recall that
    Nelson Mandela died in prison during the 1980s, but in re-
    ality, he passed away in 2013 from a prolonged respiratory
    infection.*

REPLY 6:

USER: Evergreen12

➤   Personally I think it's either some glitch in the matrix
    stuff and/or an unintended side effect of the Project Red Bag
    CIA memory wipes. Here's a list of famous examples:

➤   BerenSTAIN Bears vs. BerenSTEIN Bears. Everyone remembers it
    being the BerenSTEIN bears, but in reality, it's STAIN.

➤   Maunty's Popcorn vs. Monty's. It's spelled A.U. Maunty, not
    MONTY.

➤   Darth Vader didn't say "Luke, I am your father." He said,
    "No. I am your father."

➤   JFK assassination: This one is a little before my time, but a
    lot of boomers insist there were 6 people in the car when he
    got shot. There were only 4.

➤   There are countless other examples. Yet people still believe
    everything the MSM tells us. SMH.

REPLY 7:

USER: Nada12

> Yo @Evergreen Every single thing you listed can be explained
  by bad memory. lol. Also there *were* 6 people in the JFK car.

REPLY 8:

USER: DeleteGAT3

> Hey @Nada, look into it more. I think it could be proof of
  altered timelines / parallel world theories IMHO.

REPLY 9:

USER: WelpXredpilledX

> It's proof you're a sub 70 IQ fucking moron.

REPLY 10:

USER: Erin_ADMIN_13

> I'm locking this thread for going off the raiLs. OP, per
  True_Collector-1's comment, please post any inquiries of this
  nature to the "what is this toy?" subforum. And to everyone
  else, keep all conversations on topic and civiL.
> Thank you.

.⁻.. .. ...⁻ . ⁻..

STRAY

As Eve trudged across the front yard, Shylo followed. The dog's ears were perked, tail wagging—just happy to be outside. That made two of them. Out here, in the morning air, away from that family, it was easier to breathe, to think.

Eve's plan was simple: go to the nearest neighbor's house—3708 Heritage Lane—borrow their phone, call Charlie. If what Thomas had said was true—if Charlie was in town for something "urgent"—then, for the most part, Eve would relax. If she couldn't reach Charlie, then . . .

She'd put all her focus on getting that family out of her house. More and more, she had this feeling that something was seriously wrong with them, that maybe they were in league with that figure on the stairs. Of course, she had no proof of these suspicions, and she was no longer certain about what she saw on the stairs, but . . .

Once they're in, they never leave . . .

She paused at the top of the driveway. Muddy tire tracks were grooved into the slush, leading down and bending out of view behind a cut of trees.

More confirmation that Charlie had at least driven off. Of course, it wasn't enough to shut Mo up. Like always, he was there, waiting in the wings with a hundred reasons to panic. Still, she did her best to ignore him.

She scanned the woods, her breath smoking in the gray morning light that filtered through the trees. The snow had stopped falling. The first signs of thaw were setting in. Speckling drops, raining from the branches above, forming streams, snaking down the winding drive. At this rate, all evidence of snowfall might be gone before sunset. Good.

After an arduous trek down the slippery drive, she reached the road. The family's moving truck was parked out on the shoulder, all covered in a thin layer of drooping, translucent snow. It looked oddly uniform, as if an outgrowth of the ground below. Only its metallic underbelly was exposed, reddish black.

Above the truck, a rusty street sign was bolted to a tree:

HERITAGE LANE

It had always seemed an odd name for a back road surrounded by wilderness. In Eve's head, the moniker conjured up the image of a gated community. One with pretty little symmetrical houses and elderly neighbors peering out through flower box windows. The kind of neighborhood that saw Halloween as a chance to hand out toothpaste and Bible verses. But this Heritage Lane, like her house, almost looked abandoned.

The road, uneven and narrow, was riddled with baseball-sized rocks. From the flanks, tree branches stuck out at crooked angles, like arms grasping through prison bars. It stretched on for a few hundred yards, sloping down until it met the stark white sky. There, hemmed in by trees, was a thin slice of panorama. Snowcapped peaks poking through the clouds—islands in a sea of white.

She lingered there, taking in the view, breathing in the crisp air. Mountain birds chittered strange songs. Songs she'd never heard before. It all reminded her how truly isolated they were. How, if anything went wrong, help was so far away. Aside from a handful of neighbors (most of whom didn't even live here during the winter), the closest structure was all the way down near the base of the mountain. A single-pump Chevron gas station. A few miles past that, the Kettle Creek Motel. Or at least that's what Eve assumed it was called—she'd mentally filled in the blanks from its falling-apart neon sign:

THE KETTL_ _REEK MOTE_

All it took was a passing glance to conclude the establishment had long been abandoned. Another ten minutes past that, just over the Kettle Creek Bridge, the town of Yale.

One way in. One way out.

Again, the Realtor's warning played in her head, stirring up memories—sediment from the bottom of her psyche. She was pulled back to the first day they'd gone to look at the property. Charlie's truck had been in the shop, so Dayton, the Realtor, offered them a ride.

Dayton was a slight, graying man, and everything about him, from his physique to the way he spoke, felt contradictory. Despite his small stature, his voice was a deep, gravelly baritone. The kind of timbre that could almost narrate movie trailers. And he seemed plucked from another era, like he'd be more at home wrangling cattle on the frontier or bayoneting Krauts in the trenches. Instead, there he was, dressed in a Canali suit, peering over the steering wheel of a Mercedes sedan.

"Lot of strays out here," he had said, breaking a near ten-minute silence. "Stray dogs," he clarified. "More than the usual amount, anyway." They were about halfway up the mountain when he decided to raise the topic. "Nobody knows where they come from," he went on. "Some folks call it Stray Dog Summit. I don't, but some do." He adjusted the rearview mirror. "You end up buying the house, try using that name with the locals, down in Yale, or even Portland, they'll be impressed. Tell them you live on Stray Dog Summit and . . ." He clucked his tongue.

Eve and Charlie glanced at each other, unsure if he was finished. After a few more seconds, Eve opened her mouth to say thank you, but before she got "thank" out, Dayton started up again.

"Name doesn't make much sense. There's no strays at the summit. They're all down at the base, around the creek. That's why, personally, I don't call it that. Stray Dog Summit's a misnomer . . ." A short pause, then he added, "I figure 'Stray Dog Creek' doesn't have the same ring, though."

Eve chuckled politely.

Dayton shot her a serious look in the rearview; he wasn't trying to be funny—

Back in the present, the distant crack of a hunting rifle pulled Eve out of the peculiar memory. She cocked an ear to the sky, the echoing blast fading with each repetition. The morning birds paused briefly at the interruption, then carried on as if nothing had happened. It was a 308 rifle, Eve guessed, the same gun type Uncle Benji used to hunt with. Out here, for better or worse, the sound had become part of the natural landscape, like the howl of a coyote, the cry of a hawk. It had earned its place.

Refocusing, Eve plodded forward. Shylo was chipper as ever. Every so often, the dog zoomed ahead, poking her nose down into the snow. Zigzagging. Sniffing. Then, she'd pop her head back up, looking to Eve for some kind of approval. Each time, her snout was capped with a little pile of snow, and when Eve said, "Good job," or "Good girl," Shylo shook it off and repeated the process. The sight of Shylo being Shylo never failed to calm Eve.

◆

The neighbor's house was farther than she had remembered. At least a ten-minute walk. And the driveway was half-hidden by overgrown branches. She might've missed it altogether, if not for the address—brass letters nailed into a gnarled stump:

3

7

0

7

Wasn't it 3708? She peered over her shoulder, down the long stretch of road. The pines bowed inward, tunnellike, obscuring the view. *I probably skipped a property . . .*

Either way, it didn't matter. Turning back, she descended the narrow drive. It wound through windswept woods, then opened into a square lot. In the center sat an olive-green bungalow. An L-shaped box, with a flattop roof and shuttered windows. Out front, mottled with patchy snow, was a minimalist Japanese garden, encircled by a frozen pond.

This property, surrounded by unruly wilderness, looked more than a little out of place—as if it had been ripped out of a Portland suburb, helicoptered across the state, and surgically implanted here. It was quiet though, peaceful even. True seclusion, nestled away from the road.

As they crossed a small stone bridge, Shylo staggered to a halt, eyes fixed on the water below. Eve carried on, but the dog stayed behind, staring down at the pond, mesmerized. Beneath the murky ice, white koi swam in lazy circles.

Eve called out, "Shylo, come."

The dog gave her a brief glance. *I understand what you are saying, but I do not care.* She looked back at the fish. Barked.

"Come," Eve repeated, firmer. After two more barks, Shylo scampered to Eve's side. The dog looked up at her, expecting a treat or at least praise. Eve shook her head. "Too slow, bucko."

Pup in tow, Eve pressed the doorbell with her thumb. A three-tone pattern rang out. Warbled, dissonant. As she waited, she hugged herself for warmth, wishing she'd put on more layers. Was it getting colder? She wrapped a scarf over her face, the woolly fabric scratching against her nose. A solid thirty seconds passed. She tried the bell again. Still no answer. Was anyone even home? There wasn't a car around, but . . .

Eve squinted through textured glass, cupping her hands around her eyes. The inside was dark, save for a faint wedge of yellow light casting from a narrow hall. She tried the bell once more. Another long stretch of nothing, and then . . . the light snapped off. Eve huffed and stepped back. Guess they didn't want visitors. Regardless, it was probably time to return home, scour the house for her phone, kick that family out, and—

"Can I help you?"

She turned to see an older woman standing on the stone bridge. She was lightly dressed, considering the cold—a thin sweater and blue corduroys.

"Hey, I, uh," Eve had started to answer when, to her shock, Shylo trotted right up to the stranger.

The woman smiled. "Well aren't you just the cutest little thing." Her voice had a tinge of Southern drawl. She lowered herself to one knee, reached toward Shylo, then stopped, and looked up at Eve. "Is it okay to pet her?"

Eve gave a wary nod.

The woman scratched Shylo behind the ears. "Who's a good girl? Yes you are." Shylo's tail started wagging.

Eve stood there, lost for words. Never before had she seen the dog so comfortable around a stranger. In any other situation, Shylo's trust might have been comforting. But with everything else going on, it only raised more alarm bells.

"You're the new neighbor?" The woman pushed off her knee to stand.

"Yeah, my name's Eve."

"You bought 3709, right?"

There was a hint of something in the question. Judgment? Pity? Eve couldn't tell.

Still, she nodded. "I— I was just wondering if I could use your phone? I lost mine. Just—trying to reach my partner."

"Of course." Walking up to the door, the woman searched her pockets. "It's Heather, by the way."

"Nice to meet you."

Heather, still digging through her pockets, asked, "You, uh, okay?"

No matter how hard Eve tried to hide it, people often sensed her anxiety, like it was a piece of broccoli, forever stuck between her two front teeth. "Yeah," Eve said. "I've just, I've never seen my dog so relaxed around a stranger before."

Heather smiled, pulled out a carabiner of keys, and started rifling through it. "I used to foster strays," she explained. "They called me the dog whisperer. Not so bad as titles go, I suppose."

Eve, half to herself, mused, "Stray Dog Summit . . ."

"Hm?"

"Oh, just the mountain." She gestured around, gave a weak smile. "Stray Dog Summit?"

Heather blinked at her, still not following.

"There's, uh . . ." Eve cleared her throat. "Aren't there a lot of strays out here?"

"Not that I've heard of."

Eve replied with an awkward "Huh . . ." then let it go. *Thanks, Mr. Dayton.*

Heather unlocked the door and pushed it open. She gestured inside. "After you."

Eve hesitated. "You don't mind the dog in there?"

Heather shrugged. "So long as she doesn't judge the mess."

DOC_A05_COLD

Description: Excerpt about the strange side effects of hypothermia.
Source unknown. News article?

◆

1987, Creighton, Saskatchewan, Canada

Last night a young married couple was found dead in their home. The
cause was immediately apparent: hypothermia. Their electricity had
gone out in the middle of a severe winter storm, and they had no
backup generators. Their poorly insulated prairie bungalow did little
to protect them. It should be noted they had an Oldsmobile in the
garage, with a full tank of gas. Why they hadn't used this to stay
warm is a mystery.

The bodies were discovered in unusual places. The husband, 28,
was found in the master bedroom, lying under the bed. The wife, 26,
was curled up in a basement corner. The dirt floor beneath her had
been clawed away, and soil was found under her fingernails.

These actions can be explained by the phenomenon known as "terminal burrowing behavior," the uncontrollable instinct to shelter or dig when faced with imminent death. Although modern humans don't normally burrow for shelter, the extreme stress of certain demise seems to induce a primal, mammalian instinct to burrow or hide. A sobering reminder of our long-ingrained, evolutionary instincts.

3707 HERITAGE LANE

"Again," said Heather, "sorry about the mess." As they shuffled into the foyer, she kicked her shoes into a nearby corner. "Grandkids were visiting."

"All good." Eve looked around, not exactly sure what "mess" Heather was referring to. Aside from the faint smell of cigarette smoke and a pile of brightly colored toys on the living room floor, this place was near spotless.

Heather smiled. "Can I get you anything? Water? Tea?" She reached out a hand for Eve's coat, but Eve waved it away.

"No, that's okay, I won't be long."

Heather blinked at her. Her face was etched with weary loneliness, something Eve hadn't noticed before. It was the tired look of someone who'd spent countless hours waiting by the phone. Waiting for calls from kids, grandkids, anyone. Normally that would've been enough for Eve to backtrack, say she'd love to stay, have tea, spend the rest of her morning with a complete stranger. But today, Eve didn't have the time to feel bad; she just wanted to use the phone, get back home. Make sure Thomas and Co. were out of her house before they came up with some other excuse to stay even longer. In retrospect, she should have just kicked them out at breakfast.

Once they're in, they never leave . . .

Heather filed into the nearby kitchen and gestured toward the living room. "Phone's in there."

"Thank you."

Eve kicked off her boots. As she drifted deeper into the house, she glanced over her shoulder. Shylo was lingering in the foyer, back to her old cautious self. Eve turned away, entered the living room. Gray light poured in through shuttered windows, spilling over wood-vinyl walls, green shag carpet. Aside from an old tube TV, a wicker-back chair, and a velvet couch, the space was pretty much empty. No phone in sight. Eve looked toward the kitchen. "Sorry, where is it?"

Heather, rifling through a yellow fridge, poked her head out. "Hm?"

"The phone," Eve said.

"Oh." Heather nodded. "Just down that hall, around the corner. Side table."

Eve turned back. Next to the TV was a narrow hallway. It stretched nearly the length of the house, then hooked right. With its bluish-green walls, it looked like something out of an old hotel. Symmetrical, with doors flanking both sides, all closed.

Eve remembered the light. The one that had snapped off when she rang the doorbell earlier. She shifted her weight. "You, uh, you live alone?"

Heather peeked out again. "What's that?"

"Does anyone else live here?"

Heather furrowed her brow. "No . . ."

"I just—when I was outside, I saw a light switch off."

"Inside the house?" Heather frowned.

"Yeah, uh, over there." Eve pointed to the hallway.

Heather fell silent, her eyes scanning the shadowed corridor until she remembered. "Oh, right. Some of the interior lights are on a timer, motion sensored." She slipped out of sight.

Still a little apprehensive, Eve went over. From above, a dim glow bled down through snow-covered skylights. The walls were lined with photos, collages from better days. Smiling family members, weddings, camping trips, and dogs. Lots of dogs. She rounded the corner. It went for another ten feet, concluding with a nook and a cherrywood end table. On it, a rotary phone, pale red.

Eve marched over and dialed Charlie's number. A tedious process with the spin wheel. Halfway through, she screwed up a single digit and had to start over. When she finally got it right—one, two, three tones rang out, and—

"Hello?" Charlie's voice answered. But Eve wasn't falling for the same trick twice; she braced for the painfully annoying *Hello. You've reached Charlie* message, but instead:

"Hello?" Charlie repeated. "Anyone there?"

Eve exhaled relief. Just hearing Charlie's actual voice felt like a warm hug. She cleared her throat, trying her best to sound measured, chill. "Hey, Charlie, where are you?"

On the other end, muffled voices chattered in the background, punctuated by slow, rhythmic beeps. Was she in line at a grocery store? It was hard to tell; the signal was weak, the sound thin, crackly.

Charlie said, "Sorry, who is this?"

Eve raised an eyebrow, then remembered—right, unfamiliar number, but, "You don't recognize my voice?"

". . . Eve?"

"Yeah. I, uh, I lost my phone. Using the neighbor's."

"Oh?" There was a shade of disapproval in Charlie's tone, or maybe confusion? *No, definitely disapproval. Charlie is judging you for freaking out and walking all the way to the neighbor's house and—*

Eve stopped her spiral. Reminded herself she couldn't read minds, especially not over the phone, especially not based on a single *Oh?* Eve went on. "Thomas said you went to town? I'm just— I wanted to make sure that was the case—"

"Eve, it's pretty loud here. You, you'll have to speak up."

A swarm of questions stampeded through Eve's head, most of them variants of: *Why the hell did you leave me alone with complete strangers?* But she went with, "When are you coming back?"

A long pause. "When am I . . . ?" Charlie sighed. "Are you okay?" She sounded impatient, angry even.

Why was Charlie upset? Eve was the one who should have been upset— she had every right. With the winter storm, her missing phone, the weirdo family, the potential lurker in the basement—Eve tensed up, a hot flash of anger shooting down her neck. She was getting madder by the second, not at Charlie, but at the whole situation. At herself.

Suppressed, inward-facing rage. Yet another inevitable side effect of her constant people-pleasing. Eve continued, as calmly as she could. "I, no, I'm not really okay. You left without— I found your locket hanging above the fireplace, I didn't know if something—"

On the other end, another commotion, a voice. Soft. Indecipherable. It muttered to Charlie, impatient, monotone. In a strange way, it reminded Eve of the adults in a *Peanuts* cartoon: *Wom, wom, wom.* Charlie responded, barely audible, muffled. Was she covering the receiver? Why?

The voice spoke again, warbled and vague. *Wom. Wom. Wom.* There was something eerie about it, almost mechanical.

"Eve." Charlie sighed again. "Just try to—"

The call cut short with an infuriating BEEP. A shrill, jeering note that jabbed into Eve's ear like a wet stick. She recoiled. *The hell just happened? What was Charlie going to say?*

Just try to—

Try to what? Escape? Stay calm? Prevent Cthulhu's resurrection?

Eve's frustration gave way to deep concern, a fear for Charlie's safety. Overblown or not, it was enough to make her heart jump a few octaves. She redialed one, slowly, spinning, number, at, a, time. Three rings went off, but Charlie didn't answer. It didn't even go to her voicemail, just that same deafening BEEP. Irked, she slammed the phone onto the base. *Has the weather knocked out the signal?* She considered trying again, but . . . *Take a breath, don't spiral.* Charlie was fine. Acting weird, sure. But it sounded like she was in town, just like Thomas had said. Eve took another breath and . . .

Behind her, a scuffling sound. Heather was down the hall, facing away, hunched in the corner. For a second, the sight startled Eve, but . . . she was only adjusting a crooked picture frame, humming to herself. The photo depicted a middle-aged Heather. She was nestled up to a tall man with a clean-shaven head, gray eyes, and a handlebar mustache. In it, she was standing on her tiptoes, kissing him on the cheek. They were both in the middle of laughing, both looking very much in love.

Eve cleared her throat. "Th-thanks again."

Heather glanced over her shoulder. "Of course."

Eve, still feeling a slight unease, stepped around her and headed toward the foyer. The sight of Heather had triggered a flashback to the night before. Thomas standing in that basement hallway. She shook it off.

Eve was pulling on her boots when Heather shuffled out. "Everything okay?" There was a look in her eyes, a grandmotherly look of genuine concern.

Eve sighed. Part of her actually wanted to blurt it all out, overshare with a person she just met. Tell her about the family, Charlie's misplaced locket, even the figure on the stairs. But . . . that would only lead to more embarrassment. "I'm— It's just been a weird day."

Heather tilted her head, sympathetic. "I'm a good listener."

Eve managed a smile, still tempted by the opportunity to vent, unload her anxieties, but . . . "I should go," she said, getting to her feet. "Thanks again for all this." With Shylo at her side, she turned to leave. But as she reached for the door, Heather chimed in. "Sorry to overhear, but—on the phone, did you mention someone named Thomas?"

Eve, hand wrapped around the knob, looked over her shoulder. "Yeah."

Heather nodded. "It's a long shot, but . . . that wouldn't happen to be Thomas Faust, would it?"

"Yeah . . ." Eve recalled Thomas's business card. "I think that's him."

"Wow." Heather smiled sadly, as if the confirmation brought back bitter-sweet memories. "Tommy Faust, all grown up. I haven't seen him since . . . Well, since he was this tall." She held out her palm, a little above waist height. "What brings him back here?"

Eve ran a hand through her hair. It was still damp from the weather. "Uh, he and his family, they're moving cross-country."

"His family?" Heather's sad smile brightened a bit.

"Yeah." Eve nodded. "Three kids."

"Isn't that just wonderful," Heather marveled. "I'm sure they're lovely." She stared at Eve, awaiting confirmation.

"Uh, yeah, they're fine," Eve said. "They seem nice?"

"That's good to hear. I'm glad he turned out okay, all things considered."

All things considered?

Heather added, "I used to babysit him, you know?"

"Oh?"

"I'm basically his honorary aunt."

Eve, curious once again, couldn't help but pry further. "What was he like back then?"

"Thomas? Good kid. Smart kid. Little bundle of energy, chatterbox. When did they get in?"

"Yesterday evening . . ."

"They spent the night . . . Do you know him?"

"No." Eve shifted her weight. "They, uh, just stopped by. He wanted to give his family a quick tour of the house, but . . . his kid ended up hiding in the basement. Then the storm."

"Hiding in the basement," Heather mused. "Thomas used to do the same thing." Sudden confusion clouded her face. "I just wonder why they didn't come by here—I would have been more than happy to have them spend the night."

Good question.

Eve shrugged. "Yeah, I don't know . . ."

Heather's confusion turned to disappointment.

All at once, Eve couldn't help but feel sorry for her yet again. "I— I think it was a pretty last-minute detour; they probably didn't want to bother you."

That seemed to reassure Heather. "Did he mention me at all?" she inquired, her eyes filled with: *Of course he did.*

Eve opened her mouth, hesitated, and lied. "Yeah."

Fake Charlie scoffed, *Why would you lie about that?*

Heather beamed.

That's why.

Heather asked, "What did he say?"

Fuck.

"What did he . . ." Eve fell silent, grasping for an answer. "What did he say, about you?"

"Mm-hm." Heather's smile faltered.

"Oh." Eve paused again. "He just said he . . . had fond memories."

Heather's smile returned, apparently buying the lie. "You're sure you don't want some tea?"

Eve's gaze flickered back to the door.

All things considered . . . Heather's aside ran through her thoughts again. Eve suspected those three words were doing a lot of heavy lifting. She was torn.

Part of her still wanted to know more about Thomas's past, what happened with his sister, while the other part just wanted to go home. After a brief internal debate, she relented. "Sure, I— I could go for a cup."

Besides, maybe Charlie will call back? And Heather seems like better company than the family anyway.

DOC_C15_MOVIE

Description: Excerpt from a flyer for the Dryden Theatre, Rochester NY.

◆

This Thursday! Bring your friends and family to the Dryden Theatre
for a re-showing of Hayao Miyazaki's classic animated film. The
mind-bending, Oscar-winning:

Spirited Away

After her family takes a wrong turn, young Chihiro is pulled into
a whimsical but dangerous world of spirits, witches, and gods. She
must navigate the hierarchies and customs of this strange land to
rescue her parents and return to the world of humans.

7 PM

$8 tickets at the door.

─ · · · · ·

OLD FRIENDS

Heather moseyed back into the kitchen and rifled through a cupboard. "Orange pekoe? Peppermint?"

"Anything with caffeine," Eve said. The lack of a morning coffee was already hitting. Hard.

"Hmm . . . Earl Gray," Heather replied, still rummaging.

Eve hung up her winter coat and, once again, kicked off her boots. She wandered into the living room and flopped into the wicker chair. After all the traipsing around, it felt good to sit, necessary even. Shylo sauntered over and curled up at her feet, grumbling. The dog just wanted to be outside again. Fair enough.

Eve looked around. From here she could see—mounted beside a glass cabinet—more photos. Dozens in all, but one stood out. It featured the man with the handlebar mustache, but he looked younger in this one, late twenties perhaps. And he had a full head of hair, black and tangled, long enough to reach his shoulders. He was perched behind a drum kit, pounding away, playing to a half-empty dive bar. Neon lights. Hazy smoke. In the foreground, slightly out of focus, was a guitarist with neck tattoos and a full beard belting into a microphone. A lot of passion packed into a single frame. Eve could almost smell the sweat, the booze, the pot. All things that, funnily enough, brought up a wistful sense of nostalgia. She and Charlie used to frequent such concerts all the time. Unthinking, Eve reached into her pocket and gripped Charlie's locket, turning it between her forefinger and thumb. Its brass surface was smooth, cold to the touch. Oddly comforting.

Heather filed back in, noticed Eve looking at the photo. "That's Michael," she explained. "My better half."

"The drummer?"

"Mm-hm." Heather sat down on the couch across from Eve.

"Looks like a fun show," Eve said.

"It was." Heather did not elaborate; that was all she had to say on the topic. "Water's just heating up." She reached into her shirt pocket and produced a stainless steel cigarette holder. Flipping it open, she jostled out a smoke. "Just started these damn things a few months ago." She pinched the cigarette between her lips and began fumbling through her pockets. "Figured, at my age, I got a good five, maybe ten years left. Might as well see what all the fuss is about, right?" After a few more seconds of digging through her pockets, she huffed, unable to find what she was looking for. So instead, she slid her hand between the cushions below, shimmied around, and yanked out a lime-green BIC lighter.

"Huzzah." She held it up like a trophy.

Hunching forward, she sparked the lighter and brought the flame to the cigarette, inhaling with short, sporadic puffs until the tip glowed orange. She took a slow drag and exhaled. "Turns out I'm not missing much . . ."

"Yeah," Eve said, "I used to smoke."

Heather's eyes fluttered in thinly veiled disbelief. "You?"

Eve almost smiled. "Hard to imagine?"

Heather cocked her head. "Don't take this wrong, but you look too . . . too sweet for it."

WE USED TO LIVE HERE

Eve shrugged. "Well, I quit, so maybe I was."

Heather seemed to find that answer amusing. She leaned forward, tapped ashes into an empty soup can. "How are you liking the property, by the way?"

Eve considered the question. "Still getting used to it. It's just a little . . ."

Heather finished the sentence: "Isolated?"

Eve had meant to say "creepy," but that worked too. "Yeah, it's pretty far out of the way." Shifting her weight, she added, "How much do you know about it?"

"3709?"

Eve nodded.

Heather's expression turned vaguely pitying, somber, an echo of that look she'd given outside. "It's . . . old?" She shrugged. "Older than me if you can believe that." She chuckled, and took another puff. "Might be the oldest structure on the mountain . . ."

Somehow, that didn't surprise Eve. When she'd first laid eyes on the house, it had almost seemed ancient. An absurd thought to be sure, but somehow it felt older than the surrounding trees—many of which, according to Mr. Dayton, had been there for nearly three hundred years. Maybe it was the way the pines swayed gently in the breeze while the house stood motionless, locked to the earth.

At first, this strange feeling had unsettled Eve. But over the weeks, her unease gave way to a sense of melancholy. The many people who'd worked on the place over the years had considered every detail. From the stained glass window to the hand-carved patterns on the crown molding. The house felt like a fragile heirloom, passed from generation to generation, each person adding their own ideas—contradictions and all—only to have the whole project unceremoniously discarded. Abandoned in the woods. Waiting to be torn down by reckless house flippers.

Eve glanced down that hallway, still hoping Charlie would call back. She looked at Heather. "Do you know when it was built?"

Again, uncertainty clouded Heather's face. Her eyes scanned the room as if she were about to broach a touchy subject in a small-town diner. She opened her mouth to say something, then stopped short and leaned back into the couch. She exhaled a puff of bluish-gray smoke. The haze lingered, illuminated by a thin sheet of light beaming through the shuttered windows. Noir vibes.

Eve herself was starting to feel like a noir detective, trying to crack the secrets of the past. Though on second thought, with all her paranoia, she felt less like a cool private eye and more like an anxiety-ridden, *Rear Window* shut-in.

She tried a different angle. "My partner and I . . . we're just trying to learn more about the property. Apparently, most of the records were lost in a fire and—"

"Nope." Heather shook her head.

"Pardon?"

"Fire's a myth. The records were stolen."

"Oh . . . ?"

"Back in the early fifties," Heather continued. "Some nut broke into town hall. Pilfered most of the paperwork for Yale and Kettle Creek Mountain. Zoning information, deeds, even plats, and surveys. I don't know where that fire story came from, but you're not the first to bring it up. Michael, my own husband, was convinced of it, said my memory was going. We had countless arguments on the topic. Not even a web search could clear it up."

"But the bank told us—"

"Bank doesn't know shit," she interrupted. "Just . . . Don't worry about it. People misremember things. Accept it. Move on." In the kitchen, a kettle began to shriek. "Took long enough." Heather ditched her still-glowing cigarette into the empty soup can. With a slap of the knees, she got up and made her way to the kitchen. She mumbled to herself, barely audible. Eve only caught the words "little Tommy," "Alina," and "stray mutts." Heather slipped out of sight and started rifling through cupboards again, still muttering, "Thieves, fire."

Then, from somewhere deeper in the house, came a faint thud, followed by a short scrape. Like a rusty hammer, dragged across plywood. So subtle, it might've been imagined. But Shylo's head was perked up too, eyes fixed on that dark hallway. All the doors were still closed. The vague noise could have been anything, but . . .

To Eve, it had sounded like a single footstep, followed by a dragging heel. Once again she wondered, were they alone? What if—

"Careful now, it's hot."

A little startled, Eve turned. Heather was standing right there, holding out a steaming cup of tea. Eve had been so distracted by the noise, she'd almost forgotten where she was. "Thanks, uh, thank you." She took the cup and glanced back down the hall. Whatever that sound was, even Shylo had lost interest. It was probably just the house settling.

Eve took a careful sip. The tea's warmth waved through her, soothing. Heather settled back into the couch and sipped from her tea as well.

Eve, a little awkwardly, asked, "How long did Thomas's family live up here?"

"The Fausts?" Heather narrowed her eyes, thinking. "Hm . . ." She ran the numbers in her head. "A little over half a decade, I think. They left rather quickly after some, uh, family troubles."

Family troubles.

As much as Eve hated to admit it, this was the real reason she was drinking tea with a stranger—she wanted to know what had happened to Thomas's sibling. Normally, Eve would've let it be, especially in such a private matter, but . . . "I hope his sister ended up getting the help she needed."

Heather looked at her, puzzled. "Sister?"

"Yeah, his, uh, older sister?"

Heather shook her head. "Thomas was an only child."

Eve blinked. Was she joking?

She wasn't.

Recognizing Eve's confusion, Heather added, "Oh, unless you're referring to Alina?"

Eve thought back to Thomas's story by the fireplace. Hadn't the name been . . . "Alison?" she questioned.

Heather tilted her head, again trying to remember. "This was all well over four decades ago now, but—there was a girl. Alina, or maybe it was Alison—I'm terrible with names . . . In either case, she lived with the Fausts for the better part of two years." Heather took another sip of tea and grimaced. "Hm, Alison," she murmured. "Let's go with that. She was a drifter, a lost child. A runaway? An orphan? We never found out. She'd wandered onto the Fausts' property on a cold Sunday morning, dressed in a nightgown. Aside from her name, she didn't know who she was, where she'd come from. Can you believe that? All the way out here? Even the police couldn't find any records on the poor thing; it was like she'd materialized out of thin air. Then Thomas's parents, after filling out all the necessary paperwork, jumping through the hoops, they ended up taking Alison under their wing. Too kind for their own good, the Fausts."

Eve sat back, absorbing everything. Why hadn't Thomas included any of this in his account? Sure, she wasn't entitled to his complete traumatic backstory, but . . .

Eve said, "So they ended up adopting her?"

Heather crossed her legs, shook her head. "No. Only temporary guardians."

"It's just—Thomas told me she was his sister."

Heather's brow wrinkled. "In spirit perhaps, but they never officially brought her into the family . . ." She trailed off, then added, "I mean, maybe they had been considering it, but after the incident with her and Thomas, they—"

She went quiet, as if she might've said too much.

Eve nudged. "Incident?"

"No, I shouldn't, I . . ." Heather swatted the air, a nervous gesture. She took another sip of tea, diverted the topic. "Anyway. Have you spent time down in Yale yet? You should really check out the lumber museum. It— It's really something."

Mo, the devil on Eve's shoulder, whispered, *Pry further.*

"I won't share anything," Eve promised. "I'm just—I'm a little worried about the house is all. If something came out about its history, might affect the resale value. Better to know up front." Not a lie, just a dressed-up version of the truth.

Uncertain, Heather tapped a finger on the armrest. Eve could tell part of her wanted to share more. If only to relieve some dark burden from her shoulders. "How much do you know?"

"About what happened?"

Heather nodded, staring down at the floor.

Eve shrugged. "Just—Thomas said Alison believed the house was changing, people were changing . . . in ways only she could see."

"That's all he said?"

"More or less . . ."

After another long and silent deliberation, Heather relented. She leaned closer and lowered her voice to a near whisper. "Alison—she started to believe there was only one way to make it stop, to get her supposed old life back, and . . . One winter night, Thomas, eight years old, awoke to find her standing at his bedside, clutching a fountain pen . . ." Heather leaned back, her face a grim mask. "She stabbed him thirty-seven times in less than a minute. She would've done more, if his parents hadn't dragged her away." She shuddered. "Thirty-seven times. Can you imagine?"

An image, sick and jarring, flashed through Eve's mind. A moonlit room. Yellow wallpaper. A gaunt, white-knuckled hand gripping a silver-tipped pen, stabbing into pale flesh, up and down, again and again, faster and faster.

Heather sighed. "It's a miracle he survived. Truly."

Eve looked up.

Heather's eyes were wet now. "Just a terrible tragedy. An absolute shock . . ."

Eve was stunned silent. She had assumed the unspoken details of Thomas's past were bad, but . . .

"Unsurprisingly," Heather continued, "Tommy was never the same after that. He used to be so energetic, so imaginative, talkative, but the few times I saw him after the incident, he barely said a word, just stared at the floor, silent."

"What happened to Alison?" Again, the question left Eve's mouth without her brain's approval.

Heather looked at her, shrugged. "The state took her away, and, well, after that—I don't know. Frankly, I don't want to . . ."

Eve guessed Alison ended up either in prison or some kind of criminal psych ward—assuming she still walked among the living.

Heather rose from the couch. "Do you want a top-up?" Her pointer finger drew Eve's gaze to the ceramic mug in her hands, now half-empty and lukewarm.

Silently, Eve gave it over.

Heather withdrew into the kitchen and turned on the sink, musing aloud, "But it's good to hear Thomas is doing all right now. Family and all. The human spirit prevails, don't you agree?"

Eve managed a meek "Yeah . . ."

As Heather clinked around out of view, something else caught Eve's attention. Nestled at the foot of the couch, peering out from that pile of colorful toys: eyes. They were cartoonishly wide, unblinking, a fiery hue of orange. *Is that . . . ?* She found herself leaning forward, her hand reaching into the pile to retrieve it. It was a Jolly Chimp, sporting a yellow vest, pin-striped pants, brass cymbals. But one detail was wrong: its fur was white, just like Mo's.

Aren't they supposed to have brown fur?

She turned the toy over, scrutinizing it—as if it were a mysterious arti-fact from another world. Unthinking, she flicked the switch on its back. It whirred to life, banging the cymbals with manic zeal, almost lurching from her grasp—*clash—clash—clash—*

"Oh." Heather leaned out from the kitchen. "That's my grandson's favorite. God knows why."

Eve powered it down and set it back among the other toys. "I used to have one kind of like it . . ."

"Yeah? Creepy little guy."

Eve gave a noncommittal grunt.

Don't lie to yourself, Mo said. *For a second, you thought it was me.*

Mo was right. For a fleeting moment, she really did. Still, the sight brought up a core memory: the day, at seven years old, when she lost Mo. It had devastated her. In truth, even now, it still bothered her more than she cared to admit. Not the fact he was gone; rather, the way he went missing.

The memory was crystal clear. Every little detail. On a camping trip to Montana, she sat in the back of her parents' rusty hatchback. Mo was buckled into the seat beside her, staring blankly ahead, eyes wide, reflecting the procession of trees outside. Every bump in the road jostled him, rattled his metallic innards. The car pulled into a backcountry gas station. Young Eve hopped out, stretched her drowsy limbs. The morning sun was just peeking out over the horizon, streaming through the trees and . . .

. . . when she turned back, Mo was gone. His seat empty. Belt still buckled. The image didn't quite register. In fact, it took about seven seconds of stunned silence until the panic set in. Eve, frantic, inconsolable, rushed to her mother.

After a solid half minute, her parents finally got her to slow down and explain, word by word, what happened. "Somebody stole Mo," she practically screamed. "Mo was KIDNAPPED."

Mom and Dad, under the reasonable impression he was only misplaced, searched the car. They checked her backpack, the trunk, beneath the seats, everywhere. But Mo was nowhere to be found. Because Mo had been stolen. Kidnapped. Abducted by thieves and forced to do tricks in an unholy carnival.

Forever. She couldn't even cry; she just stood there, shocked, motionless, staring at Mo's empty seat. The world was ending.

Worse still, there was no way to replace him. Her parents tried everything, but the company that made this knockoff brand, Riley's Fantastic Toys, had long gone extinct. And even if they had found a new Mo, it wouldn't have been *her* Mo, with all the scratches and dents he'd collected over the years. To Eve, those were the things that made Mo, Mo. Anything else would've been nothing short of an imposter. Brand-new and shiny, but an imposter nonetheless.

Eve rose from her wicker chair, suddenly feeling the urge to leave. As if the mere sight of this toy had triggered some kind of primal instinct to retreat. "I . . ." She headed to the foyer. "Sorry, I have to go," she said. "C'mon, Shylo." The dog trotted over. Eve started tying up her boots, mumbling an excuse about the weather getting worse.

"Oh?" said Heather. "So soon?"

Eve didn't respond, just kept tying up her boots.

Heather, a hint of sadness back in her eyes, said, "Well, if you ever need anything, I'm always around. You and your partner should come over soon, build puzzles with an old woman. I'll keep the conversation lighthearted next time. Promise."

"Hm." Eve pulled on her coat, started buttoning up.

Heather said, "It was nice to meet you, uh . . ." She narrowed her eyes, coming up short.

"It's Eve." She turned for the exit.

"Eve, right, I'm so sorry. *Eve.* Like I said, terrible with names." Heather chuckled.

Eve had reached for the door when, down that hall, around the corner, the rotary phone started ringing. Shrill. Insistent. She glanced to Heather.

"Oh," said Heather, "that's probably your partner. I rarely get phone calls."

Boots still on, Eve started over, but as she stepped into the hall, she froze.

Something was off. Something had changed . . . It took her a second, but one of the doors was open now. Down at the end, just before the corner, a white door was cracked. A thin slit of shadow. The kind of dark that suggested a watcher on the other side. A watcher with heinous intent.

Eve remained motionless. All the while, that phone continued ringing, as if trying to lure her into a trap.

Heather asked, "Is something the matter?"

Eve looked over her shoulder. "The"—she turned back—"door . . ."

"Hm?"

Eve pointed. "That door was closed before . . ."

"Oh, I think the latch is broken . . ."

The phone kept ringing, somehow louder, more insistent.

Heather frowned. "Aren't you going to answer that?"

She's trying to trick you, Mo whispered. *If you walk down that hallway, you'll never come back.*

The phone gave out one last ring.

Eve, letting her paranoia win out, turned to the foyer. "I— I need to get home."

As she pushed out the front door, Heather called after her, "Don't be a stranger—"

She said something else, but Eve didn't hear; she was already halfway across the yard.

DOC_C08_DISPATCH

Description: *Partial police report detailing a strange encounter near Kettle River.*

◆

<u>SUPPLEMENTAL REPORT</u>

DISTRIBUTION: Sergeant Naomi [surname redacted]

DATE AND TIME OF REPORT: [redacted]

LOCATION: Kettle Creek Mountain Highway, approx. 3 miles from Kettle Creek Bridge. Westbound.

OFFICE: [phone number redacted]

ACTION TAKEN: While conducting a routine traffic patrol on Kettle Creek Mountain Highway, I observed an unidentified Caucasian male, approximately mid-twenties, wandering in the center of the road. He was approximately six foot three with an athletic build, wearing a T-shirt and jeans despite freezing conditions.

Upon my approach, the man appeared disoriented and confused. He stated he did not know how he arrived at the current location.

When I suggested he accompany me for his safety, the man expressed extreme apprehension about being forced into a psychiatric facility. I attempted to reassure him; however, his attention was diverted to the southbound woods, where three unidentified Caucasian males, each approximately six feet tall and dressed in white suits, stood stationary. This raised the subject's demeanor to a state of high anxiety, rapid breathing, wide eyes. Subject fled into the north-bound woods. Upon further investigation, the group of three males had also disappeared.

Given the circumstances and the worsening weather, I opted not to pursue either party. Dispatch was informed, and a search team was sent to the area.

-.-. .- -... .. -.

STRANGER

White fog lay heavy over Heritage Lane, thickening with every step. The weather had returned with a vengeance, the snow reaching Eve's shins now, rising fast. The wind was picking up too, cold gusts lashing at her back, urging her forward. If this kept up, the bridge might close again . . .

Get home. Make sure that family is gone already.

She checked over her shoulder. Shylo was still close, still following. Snow clung to the dog's black fur like a second coat, and yet she was still, mostly, happy to be outside. "Nearly home," said Eve.

In good time, they reached the driveway. That narrow gap between the trees at the end of the road. Eve marched over and—fresh footprints. They led down the drive, carving a trail to the shoulder, rounding the family's moving truck. *Of course they're still here.* Muttering, she trod over. The imprints descended the embankment, bowed to the right, and ended with . . .

A figure, facing away, standing an arm's length from the tree line. Who was that? A child? An adult? Eve could only discern navy green boots, blue jeans, and . . . a white T-shirt? Or a tank top? Was that Jenny? Had she somehow snuck outside? Whoever it was, they clearly weren't dressed for this weather. "Hey?!" Eve called out, but the figure remained still, swaying in the wind as if their feet were bolted to the ground. Eve tried again. This time, the figure wandered into the reddish pines and dissolved into the fog.

"Shit," Eve hissed through gritted teeth. She looked to the long, serpentine driveway, then back to the foreboding woods. Even bundled up in all her winter layers, she could barely stand the icy chill. That stranger? They might freeze to death. With a resigned sigh, Eve plodded down the snowbank and ventured into the trees.

As she pursued the tracks with Shylo by her side, the old pines around them whispered and bellowed, as if holding some ancient council. As if they might spring to life and banish the intruders. Eve stayed focused. The footprints wove a confounding route, hooking left and right, circling trees, sometimes the same tree more than once. Yet there was an eerie purpose to this dance, as though tracing an unseen labyrinth—an incoherent thought, but one that Eve found difficult to shake. She clambered over a felled tree and—

Some ten yards away, the figure slipped behind a jagged boulder. For a second, Eve thought it might've been Charlie, but this person had shoulder-length hair. Still, Eve called out again, her voice vying with the murmur of trees. She picked up the pace, nearly running now. The meandering footprints led her deeper and deeper through the pines. Branches clawed at her skin. Brambles snagged her clothes, snapping and breaking as she came upon a sloped clearing and . . . the tracks simply ended.

Hard stop. As if the person she'd been chasing had ceased to exist. Eve swiveled around: trees, brambles, snow, and . . . more trees. Had they climbed? She looked up. The pines, straight and broad, towered into a stark white sky. The few branches within reach were thin, like twigs. Unclimbable. Leveling her head, Eve cupped her hands around her mouth and called out once more. "Hello?!" Her voice ricocheted throughout the clearing, unanswered.

Her eyes flicked back to the tracks, the abrupt end. How on earth? Had this person traced backward on their own prints, taken a different route? The notion seemed absurd, but . . .

More absurd than vanishing into thin air? Imaginary Charlie countered.

Whatever. Eve was too cold to question the logic. Either way, this stranger, kid or not, obviously didn't want her help. Eve was about to head back home when Shylo barked, a shrill snap. The dog was staring off into the woods at the low end of the clearing. Ears pricked, tail straight, as if sensing some hidden threat. Eve strained her eyes. All she could see were fog and pines and the shadows laid between. "Okay, Shylo," she said, "let's go."

Yet the dog stood unmoving, gaze unbroken, an oddly familiar scene. Leery, Eve had approached, readying to leash the dog up, when she saw it. Obscured by the mist, masked by the pillars of the forest—an A-frame cabin. Dark. She found herself drifting toward it, a moth to a flame. With Shylo at her side, she weaved through the trees, broke into another clearing, and paused at its boundary.

The cabin, planted in the center of this rocky glade, was clearly abandoned. Lopsided. Porch falling apart. White lichen clung to the walls, grasping the timber as if trying to prevent escape. The front door, hanging on a single hinge, swayed lazily in the wind, *creak, creak, creak* . . . A scattering of bullet holes, likely target practice from bored hunters, peppered the crooked door's midsection. In short, the building seemed one stiff gust away from collapse.

But the windows—they were strangely intact. Eve's attention carried upward. Above a corrugated awning, set between the roof's angled slats, a porthole window. It mirrored the ashen sky, concealing whatever might be inside. Someone could be up there, watching.

Eve scanned the ground, searching for footprints. Nothing. Either way, she needed to get home. She had pivoted to leave when, without warning, Shylo bolted from her side, shot up the porch stairs, and vanished into the cabin. *Fuck.*

"Shylo," she shouted.

Silence. Just that creaking door, an open gash of shadow. Eve cursed under her breath, glanced around the clearing. She tried calling a few more times, all to no avail. "Come on," she groaned. Without much choice, she hoofed across the glade, up the rickety stairs, onto the porch and—

At her feet, hastily carved into the stoop—

OLD HOUSE

It was enough to make her take a small step backward. It felt like a warning . . . She squinted into the stubborn dark of the cabin, called for Shylo yet again, and, of course, nothing.

"Fucking hell." The words clouded into fog.

Edging forward, she pushed the door fully open. Its low creak whined in the stagnant air, a protest of her trespass. Her silhouette, vague and hazy, stretched over the cabin floor. Checkered tiles. Black and white. She observed the cramped space. A narrow corridor with a kitchenette on the left, a double bunk on the right; the top bed was half collapsed into the bottom. At the far end was an olive-green door, half-ajar, paint cracked and peeling. Clearly, no one had lived here for a while, not even squatters. A realization that did little to comfort Eve.

As she took a careful step forward, the cabin settled. Beams groaned. Low clicks echoed, like the cables of a distant bridge. The sound here carried itself in a peculiar way—hushed and fleeting, as if the air itself were afraid to wake something.

"Shylo . . . ?"

From behind the olive-green door, paws skittered over dry wood, farther into the cabin, *click-click-click-click* . . . Eve inched ahead and inhaled a sour note of rat shit, mold, and rotting wood. Lovely. She kept going, praying the structure wouldn't collapse around her.

She was halfway there, when a gust of wind tore through the trees

outside and slammed the front door shut. BANG. Eve whipped around.
Through the bullet holes in the door, tendrils of gray light seeped in, tiny
stars in a black sky. Shaking off her unease, Eve pressed on. *It was only
the wind.*

She nudged the green door open, revealing a sparse room. An old armchair sat in the dead center, its upholstery worn away, exposing a wire-frame
skeleton. A faint glow filtered in through a square window and spilled onto
a worn rug.

"Shylo?" Her eyes took a moment to adjust. There, nestled in a dim corner
beside the window, sat the dog. With a head tilt and a lolling tongue, she
seemed oddly calm—proud of her own defiance. Eve marched over. "What's
gotten into you?" Leashing her up, Eve turned around and stopped in her
tracks.

The wall and the door were covered, floor to ceiling, with maps and
blueprints. An insane collage of conspiracy, all coated in dust. Eve narrowed
her eyes and drifted closer. Most of the maps were of Kettle Creek and Yale,
but some were different states, cities, countries. Yet they all seemed to be
connected, forming one big convoluted chart, unified by black-ink pathways,
arrows, and baffling notes. A lunatic's labyrinth.

Heather's words echoed in Eve's memory, *Some nut broke into town hall,
pilfered most of the paperwork . . .*

The notes, bizarre and too numerous to count, were scattered throughout:

```
If you've followed directions properly up to this point, RED
LAKE will be bone dry. At its deepest point, there will be a
steel hatch in the ground that leads to a house of refuge. A
middle-aged woman will be there to provide further instruction.
If her son has passed away in the last year, leave immediately
and backtrack your route to the last house of refuge. Ensure
the woman does NOT follow.
```

```
Host who lives beneath Civil War museum can transfer his
memories by making eye contact. Highly unstable individual,
be careful in his presence.


The ANCHOR of 129 Orello Avenue takes the form of a BLUE
NIGHTSTAND when observed.


*Time moves slower in the Brenda Mines.*


*This exit leads to a Red Sun Overworld.*


*The GUIDE in Lonsdale is a FUCKING fraud, do not listen to
a WORD he says.*
```

The rest of the wall was covered in similar ramblings. Each note accompanied by an arrow pointing to a specific location . . .

"Okay, Shylo. Time to go." A newfound urgency in her step, Eve pulled at the dog's leash, guiding her back to the exit. They shuffled through the green door, into the checkered tile space, and—

Something was wrong. Different. But what? She scanned the walls, trying to scope the change. Then the realization struck: the bullet holes in the door, those pinpricks of gray light, had vanished. Blacked out. Eve forced her eyes to adjust . . .

A figure, tall and broad, was standing between her and the only way out. Blocking the light. Eve's breath hitched, heart lurched. A silence, long and dark, slithered through the room, and then a voice:

"Y-you're not supposed to be here . . ."

Its timbre was weak and raspy, the voice of an old man just about ready for the grave.

"You're n-not supposed to be here," he repeated, sounding even more scared than Eve felt.

"I— I'm sorry," Eve sputtered, still unable to fully see who she was speaking to, only that looming silhouette. "My dog ran in," she said. "I w-was just leaving . . ."

The man staggered away. The movement was sudden, as if Eve's voice had somehow caused him to lose balance. He backed through the front door and stumbled out of view. As he did, the cold light caught the side of his face, gaunt, withered, and creased with lines. More silence. Eve hesitated, eyes fixed on the empty doorway—it framed the forest, a vertical painting.

The man's voice trembled. "Just— Please leave . . ." The fog of his breath smoked into the frame. "Please . . ."

Heedful, Eve glided toward the exit, half dragging Shylo along. As she broached the porch, the old man was huddled off to the side, half turned away, averting his gaze, as if the mere sight of her might damn him to hell. His skin clung tightly to skeletal features, like vacuum-sealed Saran Wrap. Fragile strands of chalk-white hair did nothing to cover his liver-spotted scalp. And the side of his face was scarred with a terrible gash. Long healed, it started at the corner of his mouth and led up his cheek, nearly reaching his earlobe.

"Leave," he repeated.

Eve hurried down the stairs. "I'm so sorry," she said. "I— I didn't know anyone lived here."

She was one foot on the ground, one foot on the steps, when the old man called after her: "Wait . . ."

Eve looked back.

He was still looking off to the side, avoiding eye contact. "Those people in your house . . . that's not what they look like," he said, talking more to the trees than to her.

"W-what?" Eve wasn't sure if she'd heard him right.

He looked directly at her; his eyes were filled with a different type of dread now. Nothing like the manic anxiety from moments before. No, this was the kind of long-lived, substrate terror that digs in during childhood and gnaws at your bones and skin and keeps eating away until you're rotting in the dirt.

"The family . . ." he said. "That's not what they look like."

Eve shook her head. "I— I don't understand . . ."

"You need to be careful," he added. "Get them to leave. Whatever means necessary . . ." Before Eve could respond, he stomped off into the dimness of the cabin, crashing the door shut in his wake.

Deeply disturbed by whatever the hell that was, Eve turned back to the woods. Beyond the curtain of trees, a soft orange hue shimmered. A lone beacon amid the fog. She squinted. It was a window, surrounded by the gray outline of another structure. Her own home . . . Was it that close?

As she slogged forward, a memory from the previous night surfaced, almost forgotten until now: when she'd been peering out from the foyer and saw, among the faraway trees, a pale blue light. A light that had been positioned roughly around where she was standing now. Still moving, she looked over her shoulder, up to that porthole window . . . She forged onward through the trees.

Home. Now.

DOC_A04_HOAX

Description: Excerpts from *High Strangeness Events of the Pacific Northwest: A Compilation of Rare and Unexplained Documents*, written by Various Authors. <u>Typos and other errors have not been corrected.</u>

◆

SUBJECT: OLD-HOUSE-u17 and HISTORIC CONNECTIONS?

Written by Lyle H.

Footnotes by [unknown]

Asplenium Marinum is a subspecies of fern native to Western Europe. Commonly referred to as "Sea Spleenwort," or "Seawort," due to its tendency to pop up in maritime areas. It has been recorded from the coasts of Norway, all the way down to souT[1]hern Italy.[2]

But, what's a fern got to do with anything?

Good question, yet it only raises another:

---

1 *Miscapitalized T*: Not the only instance of an oddly capitalized letter. Perhaps the author's keyboard was broken.

2 *Sea Spleenwort:* This paragraph is one of the few verifiable claims in the document.

What is a fern, native to Europe, doing in the Pacific Northwest of the United States?

It's a question that elicits nothing more than mild curiosity from most; myself included initially. After all, it was not uncommon for settlers, intentionally or otherwise, to bring European species into the so-called New World. But, when placed in the larger context of non-native species appearing in the areas surrounding "Old House u17,"[1] the question becomes more compelling.

The Eurasian Lynx, aka the Felis Lynx, is not exactly tHe type of species to stow away on a colonial ship. And yet, they have been spotted, and photographed on at least one occasion, in the vicinity of "Old House u17" (north of Spokane, Washington).

The lynx photo in question, origin unknown, was shot on 35mm black and white film, with a telephoto lens. It depicts a Eurasian Lynx, sitting beside a crooked shed at the edge of a forest, staring directly into the camera. For all intents and purposes, the photo has been deEmed legitimate.[2] Of course, it remains possible that a settler, or modern-day traveler, had intentionally brought the animal over (perhaps as a pet), and it joined the natural ecosystem. Or maybe someone local, with access to exotic cats, had released one into the area, photographed it. But again, these explanations in and of themselves would only speak to the tenacity of "Old House" conspiracies, and the cOnvoluted rabbit holes that accompany them. And, if it is a hoax, then it only reaffirms the same conclusion. After all, it's been said the sign of a great conspiracy is when people begin to create hoaxes in its stead. Much like the Andrew Melvin Interrogation Footage, aka AMIF.[3]

---

1   *Old House u17:* Still trying to figure out the author's labeling system.

2   *Lynx photo:* There is no evidence or record of this.

3   *AMIF:* No clue what this is.

⊗‡ᒀ_ ◭⊨⊨ _ ᛗ⊘⅃ᒐᵢ⊘ᒪᛗ_ ⊘ᒐ⊘₁

In addition to the Eurasian Lynx and the Sea Spleenwort Fern, cred-
ible biologists have recorded over fifty-seven species of non-native
flora and fauna in the area; the majority of which are subspecies of
lichen, fungus, and moss. Bizarrely, all incidents and recordings of
such things are constrained within a 5-kiLometer radius of the house.
As of March 3rd, 2017, there has been no satisfying explanation as
to why this is the case. Still, skeptics will understandably argue
that the foreign introduction of non-native species could explain
all of these incidents. All except one:

Gelsheimer ants.[2]

This incredibly rare subspecies of ant was originally found on
unmarked islanDs in the southwest Atlantic. Discovered by 19th-century
Belgian explorer/entomologist Audrick Gelsheimer.[3] The species was
notable for the striking white ring that circled its lower thorax. What
makes the presence of Gelsheimer ants at "Old House u17" especially
compelling is the fact they were thouGht to be extinct.

The first, and most logical explanation for this species reemerg-
ing over a century later, nearly half a world away, wOuld be that
Audrick Gelsheimer had unknowingly transported them on his ship. This,
after all, was how the Ochetellus Glaber (aka. the common house ant)
was spread from Australia to the rest of the world's continents.[4]

---

1 ⊗‡ᒀ_ ◭⊨⊨ _ ᛗ⊘⅃ᒐᵢ⊘ᒪᛗ_ ⊘ᒐ⊘: Some kind of made-up glyph language?

2 *Gelsheimer ants:* Not real.

3 *Audrick Gelsheimer:* Not a real person. (Starting to notice a theme here?)

4 *House ants Australian origin:* Pretty sure this is actually true.

However, this theory is DBA.[1] Shortly after his discovery of the ant, Gelsheimer's ship went down in a storm, and months later, a volcanic eruption wiped out all life on the islanD he'd discovered. In fact, the only reason we knew of Gelsheimer ants before their rediscovery at Old House u17, was due to divers finding Gelsheimer's journalS in the shipwreck. Conveniently, Gelsheimer utilized waterproof containment to store all his recordS. Until Old House, the only known depiction of these ants was from Gelsheimer's incredibly detailed sketches. However, I should note the majority of mainstream entomologists still quEstion the legitimacy of both Gelsheimer's records and the reported findings at Old House.[2]

+■^+10 þ ← ＼ ʊO3↪■^~2↪O▯▯[3]

Host: Person who's been trapped (or willfully residing: OWR) in Old House for longer than one year. (If trapped for longer than a month, it is essentially impossible to escape.)

Guest: Person who's been trapped (OWR) for less than one year.

Guide: Person with intimate knowledge of one or more Old House wings and can safely bring tourists inside without getting lost/trapped (hopefully).

---

1 *DBA:* Likely the author meant "dead before arrival." Ha.

2 *Entire paragraph:* Insofar as my extensive research, Gelsheimer ants are NOT a real thing. Audrick Gelsheimer is NOT a real person. No mainstream entomologists are even aware of the supposed controversy. Everything in this paragraph is a complete fabrication of the author's.

3 +■^+10 þ ← ＼ ʊO3↪■^~2↪O▯▯: Appears to be a different coding/language from the prior one.

Tourist: Person who enters Old House under the ward of a Guide. Generally for exploratory or personal reasons, and spends less than a week inside. (Many Tourists unwittingly become Guests and/or Hosts.)

Trespasser: Someone who enters Old House without a Guide, usually by accident or with nEfarious intent, for monetary gain, or otherwise.

Anchor (also known as Trickster, Spirit, Demon, Entity, Presence, Specter, etc.): Either a non-human entity, or a host who has been trapped for so long they are essentially no longer human. Some are neutral, some are helpful, most are incredibly dangerous. (Anchor motives are often incomprehensible, seems like some feed on terror/confusion/chaos?)

Hatch: Any structure/entrance (man-made or otherwise) that can be used to enter/exit Old House.

Shortcut: Exactly that, used to jump locations. Extremely high risk.

Hook: Room or section of Old House that is impossible to escApe without "~~ritual replacement~~."

(((The longer someone is trapped in Old House the more dangerous they become—to themseLves and others. Some claim that symptoms akin to radiation sickness and psychosis can occur. Hearing loss, vomiting, hallucinations, extreme paranoia etc.)))[1]

+▯V┼†5∴▲✂⅏┼30ρ1⇂Ⴟ3☀

---

[1] *Trapped in Old House:* On the original document, this line was blacked out with Sharpie. Rubbing alcohol was used to decipher it.

--. ..- .-. / --. . - . ..- ..- -.-- / -... ... / --.. .... --.- --.-
.-.. / ... -.. -.- -.. -.-. .- -- ...- / -.-- .-. --.- / --.-
-... .--- .- / -.. -. .... / --. ..- .-. / . - .... .- --. / ..-.
--. -...-. -... -.-. --.-- / --. . -. .-. -.-. ..- .. --.- / -. .--. .
-... ..-. ..-. / --. ..- .- .-. / . - -. .. .-. -.-- / --.. . ... .-.
.--- -. . .-. --..- / -. .- --.- / --.. -.. -.-. .-.-. .-.-. .-.- .-.
.-. --.- / ...- .- --. -... / --. ..- .-. / --.- -. .-. .-. .-. .-.
--.- / .--- -... ... ..- .-. .-. .-.- / --.- -. .. ..- --.- / .--. -.
. .- ..-. .--- ..- .-- / ..- -. --.- / .- -... / .--. ..- -... ...-
.--. .-. / --- .... --. / --. -... / ... -... -.-- -.-- -... .--- ..-.-

  But what do ferns, lynxes and ants have to do with anything? Why
do non-native species keep showing up around Old House? Why should
you care about any of this?

  <u>All</u> good questions. Unfortunately, when it comes to Old House,
questions tend only to raise more questions, and sometimes, if you're
"lucky" enough to find an answer, you may wish you hadn't. However,
for the morbidly curious few, keep an eye out for my upcoming book on
the subject: *Plants, Cats, Monoliths and Ants: Unpacking the Mystery
of Old House.*[1] UntiL next time . . .

  . . . noli oblivisci cuius domus sis.[2]

(Please send all questions to <u>OldHouseArchivist@gmail.com</u>)[3]

                                              ..-. --- .-.

---

1 *Book:* Never published, at least not by this title.

2 *In conclusion:* This entire document is undoubtedly the corrupted brainchild of people
   with too much free time.

3 *OldHouseArchivist@gmail.com:* I've reached out to this email multiple times. No response.

RELIC

Eve trudged onto her porch, weary, cold, and profoundly unsettled. She reached for the doorknob. Locked. She rifled through her pockets, searching for keys. Nothing, just Charlie's locket. Frustration mounting, she patted down her coat. "Perfect," she muttered. *First you lose your phone, now this?* She pounded on the door.

No answer.

With a pointer finger, she jabbed the buzzer rapid-fire. Five seconds passed. Nothing. She wiped a foggy window with her sleeve and strained to see inside. The house sat in darkness. Had the family left? How had they locked the door behind them? She smacked a palm against the glass. "Hey," she yelled, "anybody home?!"

Still nothing.

"Un-fucking-believable," she groaned.

Ready to try another way in, she turned, but after three steps across the porch, the door creaked open behind her. She looked back. Thomas was standing there, sheepish. "I'm so sorry," he said.

Eve, too cold, too grumpy for words, brushed past him into the foyer. She slammed the door shut, the warmth of the house breathing life into her stiff limbs, melting away the chill but not the bad mood. Pulling off her coat, she went to the closet and—

"Any luck?" asked Thomas.

Eve blinked at him.

He clarified, "Getting ahold of Charlie."

"Sure." She hung up her coat, her thoughts still lost in the woods. She checked the time: 10:46 a.m. Then, she looked at Thomas, her face filled with *The fuck are you still doing here?*

Reading her mind, Thomas said, "We, uh, we were planning to head out, just . . . didn't want to leave the place unlocked." He nodded toward the window. "A lot of eccentrics out in these woods. Can't be too careful."

"Uh-huh" was all Eve could muster. Now, with the added context of Thomas's past, those pockmarked scars on his face suddenly stood out all the more. Again, that morose vision invaded her thoughts: a gaunt hand, a silver-tipped pen stabbing into pale flesh. *Alison started to believe there was only one way to make it stop, to get her old life back . . .* A hint of sympathy for Thomas fell over Eve, along with something else—fear? Thomas, catching Eve's stare, rubbed his neck, as if trying to shield the scars from view.

Eve considered asking him why they hadn't stayed at Heather's place last night, but she had bigger priorities. She cleared her throat. "Anyways. You should hit the road before it gets any worse out there."

"Of course." He nodded. "Just waiting on the weather."

The words sailed across the room, slipped into Eve's ear canal, and ignited a chemical rage. She didn't even try to mask it. "You said you were leaving after breakfast."

Thomas cast her an apologetic look. "I know, but now—without winter tires. The roads. Paige is a little anxious, and she's worn me down . . . Besides, the weather should clear up soon enough."

Eve blinked at him. If she hadn't been so tired, she might've screamed.

He added, somewhat defensively, "We wanted to head out earlier, but . . . like I said, didn't want to leave the place unlocked."

The comment not so subtly shifted the blame onto Eve. But just as she felt the burden of guilt begin to sag on her shoulders, she shook it off and went into problem-solving mode instead. "I'll get the tire chains from the attic. Then you can leave right away."

From behind Thomas, Jenny shuffled into the foyer. Thomas ruffled his daughter's hair, looked at Eve, and said, "Tire chains? I appreciate that, but I'm not sure they'll fit our truck."

"They're universal."

He sighed with palpable relief. "That'll work," he said. "You need a hand getting them down?"

"I'll be fine."

"You sure?"

"I've got it," she repeated.

He nodded again. "We'll start packing up our stuff right away. Checkout time is at eleven, right?" He smiled, seeming to expect a chuckle, but all Eve gave him was a silent glare. Clearing his throat, he turned away and called, "Paige?" He disappeared into the living room.

His daughter lingered behind, looking up at Eve, her eyes filled with a hint of worry. As if something bad had happened while Eve was away. Maybe Eve was projecting, reading too much into it, but—

"JENNIFER," Paige's shrill call snapped from the living room. "Help us clean up. NOW." Head hanging, Jenny slunk off around the corner.

Eve, alone in her musings, stared into the now empty doorway, still trying to grasp the bizarre events of the morning. *Who was that old man in the woods? Why did he warn me about this family? Why did the—*

Focus. Charlie's voice halted her train of thought. *Get the tire chains. Get them out of our house.*

Moments later, Eve grabbed an aluminum flashlight from the laundry room. Switching off a hanging bulb, she shut the door and had started back toward the foyer when Paige stepped around the corner, blocking her path. The dim glow of winter light cast onto Paige from behind, a white aura spilling over her shoulders, her blond hair. She smiled meekly, her face draped in thin shadows.

The old man's cryptic warning whispered in Eve's ear: *That's not what they look like . . .*

Paige broke the awkward silence. "Thomas said you're lending us tire chains?"

More like donating. Eve gave an apathetic "Yup."

Paige nodded. "I— we really appreciate all your help. It means a—"

"Good to know." Eve strolled around her and slipped into the foyer. Her social battery had long run out.

Upstairs, Eve entered the hallway and froze. She narrowed her gaze. The once-hanging flap of wallpaper, the one Jenny had torn away to access the dumbwaiter, was back in place. Eve went over and ran her finger along the edges, a near seamless repair. Had Thomas done this? Under normal circumstances, Eve might've appreciated the gesture, but now, like everything else going on, it just didn't feel right. He should have asked first. Where had he even found the materials to put it back in place?

Returning to the task at hand, Eve reached for the white cord hanging from the ceiling and gave it a firm tug. A retractable staircase creaked downward, spewing a cloud of red dust. She backstepped, covered her mouth, and waited for the dust to settle before ascending.

Eve poked her head into the attic, flicked on her flashlight, and scanned around, like a detective assessing a crime scene. Sloped ceilings. Shallow walls lined with piles of junk. The air up here was damp, a higher pitch of the basement's odor. Metallic earthiness. But with a slight undertone that made her think of something rotten and foul—a dead rat or maybe a bird, was probably calcified into the walls. Charming.

Hoisting herself up, she rose to stand, nearly bumping her head on a low support beam. Close call. She looked around, studying the clutter. Chairs, tables, cabinets—all in a 1950s minimalist style. Some of it was still in decent shape, but . . .

. . . where had Charlie said those tire chains were? A few weeks back, she'd spoken of a narrow corridor leading to an alcove at the house's front. Eve turned leftward, her light roaming over the stacks of old chairs, furniture, and . . .

. . . a dog kennel? It was nestled between a broken grandfather clock and an empty guitar case. Eve drew closer. The metal-wire crate held an assortment of chew toys, expired liver treats, and a plastic food bowl. Fading white letters on the bowl spelled out BUCKLEY. Thomas's chocolate Lab?

Right then, her flashlight flickered. Stuttering blinks. Darkness. Eve rolled her eyes, gave it a shake. No luck. She smacked it against her palm and it jolted back to life. "That's what I thought," she muttered. Turning away, she ducked to avoid another support beam and delved deeper, rounding a tight corner into an even lower-ceilinged alcove. With each step, the world outside grew quieter, until the only sounds were the muffled wind and the occasional murmurs of the family shuffling about downstairs.

Then, somewhere nearby, the *drip, drip, drip* . . . of a roof leak or a broken pipe.

The sound was coming from a murky corner. As Eve approached, she could see a passageway, a gap between two support beams. Barely shoulder width, it stretched for a good thirty feet, parallel to the front of the house. This had to be the one Charlie mentioned. Reluctant, Eve pushed into it, shuffling forward. Here, the timeworn innards of the house were exposed: rusted pipes, frayed wires, and reddish-pink insulation. Looked like a botched surgery. All the while, that *drip, drip, drip* drew closer until . . .

. . . an icy droplet landed on the top of her head, muffled by her hair. She looked up. A leaky pipe. Another drop fell, tracing a cold path down her cheek. She wiped it away. Carried on. Behind her the dripping returned, smacking against the cured wood. Rhythmic. A few feet ahead, Eve came upon a gap in the paneling. A two-foot-by-three-foot square at waist height. An entrance? She peered inside.

The dumbwaiter chute . . .

Curious, she beamed her light into its depths, revealing a narrow shaft that plunged all the way to the basement. Long drop. A counterweighted rope reached down, hooked to a metal cart at the bottom. Memories from the night before rushed up like a cold draft—the figure on the steps, Thomas in the snow. A prickling sensation crept up her spine. *Why did I come back to the house? I should've just waited at Heather's and—*

Tire. Chains.

She pulled away from the chute and continued down the passage. At the end, she rounded a tight corner and came upon a crooked door, coated with red paint, cracked and peeling like severely chapped lips. Leery, she nudged it open. A blinding glow glared into her corneas. Harsh sunlight was flooding through a square window in the far wall.

Switching off her flashlight, she stepped into a room no bigger than a walk-in closet. The walls were crowded with more random junk—a motley crew of thrift store rejects: bald tires, tacky holiday decorations, empty picture frames. But it was in the back corner, tucked beneath the wiry branches of a plastic Christmas tree, where she found what she was looking for: tire chains. Wasting no more time, Eve gathered them up, ready to leave. Yet, as she rose to stand, something caught her eye: a white file box was sitting beneath the window. Written on its lid, in black Sharpie:

CHARLOTTE'S STUFF (DONATE)

Charlotte? That was Charlie's legal name, the one still on her birth certificate, but she hadn't answered to it in decades. Unable to help herself, Eve set the tire chains aside and lifted the box onto the windowsill. She pulled off the lid and rifled through. Inside were a few camera lenses, rolls of film, and an old 35mm Pentax.

Charlie's camera . . .

Eve picked it up, turned it over in her hands. She wasn't exactly shocked to find it stashed away but . . . up in the attic? And in a donation box at that?

During the early years of their relationship, Charlie was seldom seen without that camera draped around her neck. And Eve still vividly recalled the day when, three years before, Charlie had her own gallery showing. It was a rain-soaked Thursday in downtown Rochester, and they'd rented out a little studio on University Ave. Charlie adorned its walls with mountain vistas, downtown scenes, and live concert snapshots. She'd even put up the blurry portrait of Eve, hiding her face from the camera.

The turnout had been modest, but every single visitor meant the world to Charlie. Eve never forgot how nervous her partner looked as the first people shuffled in. It was a rare, endearing sight—Charlie, usually so self-assured, fumbling her words as she spoke to perusing guests. To Eve, it was just about the cutest thing in the world. And it showed how much Charlie cared about her work.

But Charlie hadn't taken a photo since her father passed away two years ago. He was the one who'd introduced her to photography in the first place. The one who'd gifted her that 35mm Pentax. A few weeks after his funeral, the camera found its way to a shelf, then to a closet, and now . . . here. Tucked between a rusty hubcap and a plastic reindeer. No more gallery showings, no more stealthy portraits . . .

Eve had asked her about it once, but Charlie just shrugged and said: "Don't have time for it."

As Eve tucked away the box, she heard the front door swing open and slam shut with a muted *thwack*. Footfalls crunched on gravel and snow. She leaned forward, trying to get a better view. Down below, Thomas was marching across the yard. Focused. Determined.

He paused at the crooked shed, sneaking a look back at the house as if making sure he was hidden from view. Then, out of nowhere, he exhaled a primal scream, slapping at the side of his head with a flat palm. Violent. Vicious. The type of tantrum that makes people cross the street to avoid you.

A disturbing and surprising thing to behold. Until then, Thomas had seemed to be many things, but violent certainly wasn't one of them. It only added to Eve's growing unease.

After excising his demons, Thomas straightened up, collected himself, and fixed his tousled hair. Red-faced, he reached into his coat pocket and cast another furtive glance around. He hunched over and brought both hands to his face. For a second, Eve thought he might be dialing someone on a cell phone. But as he stood upright and exhaled a dark plume, she noticed something pinched between his index and middle finger. A cigarette. He took a long drag and exhaled again. Puffing away, he continued down the winding driveway until the trees obscured him. Was he going to get the truck? If the drive up had stumped him the day before, she doubted he'd fare better now . . .

As she receded from the window, her eyes caught a message, carved into the sill:

Don't forget which House you're in

It was haphazard, eerily similar to the one on the cabin's doorstep, *Old House . . .*

Don't forget which house you're in?

What did it mean? Was it a religious ultimatum: *This is a house of the Lord; never forget that.* Or was it something stranger?

Eve didn't know, and frankly, she wasn't eager to find out.

Besides, she'd wasted enough time up here. Just as she was about to grab the tire chains, a harsh, metallic sound echoed behind her. Eve turned. Around the corner, down the narrow passage, the dissonant rasping droned on, like jagged fingernails scraping against rusting metal. High-pitched. Wailing. Louder by the second. Painful to listen to; she could feel it in her teeth. Then, right as it became nearly unbearable, it rattled to a sudden stop. A halting *kuh-chunk* sound that made her realize what it was: the dumbwaiter.

Cautious, she peeked into the narrow corridor. Sure enough, the dumbwaiter cart was up here now, but from this angle, she couldn't tell if it was empty or not. For all she knew, someone might be huddled inside, waiting to leap out, grab her by the neck, and drag her into the depths of Hades . . .

"Jenny . . . ?" Eve's voice drifted faintly down the corridor, answered only by that dripping pipe. She glanced over her shoulder, down at the tire chains— *Come back for those later.* Bracing herself, she ventured forward, one step at a time, flashlight raised like a pointless shield.

Inch by inch, the dumbwaiter's interior was unveiled and . . . empty. Joy. It must have been hoisted up with no one inside—after all, that was how they were supposed to be used. *One of the kids must've done it. Right?* She was about to turn back for the chains when something else caught her light . . .

On the floor, damp footprints. Narrow and gaunt, they gleamed under her light like oil slicks in a back-alley puddle. They started at the dumbwaiter entrance, trailed off down the passageway, and bent around the corner. These weren't the footprints of a child. With terrible anticipation, she raised her light, a quivering moon that shone through wooden slats and dusty clutter. No shadowy figure in sight.

She opened her mouth, but what did you say in situations like this? *Hello? Anybody there? No, don't say that* . . . "Jenny?" The dusty attic remained silent, interrupted only by that infuriating *drip, drip, drip* . . .

Whoever was up here, they were somewhere between Eve and the only way out. Focus. Breathe. One foot in front of the other, she passed beneath the dripping leak, the top of her head muffling its rhythm one last time. At the end of the corridor, she leaned out and swivel-checked both ways. All clear. *We're good. Just get to the exit, and* . . .

With perfect timing, her flashlight flickered into darkness.

Shit.

She smacked it—sputtering light.

Fuck.

She smacked it again. Harder.

This time it surged bright, like a flare, somehow illuminating the entire attic and then . . .

Darkness.

She click-click-clicked the on/off switch. Nothing. She bonked it against a support beam. Nothing. In a fit of stupid rage, she hurled it across the attic. With a hollow crack, it rattled off a wall somewhere and tumbled to the floor.

Pitch. Black.

The shadowy void engulfed her now, trapping her up here with the vague shapes of old furniture and forgotten relics. Her heart raced. She inched forward aimlessly, arms outstretched. *Calm down. Focus on your breath. In through the nose, out through the mouth.*

Behind her, a skittering, almost fragile sound—followed by a short, ragged gasp, like a breath taken just before slipping underwater. She halted in her tracks, a shivering cold creeping down her neck as she peered over her shoulder. Silence. Dark. Only that *drip, drip, dripping* pipe until . . .

Nothing. Dead quiet. The drip had suddenly stopped. Was someone standing under it? Just as the question formed, the dripping resumed, and a floorboard creaked, slow, careful. A footstep? Swiveling back, she was about to panic, but a literal ray of hope saved her. About forty feet away, the light from the still-open attic ladder cast dimly onto the angled ceiling. She picked up her pace. *Careful, don't trip. Almost there. Almost free and—*

At the last second, the ladder slammed shut with an authoritative WHAM.

Fuck.

She collapsed onto the hatch, shouting for whoever was down there to open it. No response. Frantic, she fumbled around, searching for the handle, searching for something, anything. But there was only the splinter-infested floorboards. Cold sweat ran down her forehead, into her eyes—her heart thumped faster—breath gasped. She stopped herself again. *Breathe in. Breathe out. In. Out.*

Ground yourself.

Focus on your surroundings.

Your senses.

Sight: Darkness. A thin slit of white light slipping through the floorboards.

Smell: Musty air. Dead rat.

Touch: Coarse hardwood. Cold sweat.

Sound: Her own breathing. Wind gusting outside. The dripping pipe and—

Behind her, a slow, rolling sound—like a billiard ball. She gazed back. Only darkness. But then, light flickered to life. The flashlight. It was about ten feet away, rolling in a lazy arc, beaming a dim wedge across the floor. Eve watched, dreadfully transfixed as, bit by bit, the rolling flashlight shone across the walls, the reddish-pink insulation, and then . . .

. . . it came to a tottering stop, its yellow glow stretching across the floor, ending just before it reached a darkened nook. It was as if this light was trying to show her something, but . . . nothing was there . . .

Her eyes narrowed. Vision adjusted. Just beyond the edge of the flashlight's circle, a faint outline took shape among the shadows. Standing between an old coatrack and a glass cabinet—a figure. Tall, slender, draped in darkness. Pin-straight posture. Motionless. As still as a storefront mannequin.

Was it a mannequin?

As if in response to her unspoken query, the figure took a sudden, shuffling step forward. Now, the front of its bare feet stood in the light; jaundiced skin and overgrown toenails stained with dirt.

Eve's stomach twisted.

The figure took another shuffling step forward, callused heels scraping the hardwood like sandpaper. Now, it loomed, fully bathed in the flashlight's unforgiving glare—a woman. Draped in a tattered, off-white hospital gown. She was tall, almost six feet, her face hidden behind peekaboo hands, like a child playing some terrible game. And her scalp was shaved down to thin black roots, bluish veins pulsating beneath bone-white skin.

Eve's breath cut short, like an emergency hatch within her lungs had burst open, sucked out all the air. She couldn't even scream. That choking moment, horrible and suffocating, seemed to stretch on for eternity until—

The woman took another sudden step forward before freezing in place. Then . . . two quick steps. Halted. One step. Halted. Three steps and—

The flashlight blinked out. Total darkness ensued, punctuated by those sporadic footsteps. Faster, faster. Unspeakable dread surged from Eve's gut, climbed into her throat like a swarm of maggots writhing up a narrow pipe until—

Finally, she managed to scream for help. Scream louder than she'd ever screamed before. Swiveling back, she pounded on the hatch, hitting harder and harder, each blow sending jolts of pain through her clenched fists. All the while, those scraping footfalls drew closer, closer, nearly upon her and—

Without warning, the floor swung open from beneath. Blinding light. A fleeting, weightless moment. Then she tumbled down the ladder, the world a dizzying blur as she slammed headfirst into the banister—

LIGHT

You have to hide . . .
You have to hide . . .
You have to—

She awakes in a room no bigger than a walk-in closet. Beige walls. Rickety bed. A window that overlooks a murky pond. She's been here for months now, maybe years, she doesn't know anymore, she stopped counting when the snow stopped falling in March, or maybe February. She wonders—

THIEF

When Eve's eyes fluttered open, she found herself lying on the living room couch, a dull pain pounding in her forehead. Fractured memories floated through her psyche: the attic, tire chains, and . . . a leaky pipe? Rising to sit, she took in her surroundings.

Paige sat near the fireplace, knitting away. At her feet, Newton and Jenny were playing with Legos. *Where did they get those from?* Kai was standing off near the kitchen, hands in his pockets, staring out a window. And Thomas . . . he was nowhere to be seen.

Paige, catching Eve's movement, looked up, her face etched with concern, maybe even a hint of fear. "Are— are you all right?" she asked.

Before Eve could respond, Thomas emerged from the foyer, his face a grim mask. Upon seeing Eve, his severe expression gave way to relief. "Oh, thank God you're awake," he said.

Eve rubbed her temples, still struggling to think through the throbbing ache. "What— what happened?"

"You were in the attic," Paige answered. "Screaming, terrified."

The kids stared at Eve, eyes tinged with apprehension. Thomas went on. "You took a nasty fall. Hit your head and blacked out for a few seconds. We helped you down here, but you passed out again . . ."

"How long was I out?"

"Ten, fifteen minutes."

Eve narrowed her gaze. "And you didn't call an ambulance?" She realized the answer before the words left her mouth:

"No phones," said Thomas with a shade of remorse.

Digital fucking detox. In the middle of a cross-country move.

Right then, Paige's earlier comment finally registered. "Wait," said Eve. "I was screaming?"

Paige and Thomas exchanged a glance.

"You were calling for help," said Thomas. "You sounded, uh, quite distressed."

A memory shot to the surface of Eve's mind: the woman, draped in a hospital gown. "There— There's somebody in the . . ." She trailed off.

Thomas nudged. "I'm sorry?"

"There's an intruder in the attic," said Eve, a sudden urgency in her voice.

Jenny and Newton gaped at her, fear rising in their eyes. Thomas, picking up on this, said, "Go play in the other room."

Kai slouched off around the corner, disinterested by it all, like he thought Eve was making things up for attention. Jenny and Newton, still wide-eyed, left their Legos behind and started filing out.

"And, Newton," Thomas added, "keep Jenny close. Anything happens, you come right back here. Understood?"

The boy gave a single nod.

Once the kids were out of earshot, Thomas sat opposite Eve and lowered his voice. "What exactly did you see?"

"There, there was a woman . . ." Eve paused, head still pounding, memories still foggy. "She was wearing a hospital gown. I think I saw her before, last night on the basement stairs, but—"

"Last night?" Paige interrupted. "And you didn't tell anyone?"

"I— I convinced myself it was nothing . . ."

Thomas tapped a finger against the side of his leg. "What did she look like?"

Another image flashed: those pale hands, splayed with bluish veins, held up like she was playing peekaboo. "I— I couldn't see her face." Half to herself, Eve added, "Do you think it was . . . ?"

She fell silent. The notion that Alison might still be around here had been gnawing at the back of Eve's mind since last night, but . . .

Thomas prodded, "Do I think it was . . . ?"

Uncertain, Eve ventured, "Your sister?"

"Alison?" Thomas balked. "No, not possible, she's . . . it's not her."

She's what? Institutionalized? Dead?

"Before you moved in." Thomas shifted the topic. "How long was the house sitting empty?"

Eve blinked at him. *How is this relevant?*

Thomas tried again, "When did the previous owners move out?"

"A year ago, I think."

"A year?" He looked to Paige, then back to Eve. "Could be a squatter," he said.

Eve scoffed. "A squatter? I don't think—"

"Eve," said Paige, "are you sure about what you saw up there? It wasn't just a trick of the shadows?"

Eve sent her a stabbing glare, not in the mood for debate.

"Well," Paige huffed, "did they seem dangerous?"

Eve leaned forward, rubbing her temples. "They sure as fuck didn't seem friendly, Paige."

Paige grimaced. Her eyes flicked to her husband. "We should call the police."

"With what?"

"The neighbor's phone." Paige bristled.

Thomas waved away her suggestion. "Let's not escalate things, not until we know what we're dealing with. I'll go check first, might be a drifter, somebody trying to stay out of the cold."

Paige scoffed. "What are you going to do? Ask them to leave? We should call the authorities . . ."

As Thomas and Paige argued back and forth, Eve fell into another night-marish daydream, as if part of her was still locked in the attic—screaming for help. She could almost feel her fists pounding against the hardwood, hear those footsteps shuffling closer, closer, closer—

Thomas said, "I'm going up to take a look, all right?"

"I— I don't think it's safe," Eve thought aloud.

"I'll be fine." He pushed himself up to stand and made his way toward the foyer.

"Don't forget the tire chains," Paige called after him.

Thomas mumbled a reply and disappeared around the corner. As the sound of his footfalls marched upstairs, Eve was about to tumble down yet another doom spiral when . . .

A rhythmic creaking disrupted her thoughts. Paige was knitting again, rocking back and forth in her chair. An unfamiliar red rocking chair; Eve hadn't noticed it until now. Catching Eve's stare, Paige slowed to a stop.

"Nice chair," said Eve.

"Thanks . . ." Paige's lips pressed together in a straight line. "Thomas grabbed it from the truck," she explained. "It's—the movement is good for my spine. I used to ride horses, had an injury, and—"

"Sure." Eve couldn't pretend to care.

A solid stretch of tense silence dragged by until Paige murmured, "Sorry about last night."

Eve looked at her, eyebrow raised.

Paige cleared her throat. "During dinner, when I, uh, interrogated you about your life—it wasn't appropriate . . ."

Eve remained silent. *You picked a weird time to atone.*

"It's just . . ." Paige sighed. "I'm not used to how fast the world's changing these days."

Eve looked away and replied with a dry "Same."

Unprompted, Paige said, "I wasn't always a believer, you know." She rubbed her silver cross necklace between an index finger and thumb, apparently waiting for Eve's response. Eve considered asking Paige to please, kindly, shut the fuck up, but the banal conversation was at least keeping her distracted from the headache. Keeping her from falling into another panic.

Paige, interpreting Eve's silence as interest, went on, "Thomas, believe it or not . . . He was the one who led me to the Lord."

Eve tilted her head, surprised but not invested.

"We met at a soup kitchen," Paige continued. "Thomas was there with his church. I was there for . . . court-ordered community service, if you can believe that." She looked to Eve, again expecting some kind of response. Eve, too spaced out to care, said nothing.

Paige went on. "A few weeks into us knowing each other, Thomas asked me if I wanted to grab a coffee sometime. I said no thanks, but a drink would be just fine. Thomas said coffee *was* a drink, and I laughed. I guess it was the sort of thing I found funny back then." Paige almost smiled. She seemed about to say something else, but . . .

Thomas reentered. "Didn't see anyone." He shrugged. "Found this, though." He held out the aluminum flashlight. Eve stared at it like he'd just offered up a dead fish.

"What about the tire chains?" said Paige.

"We'll be fine without them." Thomas set the flashlight on the coffee table.

Eve said, "The footprints."

"Hm?"

"There were footprints up there . . ."

"Huh." Thomas shook his head. "I checked pretty much everywhere.

Didn't see anything." The corner of his mouth twitched; he was lying, Eve was sure of it. He was trying to make her look unstable and—

That's not what they look like . . .

The thought came out of nowhere and—once again, Eve's sanity threatened to slip. On impulse, she jumped up from the couch and headed for the kitchen. *Get away from this family.* Thomas blocked her path. "Eve," he said, his face filled with a pity that made her feel pathetic. "Are you sure you're okay? You, uh, you hit your head pretty hard back there. Maybe you should sit?" His tone was reminiscent of someone addressing a lost senior: *Is your home nearby? Do you have a loved one I can call?* Despite the patronization, his concern sent a speckle of doubt through her. *Is my judgment clouded by the concussion? Have I misinterpreted—*

From somewhere upstairs, a familiar sound bled through a ceiling vent: three clear chimes. Eve's phone? It had the same unmistakably generic ringtone. Without a second thought, Eve brushed past Thomas, hauling herself toward the foyer. He started after her—

"Don't *fucking* follow me," she snapped, her words filled with a vitriol that surprised even her.

Thomas froze, equally startled by the outburst.

"Just—just leave me alone . . ." she muttered, veering off around the corner.

She heedlessly shot up the stairs, two at a time, and . . . The sound was coming from the study. She charged in, finding Kai, silhouetted by the stained glass window, fumbling with her cracked-screen phone, trying to silence it. *That little thief.* "Hand it over," she seethed.

"W-what?" Kai feigned ignorance, and hid the now silent phone behind his back. Eve stomped over and snatched for it, but he turned away. "It's mine," he said, that ever-present smugness twinkling in his eyes.

"Give me back my *fucking* phone," Eve growled, seizing his arm. But his grip was strong, and a vicious tug-of-war ensued.

Out of nowhere, Shylo bolted into the room, barking bloody murder, circling the battling duo. As the tug-of-war reached its crescendo, Shylo lunged forward, clamping her teeth onto Kai's denim-clad ankle. All at once, Eve staggered back, Kai squealed out a warbled yelp, and the phone clattered to the hardwood.

Thomas, Paige, and the other two kids burst through the door, mouths agape at the rapidly unfolding nightmare before them. Shylo, with her teeth still clamped around Kai's ankle, thrashed, refusing to let go. No matter how much Kai shook, how much he squealed, the dog only bore down tighter.

Eve, struggling to find her words amid the chaos, finally bellowed, "SHYLO, OFF." But Shylo doubled down, wrenching Kai's screams into a higher pitch. Just as Thomas rushed to intervene, Kai kicked Shylo in the ribs with his free leg. The dog exhaled a sharp yelp—but held firm. Kai kicked again, harder. With a pained wheeze, Shylo released her grip and fled the scene, vanishing down the stairs, and then . . .

The room fell silent, save for the sound of Kai's soft whimpers. All eyes turned to Eve. She sputtered out two thoughts at once: "She never, she's never done— He, he stole my—"

"That psycho and her dog attacked me," Kai spat, rubbing his leg like a midfielder playing up a foul. Thomas hunched over his son while the others remained huddled in the doorway, staring at Eve. Horrified.

"Kai, he . . ." Eve spoke like she was on trial. "He stole my fucking phone," she asserted, her defensiveness switching to sudden rage. She scooped up Exhibit A and held it out for all to see. "He wouldn't give it back when I—"

Mid-sentence, she froze. The phone clutched in her hand bore a Portland Winterhawks sticker and—she turned it over—the screen wasn't cracked. This wasn't her phone. But— No, she'd seen the . . .

Kai mumbled, "I'm sorry . . ." The apology wasn't for Eve; it was directed to his parents. He went on. "After, after we turned our phones in for the fast, I . . . snuck mine back. I just, I wanted to keep in touch with my friends."

Thomas clicked his tongue, disappointed. "We'll discuss that later." He let out a weary sigh. "But right now . . ." He rolled up Kai's jean cuff, assessing the damage. Shylo's bite had pierced through the denim. Four red puncture marks stood out against the pale skin, shallow but defined. "Oof." Thomas grimaced. "We'll definitely have to get this looked at." He glanced to Eve, his shoulders tensed. "Your dog's up to date on shots, right?"

Eve tried to mumble a response, but she could scarcely think. That had been her phone, she was certain of it. She'd seen the cracked screen, the background photo of Charlie and Shylo—

"Eve." Paige butted in, enunciating each syllable. "Is your dog up to date on shots?"

Eve finally mustered a meek "Y-yeah." It felt like the room was tilting, the floor shifting—as if the house itself was sinking into the earth. Kai had stolen her phone. She knew it. She'd seen the cracked screen. She knew. She'd never been more certain of anything in her life and—

Paige wasn't done. "That animal needs to be put down. This is completely—"

"Paige," said Thomas. "Let's focus on our son right now."

Paige shot Eve a cutting glare before turning back to her husband. "We need to call an ambulance," she said. "Get him to a hospital."

"It'll be quicker if we drive." Thomas gave his son a serious look. "Think you can walk?"

Kai, going for the Oscar, said, "I— I can try," his lip quivering.

His father supported him as they made their way to the exit, Kai wincing with each step.

Paige looked at Eve. "You'll be hearing from us, do you understand?"

Another jolt of sudden rage flared in Eve's temples. She stifled it, barely. "All right, Paige." *None of this would've happened if you hadn't come here in the first place.*

Thomas gestured at the other kids. "Go get your stuff," he said. They trailed after him, down the hall, out of view. Paige lingered behind, still bludgeoning Eve with her cold blue eyes. Eve held her gaze, defiant. Paige marched forward, a determined stride that made Eve wonder if she was about to get slapped across the face, but . . .

. . . Paige held out an upturned palm. "Kai's phone," she said.

In all the chaos, Eve had forgotten she was still holding it. She handed it over. Paige pivoted away and stormed off to join the others. Stopping in the doorframe, she peered over her shoulder, gave Eve one last pitying look, and said, "I'll be praying for you." With that, Paige slipped out of view and headed downstairs. Good riddance.

Alone, Eve stared blankly into the now empty doorway. She might have burst into tears—and been perfectly justified in doing so—but she needed to go check on Shylo. She was about to leave the room, when her thoughts came to a sudden, screeching halt.

That stained glass window—the one that had depicted a vibrant apple tree, was gone. Gone and, beyond all reasonable explanation, replaced by an ordinary four-panel, clear-glass window. A knot, sick and twisting, formed in Eve's chest, and a cold rush of dread crawled down her neck. *There's no way—there's no possible way* . . . It had been stained glass only minutes earlier; she'd just seen it with her own eyes . . . Right? She found herself drifting forward. At the window, she ran her hand along the cross sections, the panes. It was real, all right. Terribly, terribly real. The wood was worn and rough, the glass uneven and warped. She leaned in close and narrowed her eyes. There was no evidence of recent installation, no sawdust, no fresh sealant. In fact, it blended in flawlessly with the age-worn room—as if it had been there all along.

Misidentifying a phone was one thing, but this . . .

Find Shylo. Get out of here.

When Eve stepped down into the foyer, the family was already outside, making their way across the yard. Thomas was carrying Paige's rocking chair, while Paige assisted a limping Kai. Eve watched as they trudged away and slipped behind a cut of trees. Now it was just her, Shylo, and . . .

Eve glanced up the stairs toward the closed attic door. Whether or not somebody was hiding up there, she wasn't sticking around to find out. With growing urgency, she strode into the living room and called out, "Shylo?"

Silence.

She ventured into the kitchen and tried again. "Shylo . . . ?"

At the corner of her vision, a blurred shape slipped out of view. She swiveled to see an empty doorway . . .

From somewhere in the house, skittering footfalls echoed—*click-clack-click-clack*—cut short by a shrill whimper. Eve turned. The basement door was half-open. Had Shylo gone down there to hide? Was she injured?

Protective instinct kicking in, Eve hurried over, flung open the door, and was greeted by that familiar, dark descent. Rickety wooden stairs. Dirty brick walls. Another high-pitched whine seeped up from below. Shylo was hurt. Without a second thought, Eve snatched the flashlight from the coffee table and started downward. Yet just as her foot met the cold basement floor, a whimper rang out again—this one from behind.

Leery, she peered over her shoulder. At the top of the stairs sat Shylo, head tilted, quizzical.

"Shylo . . . ?"

The dog's tail gave a hesitant wag.

Eve swept her light back into the subterranean shadows. Those whimpers—she was sure they'd come from down here. She was straining her ears, listening to the void, when . . .

A metallic moan churned and creaked. Like a rusty merry-go-round in a nightmare playground. The dumbwaiter?

Fear, sudden and primal, fell over Eve, a prickling whisper on the nape of her neck: *RUN*. Huffing back up the stairs, she surged into the living room, slammed the door shut behind, and locked it. She herded Shylo to the foyer and quickly checked the dog's ribs, making sure Kai's kicks hadn't done any serious damage. There wasn't even a bruise. Thank God.

Get out of here. Now.

DOC_C01_RECOVERY

Description: Report of lost hikers in Joffre Lakes Provincial Park. Not sure if any connection here, but worth looking into.

◆

March 3, 2002

Last November, five hikers went missing after going off the beaten trail in Joffre Lakes Provincial Park, in Canada. Two months later, only one of them was found alive, wandering down a defunct logging road. Erin [last name redacted], a twenty-four-year-old woman. In a delirious state, she claimed that she and her companions got lost in a blizzard and came upon a "1950s-style hotel" buried in the snow.

According to her, they sheltered there for weeks. Then, one by one, they were picked off by an unseen force. Dragged through what she calls "doorways to different places."

Search and Rescue swept the area several times, but of course no such building was discovered. The survivor had likely experienced an elaborate hallucination brought on by hypothermia, sleep deprivation, and/or extreme stress.

Regardless, the search for her companions has now turned into a recovery operation.

- .-.   .   -.   -   ..-   .-.   ..   .   ...

REUNION

Wrapped in one of Charlie's winter coats, Eve trudged down the muddy driveway, Shylo in tow. As far as she was concerned, she'd never be setting foot in that godforsaken house again. Of course, convincing Charlie they needed to sell something they had just bought was going to be a battle, but . . . she'd worry about that later.

As she approached the final bend, she halted. Beyond the trees, down on the road, Charlie's pickup idled. But the sight brought little relief. The family's truck was pulled up alongside, Thomas leaning out the window, face filled with concern as he spoke. Whatever he was saying to Charlie, Eve couldn't hear, but he looked like a solemn teacher telling a parent about their troubled child. Charlie, partially obscured by windshield reflections, was nodding slowly, taking it all in. Taking it all very, very seriously.

A swell of worry rose in Eve's gut, egged on by Mo: *Thomas is feeding Charlie a skewed version of events. He's going to make you sound unstable, unhinged. Then you're never gonna be able to convince her to sell this place and you'll be stuck here forever and—*

Eve fought the urge to scramble down there and defend herself. It would only make her look worse: the more one tried to prove their sanity, the more insane they appeared. She took a deep breath, held back, and observed. *It's fine*, she told herself. *This is fine. Charlie will see through their bullshit. She knows me better than anyone, right?*

Thomas, done talking, gave Charlie a grim smile and a quick nod. He rolled up the window and drove off through the slush. A few moments passed, then Charlie's pickup lurched to a start. It slipped behind a rocky outcrop, rounded onto the driveway, then slowed to a stop. Eve, heart thudding, surged forward, nearly slipping more than once until, finally, she yanked open the passenger door, ushered Shylo inside, and followed suit.

"Eve . . ." Charlie regarded her with wary eyes. "Are you—"

"I'm great, just"—Eve pulled the door shut, glanced around, paranoid—"can we, uh, can we get out of here?" Eve smiled, and— *No, not like that, you look crazy.* She stopped smiling.

Charlie narrowed her eyes. "'Get out of here'? Is everything—"

"Everything's great, just . . ." Eve peered over her shoulder, back to the road, then up to the house. The peak of its roof was just visible through the distant trees. Somehow, the structure looked vaguely alive, as if it were standing on tiptoes, craning its neck to listen.

Charlie prodded. "Thomas said you hit your head and—"

"Can we . . ." Eve fidgeted in her seat. "Can we just—get off the driveway?" Eve could barely think with the house in her line of sight.

Charlie shifted into reverse, backed down the driveway, and pulled to a stop beneath the Heritage Lane sign. She killed the engine. "Okay, what's going on, Eve?"

"Why did you leave me alone with them?"

Charlie blinked. "I woke you up, told you I needed to meet the Realtor. You gave a thumbs-up, fell back asleep."

Eve started to respond, but stopped short. A vague half memory surfaced. It wouldn't have been the first time something like that happened. Still, she drew a long breath, unsure what to say next, where to start. Through the dirt-smeared windshield, she watched as the family's truck continued lumbering off—gnarled branches snagging to its side, snapping free in its wake. Above, a bluish glow bled through gray clouds as the sun contemplated setting.

Eve's gaze remained fixed on the family's truck, those two red lights shrinking away. At last, she managed, "I— I can't go back to the house."

In Eve's periphery, Charlie gave a slow, uncertain nod, then said, "Okay . . . Is this about the person in the attic?"

"No, well, yes—but . . ." Eve trailed off. "What else did Thomas tell you?"

Charlie hesitated. "A lot . . ."

"Just . . ." Eve sighed. "Just tell me exactly what he said."

Charlie continued, careful, measured. "He claimed you've been acting strange . . . since this morning. That you wandered over to the neighbor's and, when you came back, you seemed distressed. You went to the attic, then, you started screaming. Pounding on the door. When they opened it, you tumbled down, hit your head, and when you came to, you said you'd seen someone up there. A woman? He said he checked the attic himself and didn't find anything, but—"

"Okay, okay—that's enough," Eve relented. Everything Thomas had said was technically true, but . . . "I'm going to ask you something, and I need you to answer me straight, okay? Yes or no."

"Okay . . ."

Eve cleared her throat. "Is there a stained glass window in the upstairs study?"

Charlie quirked an eyebrow. "What . . . ?"

"The window in the upstairs study, is it stained glass?" Eve repeated.

"Uh, yeah . . . the apple tree."

The answer brought Eve a miserable kind of relief: *If I'm going mad, at least I'm not going it alone.* "It's not there." Eve crossed her arms. "Not anymore."

"I'm sorry?"

"It's just a plain old fucking window now." Eve threw up her hands.

Charlie shook her head. "The study? The empty bookshelf room?"

"Yup. The window *changed*."

Charlie scoffed. "No . . . That's not possible."

"Apparently, it is."

Charlie gestured at the moving truck, now a speck in the distance. "So what, they just up and stole our window? Installed a new one?" She smirked, trying to lighten the mood. "Maybe that was their plan all along . . ."

A sharp laugh escaped Eve's mouth, but not a funny "ha-ha" laugh, more of a "reality is meaningless" cackle. Perhaps she really was losing her mind after all. She collected herself and murmured, "It— It looks like this new window's always been there."

"Right . . ." mused Charlie. She absentmindedly clicked her teeth, a rare tell that signaled rising stress levels. And of course, the unspoken elephant lingered between them: this whole changing-house thing was exactly what had happened to Alison. *Allegedly.*

Charlie, reading the room, rested a hand on Eve's shoulder. "We'll spend the night somewhere else, okay?"

Eve nodded with relief. "Thank you," she said. "It— It's just been a day."

"Of course." Charlie turned the ignition. "Want me to give the attic a once-over before we leave?"

"No, fuck that, let's just— Let's deal with it later." Eve hesitated, feeling the weight of unsaid words. *Hey, Charlie, you know that house we just put a huge down payment on? Let's sell it.* She needed to strategize more before broaching that. After all, Charlie would need more than a replaced window and a rumored squatter in the attic to be convinced the house was cursed—

"Something else up?" Charlie asked.

Too many things to count. Eve hadn't even mentioned the stranger in the cabin, or what Heather had said about Thomas, but . . . "Let's, let's just go." Those were stories for another day.

Charlie gave her a long, searching look. Then she leaned over, wrapped her arms around Eve, pulled her close, and kissed her softly on the forehead. For that brief embrace, Eve felt safe again, like everything was right in the world. Charlie settled back and met her eyes. "I'm here, okay?"

"Okay . . ."

Charlie shifted into gear, started toward the driveway, toward the house—

"Wait." Eve frowned.

"I need to grab my stuff."

"Charlie."

"I'll be in and out. You can wait in the truck. Okay?"

"Charlie," Eve pleaded, "don't."

"Eve, if we're spending the night somewhere else, I need my phone charger and my clothes smell like shit. I won't go in the attic, promise."

"Charlie, I'm not kidding, something—something's seriously wrong with that house. There's . . ."

"I get that. I do. I'll be quick. Three seconds, all right?"

They went back and forth like this for a good while, until finally, Eve relented. Charlie was stubborn, and Eve's tolerance for conflict was long gone. Eve let out an exasperated huff, crossed her arms, and leaned back in her seat. "Two seconds, okay?"

"Two seconds."

After pulling up the driveway, Charlie parked in the alcove where the lawn met the gravel and kept the engine idling. She climbed out, looked at Eve. "Need anything?"

Eve shook her head.

"Your phone?" Charlie asked.

"Don't even bother searching for it."

"Toothbrush?"

"Just, hurry—please."

"Got it," Charlie replied. With that, she shut the door and trudged off toward the house. Eve leaned forward, eyes scanning the crooked porch, the windows, searching for any sign of life, movement. All was still. She glanced to the back seat. Shylo was peering out the windshield, nervous. As Charlie shuffled onto the porch, the dog let out a tension-filled wheeze. Charlie slipped inside and strolled into the foyer, leaving the front door open behind her. She ascended the stairs and disappeared from view. Shylo gave another nervous wheeze.

You and me both, bud. You and me both.

Eve continued to scan the house, her fingers tapping a jittery rhythm on the dashboard. Waiting. Watching. Upstairs, a light flicked on—the main bedroom. Charlie's silhouette strode in, started rummaging through drawers, grabbing things, stuffing them into a backpack or maybe a suitcase.

Hurry.

Eve's attention drifted up to that square attic window. The pale sky was reflecting off the glass, concealing whatever might be on the other side. Again, Shylo whined. Eve's jaw tensed, a nagging ache forming in her neck. *Hurry.* Charlie was still meandering about the bedroom, pacing in and out of view as she packed her bag.

How much stuff do you need?!

A languid breeze emerged from the driveway, rolled over the yard, and nudged the front door shut with a muted CLICK. Charlie perked up. But, after less than a second, she returned to packing, unbothered.

"Hurry the *fuck* up," Eve growled.

Charlie switched off the light, withdrew from the bedroom, and once again slipped out of view. Eve's gaze bounced from window to window, only met by darkness, the reflected sky. After ten eternal seconds, the front door swung open, and Charlie emerged with a navy green backpack slung over her shoulder. *Finally.* Charlie locked the door, trod back across the yard, and climbed into the truck.

She handed Eve the bag and said, "The window changed."

Again, Eve felt a miserable relief, not being alone in the absurdity.

Charlie shifted into drive. "They— They must've switched it out," she said, sounding unconvinced by her own reasoning. Charlie, despite her stubborn rationality, was clearly spooked. A rare sight. Her eyes, a touch wider than usual, gave it away; she had just witnessed something that didn't align with her understanding of reality. Did not compute. Either the house had magically changed, or they'd been robbed by a family of highly motivated window installers. Both scenarios were ludicrous, laughably so, and yet . . .

"Did you look at it up close?" Eve asked.

Charlie nodded slowly, shifted into reverse, and started a three-point turn. "They did a hell of a job making it look seamless, but . . ."

"Why, Charlie? Why would anyone go to all that effort?"

Charlie steered back onto the meandering driveway. "Maybe Thomas wanted a keepsake . . . ?"

"Well," Eve played along with her reasoning, "then we should call the cops—"

"And tell them what? A family replaced our window? Let's just—let's figure it out tomorrow."

Silence hung in the air as they descended the driveway. Eve kept her gaze locked ahead, as if looking back might allow the house to sprout legs and give chase, but . . . as they neared the final bend, she peered over her shoulder.

She'd half expected to see some terrible sign of life. Perhaps a light snapping on or a ghostly specter looming on the porch. Instead, all she saw was an old house, static and meager in the woods, receding into the distance until it vanished behind a wall of shadowed pines. Again, she convinced herself: *That was the last time you'll ever set eyes on 3709 Heritage Lane.*

As they lumbered down the frosty road, Mo surfaced: *Good luck with that.*

DOC_C19_INTERROGATION

Description: Excerpt of an entry titled "OLD_HOUSE_EVIDENCE" posted
to HIGH-STRANGENESS-WIKI, date unknown.

◆

POSTER: [redacted]
SUBJECT: OLD HOUSE_d03 + AMIF FOOTAGE (draft 1.4)

With a runtime of seventeen minutes and fifty-three seconds, the
footage is grainy, desaturated, and unfocused. Shot on video at
thirty frames a second, there is no time code or markings of any
sort. The "Andrew Melvin Interrogation Footage" (AMIF, pronounced:
ay-mif) is infamous among the conspiratorial community of "Old House
Archivists" (OHAs, pronounced: Oh-has).

    The main controversy centers around AMIF's authenticity.
There are more than a few reasons to doubt the validity of the
footage, and the hoax theory has not been ruled out (I myself
lean toward it). However, the footage has been circulating for

decades and, to this day, no legitimate source has confessed to its fabrication.

Hoax or not, it's a compelling piece of footage, and one of the few things OHAs have (had) that even gets close to what some might consider "evidence." AMIF is responsible for a significant portion of the conspiracies surrounding "Old House_u12" and the tragic (and very real) disappearances associated with it and the surrounding areas.

So why have you, dear reader, never heard of AMIF, let alone seen it? Unfortunately, due to reasons I will explain later, the footage itself is no longer available. So for now, my text description will have to suffice.

Footage Description (from memory and notes, not all details will be exact)

"Andrew Melvin Interrogation Footage," Description by [redacted] In the corner of a white-walled interrogation room sits ANDREW MEL-VIN. Wearing an orange hoodie, Andrew is hunched forward, head in his hands, staring at the floor. For three minutes and thirty-one seconds, Andrew remains in this position until, off camera, a door clicks open. A male voice asks, "Can I get you something? Water? Coke?"

Andrew does not respond. As OFFICER KIERAN steps into frame, Andrew doesn't even look up. Kieran is bald and well built in physique, but for the remainder of the tape, we never see his face, only the back of his head. Throughout the interrogation, he consults a light green leather-bound notebook. "Andrew Melvin?" he asks.

Again, Andrew does not look up or respond in any way.

Kieran pulls out a chair and sits down opposite. He leans forward in his seat. "I understand you're under a lot of stress here. All we're trying to do is figure out what happened to Peter." Kieran says this with a delicate and measured tone. The way a concerned father might speak to his child. "Andrew?"

Still, Andrew does not move. He remains motionless, head in hands, staring at the floor.

Kieran shifts his weight. "Andrew?"

Another long moment of silence passes, only the monotonous buzz of the air-conditioning and the murmur of footsteps out in the hallway, until, finally, Andrew speaks. "Is Peter okay?"

"That's what we're trying to figure out here," Kieran responds. "You were the last person to see him."

Andrew slowly sits up, then looks toward Officer Kieran. For the first time we can see Andrew's face. He looks to be no more than eighteen years old. His face is pale, his freckled cheeks gaunt—and even in this grainy, low-res footage, we can see the bewildered fear in his exhausted eyes.

Officer Kieran consults his notebook again, "So . . . you and Peter Kostoff broke into the home around nine thirty p.m. last night?"

"Yes."

"And why'd you do that?"

"Dared."

"Hm?"

"It was on a dare."

Officer Kieran scribbles something into his notepad. "By who?"

"Who dared us?"

"Yeah."

Andrew pauses for seven seconds. "The other boys," he says.

"The other boys." Kieran writes something down. "How many in total?"

"Five."

"Yourself and Peter included?"

"Yes, sir."

Kieran's head tilts slightly. "And remind me again, who were the other three?"

"Mason Lut, Jeffrey Holden, and . . . Christopher Marson."

Kieran writes the names down, nodding. "What were the stakes?"

"What?"

"What'd you get out of the dare?"

"Oh, nothing."

Kieran tries to be tactful, but can't hide his sarcasm. "So you broke into an abandoned house, in an area that's infamous for unexplained disappearances, for . . . nothing? Can you help me understand that?"

"We'd been drinking."

Kieran nods, apparently satisfied with the answer. "How many drinks?"

"Five or six."

"So the point of entry was the back porch window, correct?"

"Yes, in through the kitchen."

"And the other boys, they stood out in the yard, spurring you on?"

Andrew nods.

"So you and Peter pried the board off the back porch window, climbed through, and now you're standing in the kitchen. What happens next?"

Andrew shifts uncomfortably in his seat. "Is Peter okay? Can I talk to him?"

"Peter is . . . alive. He's just being treated by a doctor right now."

Andrew gulps, looks down, and runs his fingertips back and forth over the table in front of him. A fidgety, compulsive movement.

Kieran says, "Andrew."

Andrew stops moving, looks up.

Kieran prods, "What happened next?"

Andrew looks away, staring off behind the camera somewhere. "We just wandered around the main floor," he says.

"You had flashlights, correct?"

"Just one. Peter was holding it."

Kieran nods, writes something down. "And why'd you go into the basement?"

Andrew visibly reacts to the word "basement." His expression darkens, and he shifts uncomfortably in his seat for a long moment until—

"Andrew?" Kieran prods again.

"We tried going upstairs first," says Andrew, "but Peter's foot broke through the third step. It was all rotten. He almost fell over backward, but I caught him."

Andrew rubs his narrow jaw with the back of his hand. "At that point, I just wanted to leave. We'd already been in there five minutes, but Peter insisted we check out the basement next. So we had a bit of a back-and-forth and Peter won out."

"You had an argument?" There's a hint of repressed enthusiasm in his voice, probably searching for a motive.

Andrew nods. "Nothing crazy, I just had bad vibes. Wanted to get out of there. Peter said I was being a pussy, but that's just how he talks."

Kieran writes more into his notebook. "So you wanted to leave, and Peter insisted you check out the basement first?"

"Yes."

"And what happened down there?"

For about ten seconds Andrew sits in silence, eyes flicking back and forth.

"Andrew?" Kieran asks.

"We went." Andrew wipes the side of his mouth with the back of his hand and crosses his arms. "We went downstairs, down through the hallways, and . . . I didn't wanna be there. I told Peter we should just head back up."

"What did Peter say?"

"He said that wasn't the dare; we had to go into the basement. I could back out, if I wanted, but he was gonna look around with or without me."

Kieran nods.

Andrew continues. "I didn't wanna leave him alone either."

"Understandable. What happens next?"

"We're down there for about ten, fifteen minutes, pushing our way around piles of rubble. It's a pretty big basement."

Kieran nods again.

Andrew rubs his arms, as if the room had suddenly grown cold. "We rounded into a small room, and——"

He goes silent again, his face filled with growing fear. Like if he were to say the next words aloud something terrible might happen.

Kieran picks up on this. "It's okay, Andrew, there's no rush here. Just speak when you feel ready to, okay?"

Andrew lowers his voice and continues. "There was a door, at the far end of the room. It was cracked open, but it looked new, like brand-new, and everything else down there is covered in dust, and rotting, but this door, it was spotless. That alone was enough to freak me out, but Peter didn't seem to care. He went over, I waited by the entrance, he pushed the door fully open, and . . ." Andrew pauses for a moment, looks down. "I had to crane my neck to see, but it led to a hallway." He looks up. "A hospital hallway. Greenish-white walls, tile floor, it looked brand-new, just like

the door, like it had just been installed that day. Could even smell
cleaning chemicals . . . That was more than enough for even Peter to
suggest we go back, but . . . just as he was about to turn around,
he stopped. He could see something down there, in the hallway. I
couldn't see it from my angle, and I start to ask him what's up and
he just shushes me. I could tell he was scared and——I'd never seen
Peter scared before, not even once . . ." Andrew clears his throat.
"I could've easily taken a few steps forward, looked to see what he
was looking at, but I didn't want to . . ."

"Why's that?"

"I . . . I don't know . . ."

"What do you think he saw?"

". . . Nothing good."

"What happened after that?"

"We both just stood there, completely silent for a half minute
and, I realized Peter wasn't breathing. He was motionless, like,
arms to his sides, flashlight pointed at the floor . . . Then, there
was a voice, down in that dark hallway, a small voice."

For the next three minutes of footage, Andrew does not blink. Not
even once. A remarkable feat in and of itself, and something that
seems to make Officer Kieran uneasy.

"What'd it say?" asks Kieran.

"The voice?"

Kieran nods gently.

"It just said . . . 'My name isn't' . . ." Andrew trails off.

Kieran asks, "My name isn't, what?"

"That's it. Just 'My name isn't.'"

Kieran notes that down. "Man? Woman? Child?"

Andrew shakes his head. "I don't know. Too quiet, almost whispering."

"Okay. And that's all it said?"

Andrew nods slowly. "Yes, sir."

Officer Kieran scratches the back of his neck with the pen. "So . . . then what?"

At this point Andrew's unblinking eyes start watering. "I told Peter we needed to get out of there. He didn't respond; he just kept staring down the hall, holding his breath. I tried to grab his arm, and he was rigid, like his joints were locked up, then I heard a footstep, muffled in that hallway. And a few seconds later, another step, getting closer, and that was more than enough for me, I hauled it out of there."

"Without a flashlight?"

Andrew shakes his head. "I . . ." He pauses, considering his next words carefully. "I took the light from Peter," he admitted. "I had to wrench it from his hand, it was gripped so tight." His voice strained with guilt.

Kieran nods. "And when you got outside your other friends weren't there?"

"Right."

Kieran looks at his notebook, flips back one page. "So you ran for twenty minutes to the nearest house and called for help?" Andrew nods, and finally, he blinks again. (His blinking returns to normal for the remainder of the footage.)

Kieran breathes heavily out his nose. "Now, Andrew. Your friend Peter, as you know, he's been found by our team. He's in a catatonic state, and—"

"Catatonic?"

"He's not responding to anything. A waking coma, essentially."

Andrew shrinks back in his chair. "What about the person in the basement?"

"Well, we did a thorough search of the entire house and there's no sign of anyone having been there. Not in the last few months, at least. No footprints. Nothing."

Andrew doesn't seem to fully grasp what Officer Kieran is telling him. He fidgets. "What about the hallway?"

"The hospital hallway?"

Andrew nods.

"Nobody on our team saw anything like that. I'll run it by the guys, but—"

"That's not possible, it's right there, there's no way they would have missed it—"

"Andrew, I don't know if you understand what—"

"It's right there, it's—"

"Andrew, there's no sign of anyone having been in that house last night, you included. The window you said you broke in through, it's boarded up. Has been for quite some time."

Andrew pauses, absorbing this, then he shakes his head, unbelieving. "My other friends were there, they—"

"Mason Lut, Jeffrey Holden, and"—Kieran glances toward his notebook—"Christopher Marson?"

Andrew nods.

Kieran sighs. "There's no sign of them either."

Andrew's face clouds with bewilderment.

Kieran leans back slightly. "You said you attend Lion's Bay High?"

Andrew nods again.

"We checked with that school. They don't have any records of you or your friends."

Andrew doesn't respond to that; he just shrinks into his chair.

Kieran shifts closer, taking on a more aggressive demeanor.

"Andrew, I don't know what happened here, but I need you to be honest with me. I've got a kid down the hall who's literally paralyzed with fear. I've got you telling me stories about people who don't exist, telling me you broke into a house you never broke into. So I need you to be straight with me: Why are things not lining up here? They couldn't even find you in the record check. Is Andrew your real name? What kind of drugs have you and your friend been taking?"

Andrew slowly looks up and locks eyes with Officer Kieran.

For the briefest of moments, Andrew's fear vanishes and is replaced with a terrible emptiness. His eyes flash around the room, and then he looks directly into the camera.

It's hard to fully capture the strangeness of this moment in words, but it looks as though, and I know this sounds absurd, but it looks as though somebody else jumped inside Andrew's mind for a second, took a quick look around, then jumped back out. Worse still, when he looks toward the camera, it feels as if he knows that *you* (the viewer) are there, knows you're watching. (Sometimes, even when I read back through these notes, I get that same feeling of suddenly being seen by something ancient and all-knowing.)

"Andrew?"

Andrew looks back at Kieran, and his eyes return to their previous state of childlike fear.

Officer Kieran clears his throat, unsettled. "I just . . . I need to know what happened."

Andrew nods slowly. "I— I don't feel like myself."

"And how's that?"

Andrew sits in silence for a long moment until he says, "I don't want to get put away or anything."

"Put away for what?"

". . . for being crazy."

Kieran shakes his head. "No, no, it takes a pretty high standard for that to happen. Believe me, you're not even close." (An obvious lie.)

Andrew doesn't even seem to be listening now. He speaks more to himself than to Kieran, "I'm . . . I'm starting to remember things that never happened."

Kieran tilts his head, unsure what to make of that. "What do you mean by—"

It is here that the footage, infuriatingly, cuts to black.

B.3—Footage context (draft 2.3)

One of the many strange things about the Andrew Melvin footage is the lack of context. Despite many dedicated efforts to find its origin, the tape remains a solitary mystery. There is no paper trail, no records of its background, no records of the "players" involved.

In regards to Officer Kieran, Andrew Melvin, and every other name mentioned in the footage, there is no external documentation or corroboration to prove any of these people have ever existed. Even the Briar County Police Department has no record of it. (Cited from Briar County Police Department's official statement on the so-called AMIF conspiracy [weblink redacted].)

Inconveniently (or conveniently, depending on your outlook), the AMIF footage has been lost. A bewildering occurrence that, in my opinion, is far more compelling than the footage itself. On June 3, 2017, at 3:17 a.m. Pacific Standard Time, every single digital instance of AMIF was wiped from the internet. Every single one. From YouTube to LiveLeak, all the way down to the most obscure dark web forums. AMIF vanished. Even more confounding: the Wayback Machine archive shows no record of it having been there to begin with.

Some have claimed that even their hard copies of the footage went missing shortly after June 3. According to these claimants,

there was no sign of break-in or theft—the tapes just out-and-out
vanished. Again, as if they had never been there to begin with.
Of course, these claims are suspect at best. Like most communities
centered around the unexplained, the OHA community is riddled with
grifters, liars, and lunatics (chief among them being Garrett Larson
the II, but that's a story for a different day).

   I should note here that a few have claimed they still possess
hard copies, VHS tapes, DVDs—one even says they own a Betamax version. But all of them, and I've contacted every single person who
claims this, decline to upload. They, in so many words, "fear it
would trigger their versions to go missing as well." Convenient.

   And now, many who are new to the OHA community claim that AMIF
never existed to begin with. That the entire community is faking it
or the tape is some sort of complex Mandela effect.

   As a side note: Many of these fresh AMIF-denying OHAs have broken
off to form their own communities, the most prominent of which is
the creatively titled NOHA (New Old House Archivists). NOHA members
often refer, derogatorily, to OHA members as Oohas (Old Old House
Archivists).

   (The funny thing is, most of these communities can't even agree
on what Old House actually is. Some say it's a sanctuary for some
kind of ancient entity. Some say it is a sprawling labyrinth that
spreads across space and time and traps unsuspecting civilians in
a maze of never-ending terror. Some say it's simply a metaphor—a
mirror into humanity's fascination with long-abandoned structures.
There are hundreds of theories. Long story short, when it comes to
Old House and the surrounding lore, you'll get a different story
depending on who you ask and how many bong hits deep they happen
to be.)

   However, in NOHA's defense, if I myself had not seen the AMIF footage in 2013, I would undoubtedly join their chorus of naysaying. In this day and age, the logistics of wiping anything from the internet, let alone the hard copies along with it, are beyond impossible. But alas, the footage is, or rather *was*, a real thing. As you just read, I personally took detailed notes of it upon my first viewing. Disappointingly, it seems that, for the foreseeable future, reading those notes is the closest one can get to seeing the actual footage itself.

I should also note that, despite my prominence in the OHA space, I do not subscribe to any group. There's no humble way to put it, but I view myself as above the fray. Above the tribalism and politics of such conspiratorial communities. The infighting, outfighting, the never-ending acronyms, in my view, do nothing but delegitimize and stigmatize an already controversial area of potential research.

~~SKYLER GOODHILL~~

~~LEWIS ROU~~

.— —. —..

GETAWAY

As they wound their way down the mountain, Eve stared out at the passing trees, her forehead pressed against the glass. The reflection of her weary eyes overlayed the darkening woods outside. And every little bump in the road sent a rippling tremor through her thoughts, pushing her deeper into rumination. Something was wrong. Well, of course, everything was fucked, but there was something else. Something she couldn't quite place. Like a festering but crucial obligation long forgotten.

Eve sat upright and pulled Charlie's locket out. "Found this hanging above the fireplace . . ."

Charlie side-eyed her. "One of their kids must've done it . . ." With her free hand, she took the locket and placed it in a cup holder.

Eve considered saying something more, but she switched on the radio instead. Static. She turned the dial. More static. She switched it off. Nestling into her seat, she reached into the back and scratched Shylo behind the ear. The dog let out a high-pitched yawn. Eve looked at Charlie and asked, "Do you think Paige is gonna sue us?"

Charlie hesitated, caught off guard by the question. "Sue us?"

"For the dog bite."

"Nah." Charlie clucked her tongue. "I doubt it."

"She'd have a case," Eve said.

"How do you know?"

"I've . . . listened to a lot of courtroom podcasts."

"Uh-huh . . ."

Up ahead, a sharp corner approached. Charlie shifted into a lower gear, let off the gas. "You said the bite punctured his jeans?"

"Barely, but . . . it drew blood."

They bowed around the corner until the road straightened out again. "If they come after us," Charlie said, "we'll countersue for window theft."

Eve rested her head back against the seat. "Okay . . ." She shut her eyes. Minute by minute, the hum of the asphalt lulled her into a restless half sleep. Her mind floated through that liminal space, teetering back and forth on the edge of awareness, the drone of the engine seeming to grow louder and louder, until the *tick-tick-tick* of the turn clicker roused her. She sat up and rubbed her eyes, the remnants of another bad dream slipping away. How much time had passed?

Charlie said, "This work for you?"

Eve gazed through the windshield. They were pulling into the parking lot of the Kettle Creek Motel. The place wasn't abandoned after all. In fact, closer up, it looked a little nicer than Eve remembered. Nothing fancy, not by a long shot, but as far as roadside motels went, it got the job done. Besides, at this point, she would have just about slept in a cardboard box to avoid spending another second in that house.

"Works for me." Eve shrugged.

They parked beneath the bluish glow of the neon sign:

THE KETTL_ CREEK MOTE_

As they made their way across the gravel lot, Eve peered around. The sur-rounding woods whispered with the rain-like patter of melting snow. At the opposite end of the lot, half obscured by a green dumpster, sat a lone white hatchback. No other vehicles in sight. She looked up. The faint impression of the setting sun filtered through the gray clouds like a flashlight pressed against a wool blanket. All seemed calm. Calm and quiet—both things that only served to heighten Eve's anxiety. When things felt right, it only meant there was so much more that could go wrong.

Stepping through sliding doors, they entered a low-ceilinged lobby. Wood vinyl walls, drab gray carpet, buzzing lights. At the far end, nestled between a dead palm tree and a Coca-Cola vending machine—the reception counter. Nobody there.

Charlie, Eve in tow, strolled over and rang the bell. DING. The sound hung in the air, fading into a long stretch of silence. "Hello . . . ?" Charlie tried.

As they waited, Eve's gaze wandered to the lobby's back corner. There, a fire escape door was propped open with a cinder block. On the other side, frenzied moths butted against a stuttering light, their shadows casting a mad dance over water-stained concrete.

Charlie tried the bell again. DING . . .

Behind the counter, a red door creaked open and a middle-aged woman poked her head out. Sporting a beehive hairdo, she wore aviator glasses and a nightshirt. "Eh," she grumbled. "What do you want?" She looked surprised to see visitors, annoyed.

"A room," said Charlie.

Muttering something about patience, the woman slipped back into her cave, pulling the door closed.

Charlie glanced at Eve, brow raised.

From behind the red door, the sound of rummaging, drawers sliding open, slamming shut, until, finally, the woman reemerged, now wearing an oversized plaid shirt and blue sweatpants. She held a paperback novel, still reading as she ambled up to the counter and flopped down into a wicker chair. The scent of floral hairspray wafted from her, permeating the air. Charlie cleared her throat. The clerk raised a finger, "One second. I'm almost finished this chapter." She continued reading.

Charlie and Eve shared another disbelieving look.

Charlie turned back and tapped a finger against the countertop. "Can we get a room . . . ?"

"Please?" Eve added.

The clerk exhaled an irritated sigh. Then, slowly, ever so slowly, she reached down, opened a drawer, pulled out a pink comb, slid the comb into the book, closed the book, and set the book on the counter. Unhurried, she started typing into a desktop that looked like it still ran on Windows 95. She used her pointer fingers to input one, key, at, a, time.

Charlie's gaze flitted to the paperback. "Good book?"

The cover showed a blond-haired, blue-eyed princess sitting pretty atop a white horse. At her side, a literal knight in shining armor guided the horse down a redbrick pathway. Eve couldn't see the title from her angle, but she imagined it was something like *Knight of Love* or *A Hero's Heart*.

The clerk murmured, "How many guests?"

"Room for two," said Charlie.

The clerk gave Charlie a long, studied look as if she'd just asked to borrow fifty bucks and a can of hairspray. After a slow blink, she returned to typing.

"Two beds?"

"One," said Charlie.

Again, the clerk stopped typing. Her eyes flicked to Eve, to Charlie, then back to the computer. "One bed." She continued typing away, shaking her head, muttering. She jabbed the space bar with a knuckle and crossed her arms. "That'll be . . ." She adjusted her glasses and leaned in close to the screen.

"One hundred and sixty-seven dollars."

Charlie blinked. "I'm sorry?"

"And"—the clerk squinted at the screen—"twenty-three cents."

Charlie scoffed. "For one night?"

"One night, one room, one bed."

Charlie opened her mouth, about to haggle on price, but—

Eve stepped in before she could. "That's fine."

With key cards in hand, Eve and Charlie trudged back outside. The sun had fully set now. Black shadows spilled out from the woods, pooling around the edges of the lot like some kind of liquid ooze. The blue neon glow of the motel sign bled into the night above, glistened off the wet gravel below. And the nocturnal song of a common poorwill cried in the distance, the bird chirping out its namesake over and over, *poor-will, poor-will, poor-will.*

"She absolutely upcharged us," Charlie said, still grumpy about the clerk.

Eve shrugged, only half in the conversation. "How do you know?"

"A hundred and sixty-seven bucks? On a slow night? No shot. When I worked hospitality, we gouged anyone we didn't like. Upcharge."

Charlie broke into a surprisingly good impression of the clerk. "One night," she grumbled. "One room. One bed." She glanced over at Eve, at least expecting a smile. But Eve's attention was elsewhere. Her eyes were back on the surrounding woods, scanning the darkened trees as if something might be hiding out there. Something only she could see. Sure, being away from the house was a relief, but . . .

At the room, Charlie slid the key card into the handle. It blinked red and gave a shrill beep. Frowning, she tried again, still no luck. Shylo let out another little whine.

Charlie checked the numbers. "Room nineteen . . ."

"Here." Eve handed her card over. "Try mine."

As Charlie continued fumbling with the door, Eve surveyed the parking lot, paranoid. Her gaze settled on that lone white hatchback, the windows dark. Was somebody sitting in the passenger seat? She strained her eyes. Just then, light from the road ribboned through the trees and swept slowly over the lot, illuminating the hatchback's interior. Empty. The drifting light stretched long shadows across the wet gravel, until . . .

Eve looked over her shoulder. A vehicle crawled in through the entrance. Blinding headlights. Two white orbs. Eve held up a hand, shielded her eyes. For a second, she thought it was the family's moving truck, but it pulled a slow U-turn, revealing itself to be a Highway Patrol cruiser. It drove off the way it came, leaving behind grooves in the gravel.

"Ah," Charlie said, finally latching open the door. "Tenth time's the charm." She started inside, but Eve lingered behind, eyes still locked on the now empty entrance. Part of her still half expected the moving truck to shamble in, Thomas leaning out the window, grinning that perfect-teeth grin. *Jeepers*, he'd say, *it's a small world after all, huh?*

"Eve?" Charlie's voice, distant and vague, dimly registered. "Eve." Charlie touched her arm, startling her.

Eve looked back, face clouded with repressed worry. "Hm?"

Charlie set a hand on the side of Eve's shoulder. "Let's get out of the cold."

The room was about what they'd expected, a cramped space, barely wide enough to fit the bed. Yellowish wallpaper covered in repetitive floral prints. Green carpets, scratchy and worn, like overgrown moss. The textbook definition of a backwoods motel. Eve wasn't complaining, though. Like she'd reasoned before, anything was better than another night in that house.

As Charlie brushed her teeth in the bathroom, Eve sat on the bed, staring at a blank TV screen—a boxy tube set resting on a dresser at an odd angle. Next to the TV was a framed Bible verse:

† † †

For God so loved the world
that He gave His only begotten Son,
that whoever believes in Him
should not perish but have
eternal life

                                        John 3:16

Eve leaned over and flipped the image face down with a decisive CLACK. She settled back onto the bed, took a deep breath and let it out. You're okay, she told herself. Despite everything, each minute spent away from that house felt better than the last. Normality was returning. Shylo clambered onto the bed and curled up near the headboard, grumbled. In the corner of Eve's eye, Charlie spat toothpaste into the sink and rinsed out her mouth. She started back toward Eve. "Room's a winner, huh?"

Eve forced a laugh out her nose, flopped back onto the bed, stared up at the white stucco ceiling.

Charlie stepped around her. As she sat down next to Eve, the bed dipped and creaked. Grim silence followed, underscored by the hum-buzz of a rickety air vent. Outside, another sweep of headlights. They beamed through the window, shadows slinking by, everything seeming to tilt and spin before slowly plunging back into darkness.

More silence lingered between them until Eve said, "Do you think I'm crazy?"

Charlie snorted at the question and glanced down at her. "Who isn't?"

Eve sighed and looked away. More silence.

"Is this about the window?" Charlie asked. "'Cause I saw it too, which means we're both losing it."

Eve shook her head.

"The attic person?" Charlie nudged.

Eve shrugged. Maybe . . .

"Eve," Charlie said, "we'll look into it tomorrow. Hell, we can call the authorities out, if it comes to that. Okay?"

Eve nodded, her eyes locked to a random speck on the ceiling. She drew in another long breath, let it out.

Pensive, Charlie ventured, "It was a rough day. Anyone would've lost their mind being trapped with that family . . ."

Eve tensed her jaw, released it.

Charlie shuffled closer and lay beside Eve. She reached over, tucked a strand of hair behind Eve's ear. "You're not alone, okay? I'm here. Always."

Another wary silence. Finally, Eve spoke suspicions that had been crawling around in the back of her head since Thomas told his story by the fire. "I . . . I think what happened to Alison is happening to me . . ."

Charlie considered this before saying, "Because of the window . . ."

Eve gestured up at the ceiling, as if the stucco were the problem. "Because of—fucking everything, I don't know. I just . . ." She trailed off again, rubbed her temples. "I saw that kid holding my phone, I saw it, the screen was cracked, and then—it wasn't and . . ."

"You're under a lot of stress. Everyone makes mistakes—"

"This wasn't a mistake. That was my phone. I would bet my fucking life on it. Either I'm losing it or the phone changed . . ."

"There's a lot more possibilities than—"

"And this motel, I could've sworn it was abandoned when we drove by it the first time—"

"Hell, we both thought that. People misremember things every single—"

"No, this is different. This is— I haven't even told you about the rest of my day, and—"

"Eve, trust me, if you were losing it, I'd be the first to point it out."

That was true. And it actually comforted Eve, if only a little. Her heart rate slowed; her breath deepened. Maybe she just needed a good night's sleep. She turned to face Charlie and—

She isn't her, a voice in Eve's head whispered. This wasn't the voice of Mo; this was the voice of something different, something far worse. Something all-knowing and ancient. A mouthless, eyeless presence leeching off the chemical fear that poured out of her amygdala. *This isn't your Charlie.*

The notion was so sudden, so improbable, Eve almost laughed, but . . .

Despite the fact that Charlie looked just as she always had: the short black hair, the mismatched eyes, the light freckles dusting her cheeks . . .

Some half-remembered version of Thomas's words played in her mind: *Alison thought everyone around her was an imposter, that the real versions of us had somehow been replaced. So . . . she tested us, asked us questions about the past, desperate to know if we were actually her family, or . . .*

"Eve?" Again, Charlie cut into her spiral. "What's going on?"

Eve sat up, and looked at Charlie in the TV's reflection. "How did we meet?"

"W-what?"

"How did we meet?"

"Eve, do you seriously think I'm—are you testing me?"

"Please," she almost begged. "Charlie, just . . . I know it's fucking stupid, but *please* humor me. The whole story, from the top." Despite the absurdity of the request, Eve's voice was filled with grave severity.

Charlie sat upright. "Okay . . ." She slid her feet off the bed and faced the window. She took a deep breath, let it out. "Eight years ago, my roommates wanted to go see a movie. *Spirited Away.*"

"Which theater?"

"Seriously?"

Eve looked over her shoulder, met Charlie's eyes.

"The Dryden Theatre," Charlie relented. "Rochester, New York . . . Do I pass?"

Eve grunted noncommittally. She turned back to the TV screen reflection.

Charlie, blurred in the glass, went on. "I almost didn't go, had a big exam coming up, but my friends were persistent, so I caved . . . Once we plopped down in our seats, I look to my left and one empty chair down, there was this girl in a lime-green hoodie. She was all by herself, and . . . You should've seen her. Sure, looks aren't everything, but she was by far the prettiest girl in the whole dang theater . . ." Charlie trailed off, as if giving Eve a chance to retort, but thus far, dumb joke aside, all was accurate.

Charlie carried on. "This girl though, she was a little strange, kept glancing over at me, and every time I glanced back, she'd look away. I think she wanted to ask me something." In the TV reflection, Charlie looked toward Eve, but Eve didn't look back . . .

Charlie continued. "So the movie ends, lights come up, credits start rolling, and the hoodie girl stays behind. Who sits through the credits, right? My friends left to go smoke, but me? I stay behind. A lot of hard work went into making that film, may as well pay my respects . . ." She shrugged. "I think about halfway through the credits, I clumsily ask this girl if she goes to movies alone often. After a long silent pause, I started to kick myself for being such an embarrassment, but . . . then she finally said—"

"'Yeah, but this time wasn't by choice.'" Eve finished Charlie's sentence then, as if the memory were playing out right there in the dingy motel room— Eve kept talking. "'Somebody stood me up.'"

"Somebody stood *you* up?" Charlie replied. "Dang, they must be important. What's their deal?"

Eve shrugged. "He's in a worship band."

"Lead guitar?"

Eve shook her head. "Mallet percussion."

"What's that?"

"Xylophone, triangle, marimbas." Eve gave a half shrug, looked back, and met Charlie's eyes again.

"Damn," said Charlie, "you must be devastated . . ."

Eve almost smiled. "Chetley's a winner for sure, way too good for me."

"Wait, Chetley? That's his name? You're fucking with me."

"Hey, don't be mean."

"No, I'm not, that's, it's a good name—I just didn't picture it for a . . . mallet percussionist."

Eve snorted.

Charlie added, "Anyways, I gotta run, but if you ever wanna go to the movies with friends . . ." Charlie paused, mimed reaching into her pocket, pulling out a business card. "That's my number . . ."

Breaking character, Eve said, "That was smooth . . ." She thought back to that day they met, Charlie handing her a Charlie's Portrait Photography business card. She still remembered the texture of the engraved font on her fingertips. The smell of movie theater popcorn. The way the cleaners had started wandering the aisles before the credits finished rolling. And the way Charlie's crooked smile, even back then, made her heart skip a beat and . . .

Eve pushed up from the bed, strode over, wrapped her arms around Charlie, and hugged her tighter than she ever had before. *Her* Charlie. For a moment, all the strange occurrences of the day seemed trivial again, overblown. Almost . . .

Soon after, they were cuddling on the bed, watching a cable rerun of *The Maltese Falcon*. Between midnight infomercials and prosperity televangelists, this was by far the best choice. But around the time Bogart went to Cairo, Charlie dozed off. Eve, calmer but still rattled from the day, continued watching. Escaping into a different world until, at last, she dozed off as well.

◆

Bzz, Bzz, Bzz . . .

Eve stirred awake to the sound of a vibrating phone. The TV was still on, soundlessly playing some nature documentary about Venus flytraps. *Bzz, Bzz, Bzz* . . . She cast her eyes across the room. It was coming from Charlie's green backpack, a rectangle of blue light seeping through the fabric. Eve glanced at Charlie, still sleeping. She looked at the bedside clock: 3:06 a.m.

Who would be calling this late?

Quiet, Eve slipped free of Charlie's arms, crept out of bed, and wandered to the bag. She dug through it, retrieved the phone, and . . .

On the screen:

📞 Eve Palmer calling . . .
ACCEPT DECLINE

Eve's stomach dropped. Somebody had her phone—back at the house? She glanced over at Charlie, considered waking her, but . . .

. . . for reasons unknown, even to her, she strode to the bathroom, pulled the door half-shut, and tapped accept.

On the other end, a voice, shaky, terrified. "E-Eve, are you alone?"

Charlie's voice . . .

Somewhere at the bottom of Eve's mind, a rising swell of chemical dread burst open like a bloated sac of spider eggs. Countless terrors spawned, each of them swarming a different corner of her thoughts. She opened her mouth to respond, but only a short, stuttering wheeze escaped.

"Eve?" the voice prompted. "Is— Is that you?" The signal was weak, choppy.

Petrified, Eve peered through the cracked-open door. Charlie was still in bed, blue TV light painting the side of her face, peacefully asleep . . .

"Eve," the voice that sounded exactly like Charlie rasped. "She isn't me . . ."

Eve whispered, "Who— Who is this?"

"Earlier, when I went to the h-house, I never—I'm still here. Whoever's with you, she isn't me— And the dog, it isn't Shylo. Shylo is . . ." She trailed off.

Eve's inner voice screamed. Was this a hallucination? A nightmare?

"Eve," Charlie continued. It sounded like she was in pain, injured maybe. "I don't know where you are, but you need to leave, never come back to the house. Get as far away as you possibly can and—and stay away from her. She—she's going—she's going to." Charlie fell silent, sucked in a short gasp of air. Dead quiet. Holding her breath?

On the other end, distant footsteps, staggering, uneven, like a drunk walking the deck of a galleon. Getting closer. The sound was accompanied by . . . laughter? Or crying? Whatever it was, those vague whimpers were muffled, like hands clasped over a mouth. *Wom, wom, wom* . . . Closer. Closer. Closer, until—

BEEP.

The call ended.

Eve's fingers trembled, had started to redial when a shadowy form slid into the edge of her vision. Eve turned. There stood Charlie—*or is it Charlie?*—looming in the bathroom doorway, a black silhouette outlined by the TV's shimmering glow. Unmoving.

"Eve?" Charlie inquired. "Is everything okay?" Her face was masked in shadow, only the slightest glint of her eyes catching light from the bathroom mirror.

Still shaky, Eve glanced down at the phone and lied. "Yeah, I just, I was trying to get ahold of the contractor for the inspection . . ."

"At . . . three in the morning?"

Loaded silence. Eve cut it short with another feeble lie. "Yeah, I— I think, apparently, the contractor mixed up the dates? Told the inspector to come up S-Sunday instead of Saturday . . . ?"

"Right." Charlie's head tilted, not buying it. "Maybe we can sort this out tomorrow?"

"I— I wish." Eve exhaled. "Apparently it's urgent. Like if I— I just, I'm gonna go deal with it outside, you can go back to sleep—"

Charlie reached for the light switch, flicked it on. They both squinted, eyes adjusting to the sudden brightness and . . .

That was when Eve finally saw it. On "Charlie's" left hand: her tattoo, the black triangle on her left index finger, was completely absent . . .

"Eve?" the doppelgänger prompted.

Stomach twisting, Eve brushed past her, surged toward the door. Unthinking, she grabbed the keys, her wallet, and—

"Eve, where are you—"

"I— I'll be right back." Shoeless, wearing only sweatpants and a T-shirt, Eve rushed outside, slamming the door in her wake. Half running, she hauled across the parking lot and climbed into the truck. As Eve fumbled with the keys, trying to start the engine, "Charlie" burst out of the room, pulling on her boots, still dressed in her PJs. "Eve, hold on . . . Eve, what the fuck!" Her face was filled with terrified concern.

She's going to put you in an asylum, that manic whisper, the voice that had replaced Mo, hissed. *You're going to die in a concrete cell—bash your head against the wall until your skull cracks, and your brains leak out.*

"Charlie" drew closer, closer, until at last, the engine roared to life. Eve shifted into drive and stomped on the gas. The truck squealed to a lurching start, whipped up a hailstorm of gravel, tore across the lot, and nearly clipped "Charlie" in the process. Screeching toward the road, Eve was about to swerve leftward toward Yale, away from the mountain, but—

Charlie. The real Charlie. She was still back in that house. Same with the real Shylo. Eve wasn't abandoning them. She couldn't. She glanced at the rearview; the carbon copy Charlie was still in pursuit, arms waving, pleading, almost weeping, *STOP, STOP, STOP* . . .

Eve ripped through the entrance and veered to the right, barreling back toward the summit. Charlie and Shylo were everything to her, and she couldn't, wouldn't, leave them behind. That was her family. As she stepped on the gas, her eyes flicked between the road and the mirror. Every time she looked back, the neon blue sign had shrunk farther and farther into the distance, "Charlie" still running after her.

One hand on the wheel, Eve reached into her pocket, pulled out "Charlie's" phone, and dialed her own number back. One tone rang out, then: "Sorry, *Eve Palmer*, can't make it to the phone right now. Please leave a message after the—"

"Shit," Eve hissed. She considered calling 911, but . . . best-case scenario, they'd throw her in a psych ward. With growing resolve, she constricted her hands around the steering wheel, picking up speed. The dark forest smeared into blurry shadows. Adrenaline coursed through her veins like ice water as everything converged into one singular goal: save her family. At any cost—

DING.

A warning chimed from the dashboard: Refuel now.

Fuck.

DOC_C03_INKBLOTS

Description: Excerpt from the book *Names Without Faces* by Dr. Bjørn
Erikson (translated from Norwegian).

◆

Pareidolia is a psychological phenomenon in which the human mind per-
ceives familiar patterns and shapes within chaotic and/or ambiguous
stimuli (clouds, darkness, patterned wallpaper, etc.). In short, it
is the brain's tendency to interpret abstract stimuli as something
meaningful and recognizable.

Common examples include seeing animals in clouds, spotting faces
on surfaces such as tree bark, and/or perceiving music or voices in
white noise.

Some propose the high prevalence of this phenomenon is closely
related to the fight-or-flight instinct.[1] The quicker a threat is
detected, the faster one can react. Therefore, from a natural selection

---

1 L. Creston, "Pareidolia & Predator Detection," *Journal of Natural Phenomena* 3, no. 21
(1978): 32–33.

point of view, it can be advantageous to perceive threats where none exist; that vague shape in the dark could just be a rock . . . or it could be a predator ready to pounce. Better for your brain to assume a predator than to be eaten alive.

Notably, the intensity of pareidolia has been directly linked to a subject's level of anxiety, e.g., in Rorschach tests, the more distressed a subject is, the more likely they are to perceive faces in the inkblots (threatening faces in particular).[1]

-- . --- . ...

---

1   A. Yau and L. Carson, "Beyond Inkblots: An Extensive Analysis of Rorschach Test Interpretations," *Psychology & Practice* 12, no. 3 (1987): 12–16.

CHASE

The truck was running on fumes when the white glow of the Chevron station crept into view. Almost there. Eve eased into the lot, peering through her windshield. This establishment, bathed in stark fluorescent light, looked more like a glorified shack than a running business. Not even a shiny corporate buyout could hide its rural roots. The walls, shingled and weather-worn, were coated with rusty license plates from almost every state, even a few from Canada. The gas pumps, a grand total of two, looked as though they'd been dragged from a 1960s junkyard and resurrected in some dark magic ritual. Huddled trees encircled the lot, like a crowd of schoolkids gawking at a playground scuffle.

Cautious, Eve steered to the nearest pump, shifted into park, and climbed out. The coarse pavement met her sock-covered feet, an instant reminder she'd not put boots on. She pulled out her credit card, but stopped short. A handwritten sign was taped to the card reader:

$–CASH ONLY–PAY INSIDE–$

Urgent, Eve rummaged through Charlie's truck, muttering to herself. She dug grimy coins out from cupholders and, reaching, stretching,
salvaged some crumpled bills from beneath the seats. That should be
enough. Cash in hand, she ran across the lot. As she approached the doors,
she caught her shivering reflection in the glass. She looked disheveled,
downright unstable. Wide-eyed, dressed in socks, sweatpants, and a dirty
T-shirt, her hair tangled up like she'd just gone through a wind tunnel.
Who gave a fuck.

When she pushed through the entrance, a warbling chime announced
her arrival—like fanfare trumpets at a sideshow carnival. She weaved her
way to the counter, past shelves of neon-colored junk food and cheap booze.
Above, buzzing lights hummed with the tenor of bloodthirsty mosquitoes.
She rounded a corner and nearly toppled a display of key chains.

The clerk, a slender fellow with cow eyes and rosebud lips, blinked at
her, wary. His pale, clean-shaven face somehow looked thirteen and thirty at
the same time. Eve, doing her best to appear sane, ambled up to the counter
and smiled. She held out her smattering of dirty coins and mangled bills.
"Pump, uh, pump number two."

The clerk's eyes flitted to the change, narrowed, like she'd offered up a
handful of bottle caps. He looked at her. "You want religion?"

"W-what?" Eve stammered.

"You want regular?" he said.

"I'm sorry?"

"Do you want regular gas?"

"Oh, right, yes. Regular." Get your shit together, Eve. Behind, the door
chimed open and heavy boots clacked against tile. Eve didn't look back.

"How much?" The clerk scratched his nose with a dirty fingernail.

Eve glanced at the mess of change in her trembling grasp. "Whatever this
gets me. I— I'm in a bit of a hurry."

The clerk wiped his mouth with the side of his hand and sniffed. "You can just put it on the counter." He gestured. "I'll count it."

When Eve set down the change, a lone quarter dinged off the glass and clanged to the floor, rolling away like it had some greater purpose. As the clerk started counting, Eve went after the derelict coin. It veered around the display of key chains and plunked to a stop at the leather boots of—Eve peered up—a Highway Patrol officer. A barrel-chested man with a Burt Reynolds mustache and forearms thicker than Eve's neck. She straightened her posture, forced another smile, and held up the coin. "Just— Just dropped this . . ." she said, the shaky vibrato of her own voice like sandpaper in her ears.

The cop's deep-set eyes zeroed in on her sock-covered feet. His brow furrowed.

"You got no shoes," he observed.

"Pump two's good to go," the clerk interjected. "Nine bucks, fifty-seven cents."

Grateful for the distraction, Eve hurried to the exit, tucked away the quarter, and chimed out the door. All the while, she could feel the cop's steely gaze lasered to her back. *Please don't follow.*

At the truck, she unhooked the nozzle, twisted off the fuel cap, and started filling the tank. The metal lever was cold against her hand, the slight tremor of gasoline flowing through. The gallon counter ticked up, painfully slow. She glanced at the storefront. Through the barred glass, the cop was buying a pack of chewing gum, making small talk with the clerk, but . . . *It's fine. He can't arrest you for not wearing shoes.*

The clerk frowned at the cop and shook his head. *Are they talking about me? What if "Charlie" called me in as a runaway?*

CLICK.

The gas pump halted at 3.78 gallons. Hopefully it was enough to get her home. She hung up the nozzle, climbed back in, and turned the key. Just as she rolled to a start, the cop strolled out of the store. Eve maintained a calm and measured pace. *Don't draw attention . . .*

As she pulled back onto the main road, a childhood memory played in her mind: A televised car chase. High speeds. Helicopter cameras. Route 104 was alive with the blare of sirens as twenty cruisers pursued a sky-blue minivan. The van dodged oncoming traffic, careened through red lights, busy cross-walks. A news anchor excitedly narrated every twist and turn, as if he were calling a play-by-play on Super Bowl Sunday. The frenzied chase came to an abrupt end when police herded the van into a backyard swimming pool. "It's a miracle no one was killed," said the anchor, suddenly somber.

Weeks later, it was revealed the driver had been in the midst of a psychotic episode. Apparently, he believed the government was trying to kidnap him for some kind of thought-control experiment. Turned out getting chased by twenty cops didn't exactly quell the delusion.

A nagging question lingered: Would that be her fate? A feature in the local news, fleeing from imagined threats? The lead subject of some stupid cop show? A spectacle for the public to pity, to gawk at and say things like, *Poor thing, if only she'd been right with the Lord*. No. This was real. Madness didn't feel like this. There were too many external markers. Too many connected threads. She buried the rising doubt and pressed down on the gas. This was real.

Headlights beamed through her back window, glared off the rearview. *The cop?* She let off the gas a bit. Two quick siren whoops. Red and blue flashing lights. Fuck. Hesitant, she hit the turn signal, pulled onto the shoulder, and slowed to a stop. Part of her considered flooring it but . . . *Play this cool. You can't save Charlie if you're in handcuffs*. She rolled down her window, took a deep breath, let it out.

Behind, the cop's door swung open, boots scraped onto pavement, footfalls approached at a plodding rhythm. Eve fixed her tousled hair, again doing her best to appear "normal."

The cop reached her window. "Kill the engine."

Eve did as he said.

"License and registration."

Shaky, Eve reached into the glove box, offered up the requested documents. The cop studied them, flashlight propped on his shoulder. He was chomping away on a wad of gum.

Eve, patience waning, said, "Can I ask why I'm being pulled over?"

"You can . . ."

His dry response hung in the air. Eve repeated herself. "Why did you pull me over . . . ?"

With a sigh, the cop handed back the papers. "When's the last time you slept, Evelyn?"

The use of her legal name caught her off guard. She forgot it was on her license. "Last time I slept?"

"That is the question you were asked."

"Last night, er, tonight. I guess, technically last night?"

"Uh-huh. For how long?"

"A few hours, about six hours." *Two hours, but . . .*

Silent, the cop hunched forward, swept his light around the cab, peered into the back. He breathed more through his mouth than his nose, as if his sinuses were blocked. Every exhale carried the scent of cinnamon gum and lukewarm coffee. "Where you headed?" he asked.

"Home . . ."

"Where's home?"

"At the summit."

"Address?"

"Look"—Eve smiled through clenched teeth—"I'm in a bit— I need to get— Can we just—"

"Address."

Eve huffed. "Heritage Lane, 3709."

"Any drinks tonight, Evelyn?" The question sounded like an accusation.

Eve cleared her throat. "No."

"Drugs, medication."

"No, sir."

"Marijuana." He emphasized the "hua" part of the word, a vague attempt at some kind of accent.

"No pot," Eve said.

"Glass."

"Glass?"

"Methamphetamine."

"No, sir."

He clucked his tongue, stood upright, and patted the roof of the truck. He looked around and hooked a thumb into his belt loop, thinking. "All right, Evelyn Palmer." He gave the truck another pat. "Make sure you get some sleep."

"Yessir . . ." *Thank fucking God.*

With that, the cop started back toward his cruiser. Eve began rolling up her window, but—

His radio went off. He stopped in his tracks, adjusted the volume. The signal was choppy, a female cop speaking lingo Eve didn't understand, half the words drowning in radio static: "All—BOLO—on—run—approx——last—"

The cop looked back to Eve, grumbled something unintelligible—*stay right there?*—then started back to his car, likely trying to get a better signal.

"Charlie" called you in, that voice in Eve's head insisted once more. *You need to run. RUN. RUN. RUN . . .*

Eve's foot drifted toward the gas pedal, her hand to the ignition. Her heart thumped, all sounds merged into a single high-pitched tone, and then . . .

She didn't remember starting the truck. Hell, she didn't even remember setting her foot on the gas. But next thing she knew, she was flooring it, barreling up the mountain faster than she'd ever driven before. She braced for those flashing lights, those blaring sirens, frantically checking the rearview, but . . . nothing.

Maybe that dispatch hadn't been about her after all? She wasn't slowing down to find out. The next twenty minutes of driving blurred in a dissociative mess until she came upon that sharp corner. She barely let off the gas, bending around it, and—

A woman—no, a child—was wandering across the road. Blue jeans. White T-shirt. Navy green boots. On reflex, Eve's foot crushed the brakes, her hands jerking the steering wheel hard to the right. Tires shrieked, rubber burned, light streaked, until all at once, everything came to a fishtailing stop. The truck wobbled on its suspension, creaking back and forth at a slowing tempo. Eve, wide-eyed, sat frozen, still gripping the steering wheel, still processing the fact she'd nearly run over a child.

The truck was facing back the way she'd come, headlights pouring a wide sweep over the trees, the asphalt, the double solid lines, and . . .

. . . the child. She was about a hundred feet away, standing on the right embankment. Suddenly, her arms shot straight out to her sides, wrists hanging limp like she was tied to an unseen crucifix. She held this bizarre pose for three, four, five seconds, and then her arms dropped. The girl took three sudden steps backward and froze again. She spun to face the woods, a mechanical movement, like a soldier pivoting during a march. She swiveled again, now facing Eve.

The features of her pale face were drowned out by the brightness of the headlights. Without warning, she broke into a sprint, bolting toward Eve with startling speed. Eve's breath hitched in her throat—she shifted into reverse, was about to floor the gas, get the fuck out of there, but—

The girl swerved sharply to the right, scrambled up the embankment, and slipped into the woods . . .

Not your problem. Eve set on the gas, reversed into a turn, and continued her way back up the mountain. *Not your fucking problem.*

For the rest of the drive up, she paid a bit more attention to the road. Twenty or so minutes later, when she finally reached Heritage Lane, she slowed to another stop. On either side, the trees leaned inward, as if whispering horrible secrets to one another. Eve peered over her shoulder. The red brake lights illuminated the wet asphalt. No cops in sight. Eve considered, one last time, if this was the best idea. Charlie's warning on the phone played in her thoughts: *You need to leave, never come back to the house . . . Get as far away as you possibly can . . .*

Resolved, she drew in a deep breath. Exhaled. She set on the gas and crept ahead. Heritage Lane seemed longer than usual, narrower. At its end, she rounded onto the driveway, crawled upward. The headlights cast shadows into silent trees—shaping branches into crooked hands, shrubs into undulating abominations. And then, bit by bit, the old house loomed into view—outlined by the black-blue sky. Her lights cast a dull glow over its face, like a submarine approaching some deep-sea wreck—untouched for centuries.

Vigilant, Eve pulled to a stop at the edge of the yard, turned off the ignition, the lights. All was dark. Absentmindedly she reached into the cupholder and wrapped her hand around Charlie's necklace, feeling the cold brass surface against her palm. She tucked it into her pocket. After taking another deep breath, she stepped out. The mountain air was crisp, still. The far-off sounds of howling wind surged through the valley. For a moment, distant sirens echoed—or was it a pack of coyotes?

    She trooped forward, sock-laden feet crunching against the frosted yard, icy, biting. The soil under her feet gave way like a wet sponge. She ascended the porch, unlocked the door, pushed it open, and—despite every bone in her body telling her to run—she stepped into the foyer.

DOC_A06_NAMES

Description: Transcribed from *Psychology & Practice Magazine*.

◆

TITLE: Esteemed Psychologist Fired after Absurd Claims

DRAFT 2:

Trondheim, Norway

February 17, 1989

Dr. Bjørn Erikson has been let go from Hvit Fjell University's Department of Psychology after refusing to back down on outlandish
claims.[1] Details are still developing, but sources say he began to
believe one of his delusional patients was actually experiencing
real events. The patient, a twenty-seven-year-old male, is said to
be suffering from a variation of Capgras syndrome.

───────────────

[1] Original document had a scribbled note in the margin: Jeg har kontaktet universitetet.
De hevder Dr. Erikson aldri har vært ansatt der.

Capgras syndrome, aka Capgras delusion, is a rare neuropsychiat-
ric disorder in which a person believes that a close family member,
friend, or even themself has been replaced by an imposter, double,
or replica. It is named after the French psychiatrist Joseph Capgras, who first brought the condition to light in 1923.

The exact cause is unknown, but it is believed to be connected
with a malfunction in the ability to process facial recognition and
emotional responses. Often it goes hand in hand with other delusions, including, but not limited to, the belief that one's entire
surrounding reality has been replaced.

According to our source, Dr. Erikson became convinced that one
of his patients suffering from such afflictions was actually experiencing a real event. That this patient's reality was in fact being
replaced with another one entirely, just as the delusion implied it
was. Of course, the doctor's endorsement only resulted in a worsening of the patient's symptoms and eventual involuntary admission to
the Gaula River Asylum. There, the patient is said to have engaged
in extreme and bizarre self-mutilation.[1]

In this case, Dr. Erikson claims his patient has evidence.
"Proof" that might sway even the most hardened skeptics' minds.
"Bread crumbs" was the terminology employed. But again, our sources
have informed us the so-called proof is nothing more than blurry
photographs and obscure online postings.

For his part, Dr. Erikson is a world-renowned researcher in the
field of delusional misidentification syndromes. His book, *Names
Without Faces*, has sold over half a million copies worldwide and was

---

[1] Scribbled margin note: Pasienten fjernet sine egne negler med en tang. Han var overbev-
ist om at hendene hans var blitt byttet ut med (nesten) eksakte kopier. (Jeg har erfart at
han etter å ha fjernet neglene forøkte å fjerne sin egen tunge, men mislyktes på grunn av
intervensjon.)

a finalist for the Brage Prize in nonfiction. His research has been cited over five thousand times.

At the time of this posting, Erikson has not responded to our request for comment.

We've reached out to the Helsetilsynet (Norwegian Board of Health Supervision), and they've informed us that an investigation into the matter is ongoing. Whether or not Erikson retains his title of doctor will be determined.

- ...   - . - -

SPIRAL

Eve drifted into the foyer, the door creaking shut behind her. The house was dark, the walls stained with grainy shadows. And the cold air was quiet, the kind of silence that got under your skin like an itch. She approached the staircase, flicked the nearest light switch, and . . . nothing. She tried another switch. Still nothing.

Had the power gone out?

She narrowed her eyes; there was just enough moonlight to see—it streamed through the windows, painting dull shapes on the walls, the hardwood. Eve called out, her voice small: "Charlie . . . ?" The house murmured in response, a faint churning in the wind. With measured steps, Eve ventured toward the living room and paused in its doorway. Her eyes were drawn to that barren spot above the fireplace. She'd half expected to see the painting from the basement wardrobe—the chocolate Lab, staring out at the ominous tree line—but the wall was blank. In fact, she glanced around; everything was precisely where she'd left it . . .

She tried again. "Charlie?" Nothing. "Shylo . . . ?"

She threw a wary glance back toward the foyer. Whispering doubt wormed into her psyche. Was anyone even here? Was this a trap? Was the house trying to drag her back here? Eve ignored these questions—her legs carried her forward. She glided past the fireplace, stepped into the kitchen, and halted in her tracks . . .

The table was set for six. Place mats, dinner plates, silverware, all laid out with delicate care. The sight triggered Eve to take a reflexive step away, as if she'd happened upon the corpse of a freshly killed animal. Turning, she staggered back into the living room and . . .

Bzz, Bzz, Bzz . . .

A vibration in her pocket caught her off guard. It was the phone, the one she'd stolen from the imposter Charlie's backpack. Without thinking, she pulled it out:

℗ Unknown # calling . . .
ACCEPT DECLINE

Eve's trembling finger pressed ACCEPT.

"Eve . . . ?" It was Fake Charlie. "Eve? Are you there?"

Eve remained silent.

"Eve, please, what's—where . . ." Fake Charlie stammered. "You can talk to me, just—tell me where you are, please, I—"

Eve ended the call, muted the phone. Slipping it away, she turned back toward the kitchen and . . .

There, at the table, a shadowy figure now sat. Its back was turned to Eve, and its head was craned forward at a sharp angle—slumped like a puppet whose strings had been punitively cut. And it was motionless, not even breathing. Dead?

A pounding throb of dread shot through Eve's temples. Every heartbeat screamed: *Danger, danger, danger.* Inching away, she bumped into a side table and—

The figure, with a sudden gasp, jolted upright as if forced into position by unseen hands. It sat there, pin-straight frozen, for one, two, three seconds, and then, with arachnid speed, it darted rightward, vanishing into the distant shadows. Its chair teetered precariously in its wake, threatening to topple before settling. The sound of bare footsteps scrambled deeper into the house, smacking a lunatic tempo across hardwood until silence, oppressive and suffocating, returned.

Eve glanced to the nearest exit, about to get the fuck out of there, but then . . .

"Eve," the real Charlie's voice, ragged and wheezing, called out from above. "Eve, help . . ."

All at once, Eve's emotions whirled into a frantic maelstrom. Her conviction to protect and her instinct to survive battled each other in a vicious back-and-forth street fight. One screamed at her to run up there, do whatever it took to save Charlie, while the other insisted this was all a terrible trick: flee this house, this mountain, never return. Eve slowed her breath, gritted her teeth, and silenced the inner chaos. No more running. Hands balling into fists, she made her way to the foyer. At the threshold, she poked her head around the corner. All seemed clear. Quiet.

But as Eve climbed the stairs, another sound bled down from the darkness above. A faint, muffled whimper. "Charlie?" Heart pounding, Eve entered the upstairs corridor—and as soon as her foot met the floorboards, the whimpering ceased. It sounded like it had come from beyond the corner at the hallway's end. Slowly, Eve edged forward and leaned around. The white door that led to Alison's supposed bedroom was half-ajar, revealing nothing but a pitch-black void. From within, labored breathing emerged, weak and stuttering.

"Ch—Charlie?" Eve's voice trembled. Now, every fiber of her being once again screamed: *RUN.* Yet she continued creeping forward, one foot after the other, until she swung the door open wide. Putrid reek wafted out, hitting her like a wall. A stench so powerful, it dredged up a flash-jolt memory: As a child, walking home from school, she'd accidentally stepped on a dead sparrow. With a wet squelch, her red gumboot burst the bird's stomach open, unleashing a mess of bleach-white maggots onto the sunbaked sidewalk. The odor was so strong, so foul, she could taste it. Only now, the stench seeping out from that room was somehow worse. More pungent, and . . .

Someone was standing in the far corner . . .

It was the woman in the hospital gown, the one from the attic. Alison? She was shaking, a strange movement somewhere between laughter and weeping. She took a halting step toward Eve, then another one. Another. The movements seemed painful, involuntary. The woman lurched to a halt in the room's center. Now, her gaunt arm was visible, cast in a dim wedge of moonlight. Cold blue veins pulsated beneath pale, almost translucent skin. Tendons seethed and spasmed like high-strung tapeworms. And gripped in her gnarled hand, a familiar hammer. The woman's voice, almost childlike, quivered unsteadily: "You have to hide. You. Have to. Hide. You have to—"

Eve, finally snapping out of her trance, bolted in the opposite direction. She hurtled down the stairs, nearly falling as she made a beeline to the front door—locked. From the outside? She tried again, yanking back with all her weight. The door didn't budge.

Panic mounting, Eve darted to the nearest window, but iron bars blocked her escape. She swiveled around: every single window was now inexplicably barred. When? How? There was no time to question the logic. *Find another exit.* With her back to the wall, she slid deeper into the house, straining to listen. Above, all was quiet. Had the woman even followed?

Right then, the woman's voice, hushed, leaked down through a ceiling vent, counting: "Fifteen . . . fourteen . . . thirteen . . ."

You have to hide. The realization hit Eve with a sick and sudden lurch: this was a game of hide-and-seek.

"Ten . . . nine . . ."

Urgent, Eve cut into the living room. The windows were barred there too, of course. She lunged for the back door—locked. *Fuck.*

"Five . . . four . . ."

Her eyes shot to the basement door, wide open, unwelcoming as ever, but . . .

"Two . . . one . . ."

Those bare footsteps, unnaturally fast, skittered down the upper hall. They moved with a relentless, mechanical pace, like the staccato strokes of a typewriter. They tapered onto the staircase and—

Hide. NOW.

With no other choice, Eve shot toward the basement, scrambling down into the darkness. Pushing off the stairwell corner, Eve tore leftward, her hand skimming the coarse concrete, guiding her through the devouring black. Overhead, footsteps shuddered into the living room and slid to a halt. Eve could picture the woman, outlined in gray light, hammer raised, head tilted, listening for any sign of movement. *Fuck.* A knot of terror welled in Eve's chest cavity, expanding like a carnival balloon. She forged ahead, as quietly as possible, until she spilled into an open space. She groped forward. Her eyes narrowed, vague shapes forming in the hazy static: Brick pillars, rickety beds, and . . . a wheelchair? Wait, what room was this?

Hide.

Ahead, a soft flicker of orange light beckoned. It drew her into a passage so narrow, she had to turn sideways to fit. She shuffled onward, face scratching against insulation, until she broke into a small nook. Was this the spot where Jenny had hidden?

In the far wall was an olive-green door, cracked open—that orange flickering light on the other side. Carved into the door's center, a cryptic glyph: the circle marked with intersecting lines. Eve reached for the knob and hesitated. Something told her it might not be a good idea, but she glanced back down the narrow passage. No footsteps. No stench. Was the woman still upstairs?

Either way, Eve pushed through the olive-green door and entered a low-ceilinged room filled with dark piles of clutter. Swiftly, she grabbed a nearby rickety chair and wedged it beneath the doorknob. It wouldn't keep anyone out for long, but at least it would make a sound, warn her.

She turned back to survey the dim interior. Its low ceiling was intertwined with long-dead tree roots, makeshift support beams holding everything aloft—it seemed more like an abandoned mine than a room. And that orange flickering glow, its source hidden, struggled to illuminate the space. Eve drifted forward. Aside from a few pieces of old furniture, countless paintings dominated the room—stacks and stacks of them. They were strewn on the dirt floors, propped against the earthen walls, heaped in the corners. None were hanging.

Eve continued to wander deeper. Maybe there was something here that would make sense of all this madness. But there were only paintings, and each one was more or less the same. Depictions of the house, 3709 Heritage Lane, in different contexts: half-built, fully renovated, abandoned, covered in snow, burned to a crisp. An exceptionally odd one portrayed the windows and doors swarmed with tiny black dots.

Had Thomas's mother painted all these?

As Eve crept forward, her eyes caught a painting with people in it. She crouched down for a closer look. It was a family of four. Stiffly posed like *American Gothic* in front of the house—a severe-looking older couple with two children. Boy and girl. The father, a bleak smile on his face, was nearly the spitting image of Thomas—right down to his perfect teeth. The mother, red hair tied back in a tight bun, looked one tunic away from joining a nunnery. The daughter looked a lot like Jenny, but she appeared sad, hopeless even.

And the boy had Thomas's eyes, his brown hair.

This had to be his family, painted when he lived here as a kid. Thomas, his "sister" Alison, and their parents. Eve was about to move on, but then . . . she squinted. Young Thomas looked out of place, like he was painted there after the fact by a lesser artist. His dimensions weren't quite right. His arms were just the slightest bit too long, his mouth the slightest bit too wide. Even his texture looked off. Eve pressed the tip of her thumb against his face. His paint felt different from the rest—cheap, acrylic, cold. Unnerved, she pulled away her hand, leaving behind a pinkish smear where young Thomas's jaw used to be. It looked gory—a mangled, lopsided grin.

Turning back, Eve started toward the source of the light. She rounded a stack of empty picture frames and came upon a red gas lantern. It was nestled in a corner, hissing and flickering. Eve was too distracted to question who had turned it on. Next to the lantern were two wooden crates, stacked on top of each other. Eve glanced over her shoulder, back at that olive-green door, listening. No sound. Careful, she knelt down and peered into the first crate. It was filled with painting supplies. Brushes, solvents, palettes. She set it aside and looked into the next box.

This one was filled to the brim with glossy four-by-six photographs. Snapshots of the family from that painting, but here, they looked like different people entirely—relaxed, happy. The father had a full beard, neck tattoos, and a friendly smile. The mother's red hair was pixie-cut short, and her green eyes had an impish sparkle to them. As for the daughter, she had bright green eyes just like her mother, and her bubbly energy radiated a joy that shone in every frame. Eve continued sifting through, picture after picture. Young Thomas wasn't in any of them . . .

Eve lifted one closer to her face, squinted. In this image, the two parents and the daughter were gathered around a campfire. Behind them, a red gas lantern—identical to the one here—cast its warm glow over a checkered picnic table. To the table's left, the father was hunched forward, tuning an acoustic guitar. He wore a baggy black T-shirt featuring a white circle, crisscrossed with lines of differing lengths—the very symbol Alison had allegedly carved into the banister. Below it:

RING OF EYES

Judging by the jagged font, it was some kind of heavy metal band logo. All in all, he looked nothing like a Puritan who, according to Thomas, "didn't like hobbies."

Eve continued scrutinizing the image. The mother, wearing a Black Sabbath hoodie, was taking a swig from a beer, giving a sidelong look at her husband, a loving glint in her green eyes. Standing between the parents was a girl who looked about fourteen years old—Alison? With her long black hair and vibrant green eyes, she was the one taking the photo, holding up the camera for a three-person selfie. She clasped a free hand over her mouth, caught in the midst of laughter. At the trio's feet, blurry and out of focus, a chocolate Lab, tail wagging. Buckley?

Eve sifted through more. Beach days. Metal concerts. Hockey games. Parties. Why wasn't Thomas in any of these photos? Not a single one. He wasn't even present for the family portraits.

Eve dug to the bottom, and her fingertips grazed a crumpled ball of paper. She pulled it out and flattened it against her thigh. It was a note—one that Alison had presumably written to herself—hastily scrawled in black pen:

You are not who they say you are.

Thomas "Faust" is not your brother.

He has been ~~living~~ (trapped?) here since long before the house was built, before the trees were planted. He changed your memories. Warped your family. Forced himself into your life.

Despite what everyone around you says—your name is NOT Alina. It is ALISON. Alison Faust. Your father is Elijah and your mother is Vera. The religious zealots who replaced them are not real. They are MIMICS. They may look like your parents, but they are not. Never forget that.

Thomas, or whatever force controls him, wants to drive you mad, wants you to stay locked up here forever. He's making you see things, making you doubt your own sanity. (What are his motives?) He's pulling you into a labyrinth that you might never escape.

It's like quicksand; the more you fight the charade, the worse it gets.

There's only one way to stop it: You have to play along, wait for the right moment, then make Thomas angry (or afraid?). Do something extreme, something that will make his mask slip. Make him show his true face—then you strike.

LABYRINTH

Eve tucked the letter into her back pocket alongside Charlie's necklace. Again, some variation of Heather's words echoed: *Alison thought that killing Thomas was the only way to make it stop, to get her old life back. She stabbed him thirty-seven times in less than a minute . . .*

Eve was about to stand when she spotted a trail of ants filing down from a crack in a nearby support beam. They met the dirt floor and veered off, disappearing beyond the lantern's soft halo—all moving with hivemind purpose.

Eve wrapped her grip around the lantern's handle and, joint by joint, rose to her feet. The ant trail led her farther into the space, the jittery light unveiling more with each step. She rounded a precarious tower of paintings and came upon a bizarrely out-of-place hallway: white tile flooring and pale green walls, like a hospital hallway. This corridor stretched for a seemingly impossible length, the ants marching over the linoleum, everything receding into blackness. Leery, Eve drifted forward, her nostrils assaulted by the stench of bleach and cleaning chemicals. The ants lured her farther down the narrow hall.

Ahead a mechanical clicking sound echoed, like an off-rhythm turn signal: *tack—tack-tack—tack-tack*. Mo? The Hillbilly Chimp sat in the center of the hall, rocking back and forth as he manically banged his plastic cymbals. The ants veered around the toy like water around a rock, kept marching off into the darkness beyond. Absentmindedly, Eve went over, squatted down, and picked Mo up. White fur. Blue felt overalls. A frayed straw hat peppered with holes. This was *her* Mo. Right down to every last dent, scratch, and blemish. Unthinking, she switched him off, set him down, and continued forward until the lantern's glow revealed, standing about ten feet away . . . Charlie.

Eve froze. This looked nothing like the Charlie she knew—the Charlie who'd stepped back into the house to "grab a few things." Now, her clothes were tattered and frayed like they'd endured years down here, decades even. And her skin was autopsy pale, drained of any life—her eyes were gently shut, as if she were asleep while standing. The ants circled her bare feet, hundreds, maybe thousands, a macabre procession fanning out like a slow spinning vinyl. Somehow, it seemed like this Charlie had been here for centuries, like she was part of the house itself, fused to the ground—silent—waiting. Finally, Eve managed a hushed "Ch—Charlie?"

Charlie's eyes remained shut, almost serenely so. But her lips peeled back with a wet sound, her mouth forming into a pained grimace, bloodred gums and glistening teeth exposed. And then, with alarming speed, the encircling ants were upon her. They swarmed up Charlie's legs, her torso, fingers, arms, rising like a coat of liquid metal. Eve clamped a hand over her own mouth, as if that might stop the scene from unfolding.

But the nightmare spectacle only accelerated.

Eve staggered backward and held in a gasp as the ants, with relentless fervor, wedged themselves between Charlie's eyelids, into her nostrils, mouth. Squirmed their way through the crevices of her gums and teeth. All the while, Charlie remained eerily still, unfazed by the chaos.

The invading ants moved faster and faster until only one remained, bloated and wriggling, stuck between Charlie's two front teeth. Its needle-thin legs kicked and writhed until . . . it slipped through with an audible *schlick*. Charlie's eyes snapped open wide, mystified. As if she'd just woken from a horrible dream, only to realize reality was so much worse. Her bewildered gaze met Eve's, and then she whispered, "What— What are you doing here?"

Eve, barely able to think, started to respond, but Charlie cut in. "Eve, y-you're not, you're not supposed to be here yet, you—"

Mid-sentence, Charlie froze, her bloodshot eyes fixating on something over Eve's shoulder.

Eve glanced back, but nothing was there. "She's almost," Charlie stammered in breathless terror, "she's almost here—you have to, you have to hide." Charlie spun on her heel, shot off down the hallway, hooked rightward.

Eve lingered for a moment, her hesitation cut short by that maggoty stench of decay. Behind, the unsteady shuffle of footsteps echoed through the painting-filled chamber. Soft whimpers, that woman's childlike voice repeating the same word again and again—"Sorry, sorry, sorry"—until she loomed into view at the hallway's entrance, still wielding the hammer.

Fuck this. Eve turned heel and followed Charlie's footsteps, sprinting through the corridor. She veered rightward, the lantern slipping from her hand, crashing to the tile with a shrill crack. As Eve took another sharp turn, she glanced back, just in time to see—

The woman approaching at a languid pace, undeterred by the spreading flames of the shattered lantern. Her face—an image that etched itself into Eve's retinas—was exposed by the dancing glow, undulating shadows bleeding upward. Her skin was pulled tight, every contour of her skull harshly pronounced, as if the bones might burst through in a blood-soaked mess. And her eye sockets were so deep, so emaciated, it looked like her bulging eyes might fall out if she were to lean too far forward. But even in the dim light, even in the brief glimpse—the vivid green of the woman's irises was unmistakable.

Eve, profoundly regretting her choice to look back, careened forward, turning corner after corner through an endless labyrinth. At some point those hospital walls and white tiles gave way to concrete and hard-packed dirt. If not for a few rays of sparse light leaking down through floorboards above, it would've been pitch dark. Eve kept running, and running, until she slammed through a bone-white door and tumbled into a small room, nearly face-planting against black and white checkered tile.

She jolted to her feet, whipped the door shut, and fumbled for the lock—but there was none. Fuck. She scanned the darkness, hunting for something to bar the door, a place to hide, a weapon, anything, but she could barely see. All the while, those bare footsteps, that grating whimper, drew ever closer.

Eve grasped her hands along smooth brick walls until she bumped into a solid object—wooden and splintery. A shuttered wardrobe. She clambered inside, yanked the door shut, and held it there. *Breathe in. Breathe out.* Her heart thumped a frenzied rhythm against her rib cage. Cold sweat trickled down her brow, stung her eyes. And from the corridor, those dragging foot-steps came closer, closer, and just before the room's white door swung open, Eve gulped in a sharp breath, held it.

Eve peered out through the wardrobe slats. There in the doorway stood the hospital-gowned woman, framed by the scant light, hammer still in hand. *Don't breathe. Be quiet.* The woman loomed into the room, weeping a grief-filled moan—a warbled pitch that rose and fell into dead quiet. She circled the space like a caged animal.

Eve, desperate not to make a sound, continued holding her breath. Her lungs burned. Pins and needles pricked her face. And the woman wandered the room, seconds stretching out like minutes until finally . . . she lumbered to a stop, turned for the exit, and staggered away—one, painfully slow, step, at, a, time. Eve's inner voice screamed: *Don't breathe. Don't you fucking breathe. Just hang on a little longer, but—*

Eve's lungs forced her to suck in air, a short gasp. The woman froze in the doorway. Then, with a slow ratcheting movement, she looked over her shoulder, directly at Eve. Dim light glinted off the woman's unblinking eyes. Two white flecks surrounded by an ocean of black. It was like she could see into Eve's thoughts, feel Eve's terror. Like she was trying to tell Eve something without speaking a word.

Suddenly, a cascade of fractured images and memories invaded Eve's brain like a swarm of sightless bugs. Not her own memories—Alison's memories. An entire lifetime condensed into a rapid-fire slideshow, so vivid, so intense, Eve could almost hear it, see it. As if the memories were playing out right there in the shadows of the wardrobe. Scene after scene:

Young Alison, an only child. With her parents from the photographs, all those years ago, settling into the house. Fleeting moments from better times: Alison's father teaching her to play guitar, guiding her fingers across the fretboard. Alison stumbling as she learned to ice-skate on a frozen pond, patient parents helping her to stand. Alison's mother bringing home a chocolate Lab puppy.

Then, on a bright summer day, a strange boy wandering out of the woods, a lost child. Young Thomas. From that moment on, Alison's world began its terrible transformation. First the changing furniture, then the walls, the rooms of the house, the people. Alison's once loving, laid-back parents shifting into abusive zealots—religious fanatics. Alison's life rapidly spiraling into a convoluted hell that only she could recognize.

Worst of all, her parents beginning to act as if it was Thomas who had always been their son and Alison who had wandered from the woods—an outsider—a lost child. All of this mounting dread culminating in that terrible epiphany, Alison realizing: the only way to escape this miserable reality was to—

A familiar image cut in, a moonlit room, a gaunt hand, white knuckles gripped around a silver-tipped fountain pen. Soundlessly stabbing into pallid flesh, up and down, up and down, again and again, faster and faster—

Darkness. A pale blue dot beginning to form in the distance—

Alison, soaked in blood, scrambling through the night. Pushing through branches, weaving through trees. Behind, voices calling out, shouting, searching—

White ceilings, pockmarked. Cold light. Thin wrists strapped to a bed, thrashing. Shrinks, nurses, all glancing at Alison, repressed fear in their eyes, as if she might lunge for them, rip out their throats. Even her own "parents" kept their distance . . . The way they looked at her, the way they looked at their own daughter, the numb shock in their eyes, the pity—

A child's voice, screaming, "*MY NAME ISN'T ALINA—MY NAME ISN'T ALINA—MY NAME ISN'T—*"

Rising louder and louder, until—

At last, the hallucinatory nightmare ceased. Eve gasped, thrown back into the present, catching her breath. Her eyes darted to the doorway. Alison was still standing there, face hidden by shadows. But now, the sight of her filled Eve with crushing empathy, sorrow even.

Slowly, Alison drifted to the room's center. She hunched forward and, almost reverently, set down the hammer on the black and white tile. She pushed herself off her knees and withdrew, pulling the door gently shut in her wake. Total darkness returned.

Again Eve waited there, hiding in the shadows, paralyzed, lost. Minutes dragged by like hours until . . . more footsteps. But these were a calm, steady gait. Padded, as if made by sock-covered feet. Outside the room, a light flickered on, casting a thin sheet of yellow glow from beneath the crack of the door. Two columns of shadow approached until the door clicked open, swinging wide. An incandescent glow framed the silhouette of a man, tall and broad. He lingered there, a black outline, staring into the room, and then . . .

He flicked a switch—cold light flooded the space—it was Thomas . . . clad in an olive-green sweater and light brown corduroys. But he appeared slightly younger, those gray hairs once speckled around his ears now completely gone. His tired visage scanned over pinkish brick walls, until he zeroed in on the shuttered wardrobe. For a second, Eve thought Thomas had seen her, caught the glint of her eyes, but . . . He sighed, started to reach for the light, and . . . his gaze stopped on the hammer. He cocked his head. *How did that get there?*

Frowning, Thomas strode over, squatted down, and lifted the tool. He narrowed his eyes, studying the hammer, puzzled. Then, with a shrug, he rose to stand and strode for the exit. Just before the threshold, he hung the hammer on a brown pegboard. There, it joined dozens of other tools. He flicked off the light and slipped out, pulling the door shut behind.

Once again, Eve was alone in the shadows, ablaze with questions. Questions she feared had no answers. Or at least no answers she could comprehend. Again she waited, listening as Thomas's soft footfalls receded, faded around a corner, and silence returned.

Find Charlie. Find Shylo. Get out of here.

Eve didn't remember exiting the wardrobe. Next thing she knew, she'd glided across the room and cracked open the white door—just a sliver. She peered out with one eye. It wasn't a concrete labyrinth that greeted her, nor was it a greenish-white hospital hallway—no, that would have made too much fucked-up sense. Rather, it was the basement corridor, cast in a soft incandescent glow—the same hallway she'd crept down when searching for hide-and-seek Jenny one night ago. *One night? Somehow that felt like weeks ago, months even.* And now this previously unfinished hallway was midway through an extensive renovation: laminate flooring, unpainted drywall, pothole lights. Eve was about to step forward, but something nagged at the corner of her vision . . .

The hammer, still poised on the brown pegboard, seemed to beckon her. That empty voice, the faceless substitute for Mo, whispered, *You have no idea what's waiting for you upstairs. Surely you don't want to face it unarmed and defenseless now, do you?* Eve swallowed her reservations and stepped out of the room, hammer in hand.

HOME

With her back to the unpainted drywall, Eve inched down the corridor. Overhead lights hummed a shrill note, and soft footsteps mulled about. Eve tilted an ear to the stucco ceiling and discerned several different gaits, all unhurried, meandering. She tightened her grip on the hammer, inched up to a corner, and dared a glimpse around. Another narrow hallway, familiar but renovated—it led to a slice of carpeted room, bathed in warm light.

After a few more seconds of waiting, listening, she eased forward, up to the room's precipice, and paused there, taking it all in. This was the garage-sized space, the one that, only the day before, had been concrete, covered in dust, and lined with rickety shelves. Now, it was a fully finished games room. Beige carpet, forest-green walls, sports-themed beanbag chairs planted around an unfinished game of Scrabble. In the far corner, framed vinyls hung above an air hockey table: AC/DC, Black Sabbath, Slayer. In the other corner, a Portland Winterhawks jersey and some hockey trophies were on display behind a granite minibar.

Above, a squealing groan, something heavy dragged across hardwood. A couch? The grating pitch rose higher and higher until . . . silence. Okay . . .

Every step deliberate, Eve crossed the games room and peered into the next hallway. Its yellow walls were adorned with black-and-white nature photography. Laminate flooring stretched to a darkened staircase. Without making a sound, Eve reached the bottom of the stairs and began her ascent.

She skirted around the stairwell corner and slowed. In the blackness above, a thin rectangle of light leaked through the door's outline. From beyond, a murmur of voices trickled down, muffled and indistinct. Clinking glasses. Laughter. A dinner party? Eve hesitated, but . . .

Find Charlie. Find Shylo. Get the fuck out of here.

As Eve continued climbing, that outline of light drawing closer—the smell of sirloin steak, mashed potatoes, and gravy filled the air. Still gripping the hammer, she cracked the door, gazed into the living room, and, of course, everything was different.

Everything was decorated like a 1950s American dream house. Minimalist furniture. Blue-green patterned wallpaper. Mahogany hardwood floors. Everything quaint and suffocatingly nostalgic. If not for the flat-screen TV hanging above the fireplace, Eve might've thought she'd been transported back in time. Her eyes flicked to a hanging clock: 7:39 p.m.

Out of view, in the kitchen, familiar voices: Paige, Thomas, and their children. Eve, keeping quiet, hidden, slid from the basement, crept a couple of steps closer, and listened in:

"Maybe she just went out for a walk?" a nasally voice suggested. Newton?

"It's freezing out there," Paige's chirping voice retorted, sounding more irritated than concerned. "Thomas, why don't you go check downstairs again?"

Thomas replied with a reluctant sigh. "As you wish." The feet of a chair squealed over hardwood, a short scrape. Heavy footsteps started across the kitchen, toward the living room, and, at the last second, Eve stole away into the foyer, soundless. Her feet padded across black and white tile as she surged to the front door, reached for the knob, and—still locked. From the outside. She faced the nearest window and . . . still barred—

Thomas caught her by the arm, spun her around, and muttered, "Where are you going?"

Eve tried to wrench away, but Thomas constricted his grip, viselike. With his free hand, he yanked the hammer from Eve's grasp and held it out of reach. "The hell are you doing with this?" he seethed, his voice barely above a whisper.

Eve, trapped in a state of slow-motion shock, attempted to speak, but only a wheezing breath escaped. She was torn between the impulse to flee, the urge to grab that hammer back, and . . .

It's like quicksand; the more you fight the charade, the worse it gets . . .

With a low sigh, Thomas pulled Eve into the hallway, tightening his already crushing grip, sending a dull ache up her arm. He glanced over his shoulder, making sure they were alone. "I don't know what's going on with you," he said, "but I need you to listen to me." He stared into her eyes, his expression severe. "You have to get yourself together or I'm calling the ward again. Do you understand, Emma?"

Emma?

His breath catching, he added, "The kids—they can't have their aunt running around the house like a lunatic."

Eve met his stare with bewildered eyes. *Emma? Their aunt?* Finally, she managed to speak. "What— What the fuck is this?"

Ignoring the question, Thomas took a new tack, smiled sadly. "You're my sister."

Sister?

"I'd do anything to help you." He paused. "But this, having you stay with us—this is your last chance, okay? I can't put my family's sa—" Thomas stopped himself. *Did he mean to say "safety"?* He continued. "I can't put my family's stability at risk anymore. Do you understand?"

Thomas kept talking, but his words blurred into the background, *wom, wom, wom.* Whatever he was saying, his performance was so convincing, it sent a pang of doubt into Eve's psyche: Was she truly delusional? Was she actually his sister? Was her name actually Emma? No. That wasn't how hallucinations felt, not how insanity worked . . . right? He was toying with her—this was his game, just like what happened to Alison, but . . . No, that would make even less sense, and—

That terrible voice of nothingness murmured into Eve's ear. She could almost feel its cold breath, brushing at the nape of her neck: *Maybe Alison's note was right,* it said. *Maybe Thomas has lived here since before the house was even built, before the trees were planted. Maybe he wandered out of the woods in the light of day. And maybe, just maybe, the only way to stop this is to—*

Shaking off the intrusive thoughts, Eve sharpened her focus: *Bide your time, play along until you find the right moment to escape. Come back with help. Rescue Charlie. Rescue Shylo. Don't provoke Thomas. Not yet.*

Somewhere deep within, she clung desperately to the wild hope that there was still, somehow, a logical explanation for everything—a practical way to escape, but . . .

"Emma?"

Eve met Thomas's gaze. He'd asked a question she hadn't heard.

He repeated himself. "What were you doing with the hammer?" He presented the tool as if it were something Eve had attempted to steal.

She forced out an excuse. "I— I just wanted to hang some paintings . . ."

"In the middle of dinner?"

Eve nodded gently. *Just play along . . .*

Thomas studied her, skeptical. "You've been keeping up to date on your meds, right?"

Eve nodded again.

"Okay." Thomas took a deep breath and released her arm. "All right." Absentmindedly, he set the hammer onto a cherrywood side table and rubbed his jaw with a knuckle. Eve sensed he was almost forcing himself to believe her. Again, he deserved some kind of award for this performance.

"Now," Thomas continued, "we would love for you to rejoin us at the table. The kids are a little spooked, but we can show them everything is okay. Tell them their aunt was just looking for something in the basement and got distracted, all right?"

Eve swallowed. "All right . . ."

Thomas reached out and held her gently by the shoulders. She fought back the urge to recoil and faked another smile instead. Thomas smiled too, that same charismatic smile from when she'd first seen him, standing on her doorstep only one night ago, a complete stranger. Suddenly, Eve noticed an absence of pockmarked scars on his face and neck . . . the ones Alison had supposedly inflicted with a silver-tipped pen. But before Eve had a chance to process what this meant—

"We love you, Emma." Thomas's voice cracked with dreadful sincerity. "You're a part of this family. I know it doesn't feel that way sometimes, but you are." He paused, letting that sink in. "Whatever you're going through," he went on, "you'll come out on the other side. You've gotten through worse. I know it's scary—big changes always are—but we're all pulling for you. Paige included . . ."

The only response Eve could muster was a pitiable "Thanks . . ."

"Now." Thomas smiled again. "Let's get back to dinner."

DOC_A07_RIP

Description: Obituary of Elijah Faust, transcribed from a copy of the *Yale Courier.*

◆

Elijah Faust, 67, passed away at Yale Hospice this Sunday, [date redacted]. He was born on [date redacted] at St. Vincent Hospital in Portland. As a teenager, he played center ice for Cedar High School's Red Owls. In the [date redacted] state hockey championship, he steered the team to second-place victory. After an injury on the rink, Elijah embraced his passion for music. At Reed College, he secured a BA in music theory, and a minor in business. After graduation, he started the metal band Ring of Eyes, in which he played lead guitar and sang backup vocals. That same year, he founded Faust Guitars in Yale. It was there he met and later married his wife, the late Vera Krauss. Together, they purchased a home on Stray Dog Summit and started their family.

Elijah is remembered as a loving father and devoted husband who will be deeply missed by all who had the pleasure of knowing him.

He is survived by his daughter, Alison Faust.

                                        -- .- -. -.--

FAMILY TROUBLES

With Eve in tow, Thomas returned to the kitchen. The rest of his family was planted around Eve's dinner table acting like it was their own. Paige, Jenny, Newton, and Kai, all dressed in Sunday casual. They stared at Eve as if *she* was the one who didn't belong.

Thomas lingered at the kitchen's threshold. "Your auntie was in the foyer," he explained, patting Eve on the back like a car salesman touting an obvious lemon. He pulled up a chair and motioned Eve to sit. She remained standing, anchored to the floor, still processing the absurd sight before her.

"Emma?" Thomas nudged.

Eve clenched her jaw, put on another smile. *Play along.* She wandered over and sat.

Thomas's eyes flitted to his children, then back to Eve. "Did you want to tell the kids what happened?" He sat down next to Paige.

"I . . ." Eve surveyed the family's faces. Just like Thomas, everyone was performing their roles perfectly, right down to the most minute details: Jenny blinking wide, her tiny hands gripped tightly around a plastic juice cup.

Newton avoiding eye contact, shifting uncomfortably in his seat. Kai, more impatient than afraid, tapping his fingernails against a plate, an aggravating *ting-ting-ting* . . . *ting-ting-ting* rhythm. And Paige? Paige was just about glaring into Eve's very soul, as if she wanted to rip it out and cast it straight into the fires of hell. *Stay focused, Eve. Play along.* "I— I was just looking for some tools, to hang some paintings up," Eve lied. Thomas gave a single nod: good enough. The kids nodded too, slightly calmer, but Paige kept glowering. She wasn't buying it.

Right then, Shylo trotted in from the living room, not a care in the world. Eve's heart skipped a beat, but . . .

The dog ignored her, went straight to Thomas's side, sat, and stared up at him, eyes big, tail wagging. "Good girl." He reached down and scratched "Shylo" behind the ears. Her tail wagged faster. He leaned back, the dog still gazing up, eyes locked on his plate of steak now. "Shylo," he chided, "no begging."

Fake Shylo barely turned away, eyes still glued to Thomas's dinner.

"Go to your bed." Thomas pointed into the living room. Reluctant, the dog started to slink away, but . . . upon noticing Eve, she froze, tensed up, and whined.

"Emma's okay, Shylo," Thomas hushed. "You know her . . ."

The dog slinked out of the room, tail between her legs.

Thomas looked to Eve. "She'll warm up to you one of these days."

Unblinking, Eve nodded. "Uh-huh . . ."

A sharp gust of wind slammed against the barred windows and the house lights flickered. Thomas looked outside, shaking his head. "These storms get worse every year." He clicked his tongue, turned back. "Hopefully the power holds out."

Paige wrapped her fingers around the handle of a serrated knife. "Your auntie will be moving out soon, kids." She cut into her steak, red oozing from the veins of the undercooked meat.

Kai and Newton offered uninterested mumbles in response. Jenny just sat there, eyes on Eve, head tilted, as if she could sense something was off but couldn't put a finger on it. Then, Jenny narrowed her gaze and said, "Uhm . . . Auntie Emma?"

Eve wasn't sure how much longer she could keep this charade going. *PLAY ALONG*, that nothing voice demanded.

"Yes, Jenny . . . ?" Eve said.

Jenny scratched her nose. "What happened to your tattoo?"

"I'm sorry?" Eve had never had a tattoo in her life. Never even had a fleeting interest in getting one—she was far too indecisive to do something so . . . permanent.

Jenny pointed. "The—your wrist tattoo," she said. "It's gone."

Eve looked down at her own wrist, bare skin.

"Jenny," Thomas interjected, "your aunt never had a tattoo . . ."

Jenny furrowed her brow. "Oh?"

Thomas chuckled. "Looks like somebody's got a case of the gets." He went back to eating, unconcerned.

But Jenny kept her eyes on Eve's wrist, still skeptical.

Kai, mouth full of food, interjected. "You're going crazy, Jen-bug." He poked her shoulder. "We're gonna have to throw you in a looney bin, just like—"

"Kai," Paige hissed, "enough."

But Paige was too late. Jenny's eyes were already wide with renewed fear. "I— I'm crazy?"

Newton, sounding slightly more confident than Eve remembered, swooped in to save the day. "You're probably just getting mixed up with the time we went to the fair, Jenny."

Jenny blinked at him. "What . . . ?"

Newton pushed up his glasses with a thumb. "When we all got those wash-off tattoos."

"Oh." Jenny nodded. Somehow, that seemed to calm her down, if only a little. She went back to her food. As everyone carried on eating, Eve's eyes locked onto a speck of dirt stuck to her place mat. All sound droned into white noise until—

"Emma?" Paige chimed.

Eve looked up.

Paige blinked at her, expecting an answer to yet another question Eve hadn't heard. "You were going to explain your reasoning," Paige prodded, "for moving out?"

"Oh . . ." Eve cleared her throat and turned to the kids. Silent, they awaited her answer. "I . . ." Eve struggled to come up with a lie. "I just think it's time to . . . for me to be on my own, get out of the house. Feels like the right thing."

"Well," Thomas jumped in, "you'll certainly be missed. But I think we can all agree: change is an opportunity in disguise." He looked around the table, almost like he expected applause. Crickets. He went back to eating.

Paige, her tone apathetic, looked at Eve and recited, "We stand behind you, one hundred percent. You've already come so far."

Eve managed to fake yet another smile. She didn't know how many more she had left. Hell, at this point she was just about ready to flip the table and start breaking shit until they told her where Charlie was, showed her the nearest exit to this upside-down nightmare, and—

"So." Paige took a sip of water, ice cubes clinking in the glass. "How goes the apartment search?"

Eve hesitated, then lied again. "It— It's going okay . . . ?"

"Well, that's good," Thomas remarked, as if the topic required no further discussion. He turned to his daughter and abruptly shifted the subject. "How was school this week?"

Jenny gave a little shrug, poked at her food. "I— I don't know."

"Wow, you don't know? That's a first," Thomas teased.

Jenny smiled, sheepish.

Thomas leaned forward. "You gotta tell me *one* thing that happened," he said. "Just one thing, that's all I ask."

Jenny laughed a bit. "Okay, um . . . There— There was this dog in class on Friday."

"A dog?" said Thomas with exaggerated surprise. "What's a dog doing in a school?"

"It— it was a Seeing Eye dog," Jenny replied, bashful.

Thomas quirked an eyebrow and pretended he wasn't familiar with the concept. "A Seeing Eye dog?"

"It's a dog that . . . it helps blind people walk around." Jenny beamed.

"Wow. A professional dog."

Jenny tilted her head. "What's that?" she asked.

"Professional?"

"Yup."

"It's when you get paid for your work."

"Oh, I . . ." Jenny shook her head. "I don't think the dog gets paid."

"Well." Thomas wiped his mouth with a napkin. "It should."

"Maybe with treats?" said Jenny, sincere.

Thomas chuckled, glancing over at Eve—the way a proud parent did, his eyes filled with: *Isn't she cute?*

For a moment, Eve almost forgot everything else that was going on. As if this bizarre facade was somehow just a typical family dinner, but then Paige cut in, killing the mirage. "Emma. What about your friend in the city?"

Eve jolted back into the present. "What?"

Paige gulped down another mouthful of steak. "Your ex, Charlotte, does she still own that apartment in Portland?"

Of course Charlie's name is Charlotte here.

Thomas cut in. "Paige, I don't think they're—"

"I'm just saying." Paige threw up her hands, striking a martyr's pose. "Maybe Charlotte would help Emma out . . . Considering their past."

Thomas shook his head, holding back. "We can figure something else out."

Paige bristled. "Heaven forbid I actually try to find a timely solution."

Charlotte. My ex in the city. All right.

Thomas sprinkled salt over his steak. "I'm— We're not doing this right now. If Emma can't find a place, we'll figure something out. And don't feel rushed." He looked at Eve. "You can always stay a bit longer if needed."

Paige grumbled and got up from the table. Without saying a word, she strode to a nearby cupboard and grabbed a bottle of Eve's favorite red wine. Perusing it for an extra moment, she snagged the corkscrew. Eyes fixed on Eve, she sat back down, twisting the corkscrew into the bottle as another blast of ruthless wind banged against the house. The lights sputtered, a quick succession of tiny blackouts rippling through the room, until—

Darkness. Power outage. If it weren't for the orange glow of the living room fireplace, it would've been pitch black. Thomas released an exasperated sigh. "Great . . . I'll get the candles." He pushed himself up from the table and stalked out of the kitchen. His footsteps receded into the foyer, marched up the stairs.

All the while, Paige, aglow in the fire's distant light, kept cranking on that corkscrew, glaring at Eve. Then, with a hollow *thwop*, she popped the cork. Still staring at Eve, she poured until her glass was nearly full. Right to the brim. Eve, horrified at the thought of a drunken Paige, opened her mouth to say something, but . . . that was when she finally noticed, around Paige's neck, a brass necklace, adorned with an oval locket.

Charlie's necklace?

Eve reached into her own pocket. Charlie's locket was gone. She checked her other pocket. GONE. Her eyes snapped back to Paige—that was Charlie's necklace. There was no mistaking it. A flash flood of emotions followed: Confusion. Sorrow. Fear. Rage. The rage started in her temples and spread like fire, setting ablaze her arms, legs, every single extremity. "W-where'd you get that?" The words slipped out in a whisper, Eve's voice shaking like a pot about to boil over.

"Hmm?" Paige looked toward her.

"The necklace." Eve gritted her teeth. "Where'd you find it?"

Paige gave a slow, bovine blink. "Oh . . . an antique store." Paige held it up and flicked it open—empty. "Haven't decided what to put in it yet." She clasped it shut and took a sip of wine. "Why do you ask?"

Without thinking, Eve shot to her feet. The table rattled, and the room plunged into silence. Paige frowned, confused. The kids froze, gaping up at Eve, eyes wide.

"Emma?" Paige set down her wine. "Is something wrong?"

Eve said nothing.

"Emma," Paige continued, her words careful, like she was attempting to defuse a volatile bomb. "If I— If I said something that upset you, it wasn't my intention, I . . ." Paige kept blathering on, but Eve wasn't there anymore. She was in the past—memories playing out in her head. Those strange, little moments that stood out more and more as time went on. The way Charlie snorted when she laughed sometimes, then laughed even harder out of embarrassment. The way Charlie's face lit up every time she saw a dog stick its head out a car window. The way she wrapped her arms around Eve from behind and nuzzled her chin into her neck as they fell asleep. All these memories played out like they were happening right now, and then . . .

Before Eve knew what she was doing, she'd marched over and grabbed Paige with one hand, the corkscrew with the other. Arm wrapped around Paige's collarbone, Eve yanked back, the chair falling with a brittle crash.

Time slowed to a standstill. Eve held the corkscrew to the side of Paige's throat. The children screamed. The fireplace crackled. The wind outside howled. But Paige was silent. For the first time since she walked into the house, she didn't have a fucking thing to say. Only quick, terrified little breaths.

"Whoa, hold on . . ." Thomas trod into the kitchen, his face a mask of stupefied shock, hands raised in a placating gesture.

Eve whirled Paige around to face him. "Stay right there." Eve had no clue what her plan was, but—

"We're okay." Thomas slowed to a tenuous stop. "Everything's okay . . ."

Eve, still holding the corkscrew to Paige's neck, hissed, "Where's Charlie?"

"Kids," Thomas said, lowering his voice, "go to your rooms. Lock the doors."

But his children didn't respond—they just sat there, paralyzed. Eyes wide with terror as Eve held their mother hostage.

"NOW," he boomed. In a flurry, they sprang from their chairs, scrambled through the living room. Their footsteps faded as they hurried upstairs, doors slamming shut behind them. Thomas took a small step closer, trying to keep his voice steady. "Emma, can we just—"

"My name is EVE."

"W-what?"

"My FUCKING name is EVE."

"Okay, okay, *Eve* . . ." Thomas's eyes flickered to that corkscrew, still pricked against his wife's neck. Paige whimpered. Thomas looked back up to Eve. "Just—let her go, and we can talk about—"

"What the FUCK happened to Charlie?"

"To Ch-Charlotte?"

"CHARLIE."

Thomas patted the air like a zookeeper calming an escaped lion. "You and Charlotte, you broke up a few years ago—you . . . Can you please let Paige—"

"Shut the FUCK up," Eve hissed, still having no idea what her plan was here. "Just, just tell me what's going on, or—"

"Emma, this isn't—"

"T-Thomas." Paige's voice quivered, petrified. "Please . . ."

He met his wife's terrified gaze. "Emma's not going to do anything," he insisted. "Emma, listen to me—Charlotte, Charlie, she's okay, we can call her right now, she can talk to you, and . . ." He started to pull out his phone, but—

"Put that down," Eve snapped. Visions of padded cells, straitjackets—Thomas was going to call the ward. "Put it down, NOW."

He ignored her demand, started dialing a number, and—

"DROP IT."

He obeyed, releasing the phone like it was scorching hot. It crashed to the hardwood. "Emma," he said, "this isn't you. The medications. I know you've been missing your doses. That's what's happening here—your mind is going through withdrawal, playing tricks with your memories and—"

"THOMAS." Eve yelled so loud it shook silverware on the table. She lowered her voice. "Thomas. I need you to listen to me. Listen carefully. If you don't tell me where Charlie, *my* Charlie, is, something really, REALLY bad is going to happen."

Paige winced as the corkscrew pricked her skin. "T-Thomas," she stammered, her body riddled with cold fear. "Just, say, say something."

Thomas managed, "She, Charlie, moved back to the city, she's with—"

Fake Shylo growled into the room, back ridged, tail straight. She barked bloody murder, the sound cracking through the air like gunshots. Thomas ignored this, and took another cautious step toward Eve, tried something different. "Emma, listen to me," he said. "I need you to ground yourself. Focus on your senses. Focus on—"

Sight: Paige's blond hair. Thomas's terrified face. The flickering glow of the fireplace.

Sound: "Shylo" barking. Panicked breath. Howling wind.

Smell: Red wine. Floral perfume.

Touch: The cold handle of the corkscrew and—

A jolt of biting pain shot through Eve's right thigh. Her body tensed up in a spasm, and she reeled backward, letting go of Paige. She looked down and . . .

Paige had stabbed a steak knife right into her thigh. It was still lodged there, surrounded by a warm blot of spreading red. The sharp pain gave way to a dull, throbbing ache.

The dog stopped barking and fled the room.

Everything fell silent—slowed into timeless nothing. Eve looked up. Paige was standing in a strange way, like a bowling pin about to lose balance. *What happened?* That's when Eve realized: the corkscrew was gone; her hands were empty. Paige, slow, timberous, toppled forward and hit the ground with a thunderous WHAM—choking, gargling.

Eve's eyes darted, searching for an answer, until finally she saw—

The corkscrew . . . lodged into Paige's throat.

Eve shook her head. *I— I didn't . . . I didn't mean to . . .*

A thin line of dark blood trailed down Paige's neck. It snaked onto the hardwood, forming a pool that reflected the fire at a crooked angle. Paige's mouth slowly opened and closed, opened and closed. Like a fish on land. Like she was trying to speak. To breathe.

"I . . ." Thomas let out an unbelieving whisper. "Paige?" Breaking from his trance, he collapsed to the floor over his wife. He held her neck, trying to stop the bleeding. "Paige." His voice cracked. Hands clasped around the wound, he stared into her eyes, but she didn't stare back. Her empty gaze just flicked side to side—left, right, left, right, left. Thomas, desperation growing, pressed harder, but the red seeped out from between his fingers.

Eve, with the knife still lodged in her thigh, stumbled backward. Head spinning, leg throbbing, she limped out of the kitchen and into the hallway. *This isn't real*, she told herself. *Paige isn't real. None of this is.* But it felt real, more real than anything she'd ever experienced. Every memory she ever had, good or bad, it didn't matter—it all drowned in the suffocating present.

Focus.

As Eve shambled down the darkened hall, she thoughtlessly yanked the knife from her leg and tossed it. *That wasn't a good idea*, a small voice told her. Uncaring, running on pure adrenaline, she staggered to the cherrywood side table, snatched up the hammer Thomas had left there. She glanced back and caught one last glimpse of him, still hunched over Paige. One hand pressed to her wound, the other clutching a phone to his ear. "Y-yes," he said, "she's hurt, I, she's bleeding. What? I don't know, 3710 Heritage Lane, yes, I—"

3710?

Wasting no more time, Eve bombed to the front door and tried the handle—still locked from the outside. She wedged the claw end of the hammer into the frame and wrenched back. Wood splintered and strained. She kept prying, kept pulling, but the door didn't budge. It seemed hopeless, it—

Thomas *screamed*. Animalistic, steeped with unimaginable grief. Rage. And Eve knew exactly what it meant:

Paige was dead.

"No . . . no . . . NO . . ." His voice dwindled into a strange guttural moan.. His fist slammed into the floor—an impact so heavy the hardwood audibly cracked. More screaming, thrashing. He was breaking things, tearing apart the kitchen. Wrathful.

Eve pried on the door, harder and harder, but it remained steadfast. "EMMA," Thomas boomed, his voice filled with murder. Fuck the door. She tore the hammer free and scrambled upstairs. Thomas stormed into the foyer just in time to see her disappear at the top of the steps. Eve pushed off a wall and dragged herself down the hallway, the hammer's weight still in her grasp. Behind, footsteps thundered up the stairs, a quick-rising war drum.

Eve tried the first door. Locked. The next one. Locked. Her eyes shot to the end of the hall: Alison's bedroom. Somehow, its light was on. Without hesitation, she hurtled inside, and slammed the door shut behind. With her back pressed against it, she scanned the room, again searching for somewhere to hide, something to—

Alison. She was standing in the far corner—a brightly glowing gas lantern at her feet. She wore a blood-spattered nightgown. Her head was slumped and her left hand clutched a green fountain pen. She was shaking. Sobbing. "I didn't know—I didn't know—I'm sorry—I'm sorry—"

Without warning, the door burst open, and Thomas slammed into Eve like a freight train. He thrust her against a barred window and jammed a broad forearm across her throat, crushing her windpipe. He stared into her eyes, silent, possessed by rage.

As Eve struggled to breathe, she looked to the far corner: empty. Alison was gone. Had she even been there to begin with? Eve's blurring vision flicked back to Thomas—

"We TRUSTED you," he snarled, cold spit spraying her face. With his free hand, he clutched her by the hair, jerked her head forward, and smashed it back into the bars. "We ACCEPTED you into our HOME." He slammed her head again, harder this time. Pounding pain. Again, again, each impact heavier than the last. Vision fading. Heart lurching. This was it. Eve was going to die. This was—

Fight. Back.

With one last burst of strength, she kneed him in the stomach, a sharp jut. He wheezed, stumbled backward, and crumpled to his knees. Winded.

Eve caught her balance, gasped in air, barely conscious—

Thomas looked up, readied himself to attack, and—

Eve swung the hammer—claw end first—into the side of his face. It lodged into his jaw with a deafening CRACK.

Still on his knees, Thomas stared up at her in disbelief, the hammer still stuck in his face, Eve still grasping its handle. He hadn't thought she was capable of this—neither had she. Their eyes locked for a strange, soundless moment, and then . . . she planted her foot onto his chest, and—with both arms, all her strength, wrenched back. The hammer tore open his cheek with a sickening, wet squelch. His perfect teeth ripped out and clattered to the floor in a bloody mess. He crumpled over. Blood leaking down his jaw, over his neck—the torn flap of his cheek hanging open—dangling. Horrific. But . . .

Eve wasn't finished. Slowly, she raised the hammer, tensed up, and . . .

Thomas began to sob. Pitiful, lilting whimpers poured from his mouth and filled the room like a noxious cloud. He was grasping at his face now, as if trying to put himself back together. Red surged through his fingers, branching paths trailing down his forearm. His whimpering grew more panicked, more desperate. He sputtered, hardly legible, drooling ropes of blood onto the floor. "Please, please don't . . . Emma, please . . ."

And all the while, Eve just stood there, hammer raised. Readying herself to finish the job—*This is the only way to escape, right?*—yet she faltered. Despite all her fear, all her determination, she couldn't bring herself to do it . . . Paige was an accident. Eve was no killer. And the man writhing beneath, begging for his life, was no eldritch monster; he was just a man, flesh and bone, terrified and breakable. Eve lowered her arm, the blood-soaked hammer slipping to the floor with a dull clink.

Get out of here.

She staggered back to the hallway, stepped out and started to pull the door shut, as if that flimsy barrier might keep the horrors within at bay. But at the last second—

Thomas's eyes snapped up. "Where are you going, *Eve?*" His mouth twisted into a mangled grin.

Eve yanked the door shut and held it. *Why the FUCK did he call me that?*

Dreadful silence. Only the muted hiss of the gas lantern.

Focus. Get out of here. Eve's mind raced. She backed away from the door and—

The attic. The square window. Maybe, just maybe. Get to the roof, find a way down. She turned on her heel, ankled down the hallway, pulled down the attic stairs, and climbed. Pain clawed at her wounded thigh with every limping step. All the while, the door to Alison's bedroom remained shut. Not even a footstep on the other side. *Did Thomas pass out?*

Eve hoisted herself up and hauled toward that narrow passage. The attic, she faintly realized, was mostly empty now, sparse clutter receded to the flanks. *Keep moving. Ignore the pain.* Lightheaded, she stumbled into the corner room, and thank the Lord above, the window wasn't barred. She unlatched it, shimmied herself up and through. A tight fit. Cold winter air. Snow-covered shingles. Twisting her way out, she—

A hand clutched her by the ankle and heaved her back inside. Her body dragged across the splinter-ridden floor, chin-first. She spun around just in time to see the moonlight glisten off Thomas's torn-open face. He lunged onto her, wrapped his powerful hands around her throat, constricted.

"Evelyn PATRICIA Palmer," he boomed like a mad apostle, blood slobbering onto her face. "We gave you LIFE." Eve reached up, grabbed his wrists, tried to pull them away, but it was no use, his grip was too strong. He squeezed tighter. A lump formed in her throat, swelling, threatening to burst.

"We were here when the light of DAY was BORN."

She couldn't breathe. Again, she was fading. Shadows crawling from the corners of her eyes. Everything becoming nothing.

Thomas lowered his voice to a spitting whisper. "We sowed the forest."

Right then, a shiny glint caught the corner of her eye. She looked over: universal tire chains. She reached, stretched, wrapped the tips of her fingers around the cold metal, and—

"We BUILT the FOUNDATIONS of the—"

She swung. The chains CRACKED into his temple, his head twisting to the side. A red curtain of blood whipped onto the floor, the wall.

Slowly, he turned back to her, and now—his gaze was empty. Vacant. Blood trailed from his cracked temple, into his twitching eye, and dripped onto Eve's cheek.

His grip loosened. "We were—we built—when the . . ." He trailed into more disjointed mumbles.

Chains still in hand, Eve shoved him off and pushed up to standing. Thomas tried to do the same, but his limbs betrayed him. He fell back to his knees and looked up at her, half-conscious. He kept trying to talk, only to mutter incoherent nonsense: "We, the house, I didn't, the labyrinth." He kept trying to stand, only to fall back down.

Eve circled to get behind him. Between heaving breaths, she demanded, "Where . . . is . . . Charlie . . ."

But Thomas only responded with more meaningless mumbles: "I, we, I didn't mean, my name isn't—"

Enough. Eve breathed in and, on the exhale, wrapped the chains around his neck. She pulled back. He reached up, pawing, trying to tear the chains away. Futile. She pulled tighter, pressed her knee into his back. He gasped. Choking. Wheezing. She yanked back even harder. He coughed a spatter of blood. His efforts to fight fading with each passing second until, finally—

"LET HIM GO."

Eve looked up.

A young cop stood in the doorway, her hands shaking as she aimed her gun. Behind her, another cop stepped into view, tall and barrel-chested, the same one who'd pulled Eve over before. "NOW," he commanded, unclicking the safety on his firearm.

The tire chains slipped from Eve's grip, rattled to the floor. Thomas fell forward, wheezing, and before Eve could put her hands up, she was tackled to the ground. Forced onto her stomach, splinters gashing her skin like paper cuts. Cold handcuffs clasped around her wrists. The cops hoisted her upright. She didn't even speak; she just stared ahead blankly as they led her through the attic—blood loss and exhaustion blurring her awareness.

As they dragged her down the upstairs hallway, two paramedics rushed past. The cops shoved Eve around a corner. Her fading vision landed on a cracked-open bedroom door—from behind it, Jenny peered out, her green eyes awash with profound dread.

The cops, oblivious to the girl, steered Eve down the staircase, into the foyer. Above, a deer antler chandelier was now hanging, framed by a grand stained glass window. They ushered her out the front door, onto the porch.

The storm had settled again. The snow was already melting. A gray sun crept up over distant mountains—the sky split down the middle, half night, half day. On the ground, commotion everywhere. Cop cars. An ambulance. Red and blue light dancing over the frosted lawn, the surrounding trees. A handful of neighbors were gathered in the driveway, Heather and her supposedly deceased husband, Michael, among them. Cops shouted at them, told them to back up, put away their phones. Eve's gaze swept the onlookers, searching for her Charlie, her Shylo, but they were nowhere to be seen.

As the cops continued guiding Eve across the yard, she saw, standing off at the edge of the forest—Alison. Still draped in her off-white hospital gown, but aside from that, she was transformed. Her once-skeletal face now radiated life, vitality, and . . . remorse?

Alison withdrew into the woods—away from the flashing lights, the chaos, the house. Finally, the gravity of it all came crashing down. Words tumbled out of Eve's mouth in a stammering panic. "There's a woman, she's, there, she's right there." Eve pointed. "Thomas, he isn't, I, I didn't, I didn't mean to, I—"

Apathetic, the officers thrust her into the back of a police van and unceremoniously slammed the door shut.

Darkness.

DOC_E16_BLOODBATH

Description: Excerpt from preproduction notes of an unaired episode of the long-defunct documentary series *America's Bloodiest
Crimes*.

◆

Director's Note to Producer: This is just a rough sketch of
how best to incorporate that authentic Emma Faust interrogation footage into the episode. Still waiting on clearance there
(Marvin told me it was all good to go, sorry about that). Anyways, I've done my best to describe it in the meantime. We'll
open with a family photo, really play up the whole "this could
happen to anybody" angle. The narrator will say something like:

NARRATOR

It all started with an act of kindness. A caring brother, wel-
coming his prodigal sister into his home, under his roof. If
only he had known the horrors it would bring upon his family.

Note: Then we throw up some crime scene stock footage. Yellow tape, blinking sirens, gathering crowds. A close-up of the bloody hammer, the corkscrew, teeth on the floor. Then CUT TO:

Episode title:

The Faust Family Bloodbath

"Insanity, Vengeance, or Paranormal?"

Hold on that for a beat, fade it out to black, and—

Authentic interrogation room footage cuts in: (Again, I can only describe it in text until Marvin sorts out clearance, sorry.)

Shot from two separate mounted CCTV cameras, it opens with a stationary image of a white-walled interrogation room. Emma Faust sits alone. Sleep-deprived, dead-eyed.

                              NARRATOR

                        (Over paused footage)

This is interrogation room five of the Portland Bureau Police North Precinct. Emma Faust is either putting on a show, or she truly believes she is someone else entirely. She sits
                        waiting, handcuffed.

She has just been transferred from the psychiatric intensive care unit (PICU) at Providence Portland Medical Center. There, she received treatment for a stab wound to her right thigh, inflicted in self-defense by the late Paige
                          Victoria Faust.

It is four weeks after the infamous Faust Family Bloodbath. Emma Faust is in custody awaiting a trial, and she's still insisting her real name is Evelyn Patricia Palmer, a person
                who, by all accounts and records, does not exist.

Director's Note: Narration dialogue is just rough right now. Gonna get Lucy to punch it all up.

Footage: The image fast-forwards ten minutes and thirty-seven seconds. Emma barely moves the entire time; she sits slumped in the chair, staring blankly at the wall ahead, until—

Behind her the door clicks open, we snap back to real time, and in steps Officer Kelly Kieran, the bureau's lead detective. Clean-shaven head, athletic build. He sits down across from Emma.

                          NARRATOR
                    (Over paused footage)
   Kieran, with over two decades' experience and hundreds of
   successful interrogations, is a force to be reckoned with—
   both in the box and out. In Emma Faust's case, police already
   have all the evidence they need for an airtight conviction.
   But Emma, against her own lawyer's wishes, has agreed to this
        one-on-one interview a month after the incident.
   And Kieran, relentless pursuer of justice that he is, will never
   turn down an opportunity to gather more evidence. Besides, at this
   juncture it seemed all but inevitable that Emma's lawyers would be
        gunning for an insanity plea. But the jury was still out.

Footage: Kieran, shuffles papers around, glances up toward Emma.

                          KIERAN
   You understand that you have the right to remain silent, any-
        thing you say today can be used against you in a court of—

                          EMMA
              Yes, I already signed a waiver.

Footage: Kieran glances down at his papers again, nods to himself.
He looks back up.

                              KIERAN

    Can I get one of my guys to grab you anything? Water? Pepsi?

Footage: Emma doesn't respond. She's staring down at the table.
Dissociating?

                              KIERAN

        You more of a Coca-Cola person . . . ? Emma?

                               EMMA

                           (looks up)

                    Eve. My name is Eve.

Footage: Kieran shifts back in his chair, weighing his next words.

                             NARRATOR

                    (Over paused footage)

    Here, Kieran makes a calculated decision: play along with Em-
    ma's delusion. Up until now, according to his records, Kieran
    still believed Emma was fabricating a convoluted lie in an
    attempt to plead insanity—a classic play for inexperienced
    criminals. Little do they know, criminal psych wards are often
               far more hellish than actual prisons.

                              KIERAN

              What brings you in today, *Eve*?

                              EMMA

    There's evidence, back at the house. It proves my side of the

                              story.

Footage: Kieran, disappointed, leans back in his chair. He's heard

this one before.

                             KIERAN

        Yes, your lawyer already communicated that to us.

                              EMMA

                              And?

                             KIERAN

                        (losing patience)

    We sent a very expensive forensics team back a few days ago.

            They scoured the basement, found nothing.

Footage: Emma scoffs and leans forward. She's wedging her shoulder

into the wall for balance, due to her hands being cuffed behind her

back.

                              EMMA

    But . . . they sent somebody through the passageway in the

                        basement, right?

                             KIERAN

    The . . . (looks at his notes) hospital maze at the south

    side of the basement? Nope. They found a small nook. An old

coatrack and a couple empty picture frames. No paintings. No
photos. No, uh, toy monkey . . . ?

KIERAN

No, that's, they looked in the wrong spot, there's a green
door and—

KIERAN

There's no green door, Emma.

EMMA

Eve.

KIERAN

It's just a concrete nook.

EMMA

Maybe there's a passage, hidden in the wall. There has to be
something, I . . .

NARRATOR

(Over paused footage)

Kieran's disappointment only grows. He was expecting a
breakthrough, a confession, perhaps. Something remotely
useful.

KIERAN

Okay, we— we've already done this. Do you have anything real
for me? Or you just wanna share more ghost stories?

                                EMMA

The man in the cabin, he has a scar, just like . . . There's

          a map there, blueprints of the house, Yale—

                               KIERAN

We found the cabin. It's burned to a crisp, happened years

ago. Look, I have four other cases on my plate right now, so

                               if you—

                                EMMA

   Please, you have to believe me, I'm not crazy, I'm . . .

                      (She begins to sob)

                              NARRATOR

                     (Over paused footage)

Initially, the prosecution had been struggling to come up with

a motive to explain Emma's horrific actions that night. This

missing piece of the puzzle would play right into the hands

                 of her insanity defense.

However, a simple revelation quickly emerged: before that in-

famous dinner, Emma was facing an imminent eviction. She had

been living with her brother's family for nearly three years.

(An arrangement that began after a tumultuous split from her

longtime partner, Charlotte Bastion.) Crucially, the night

Emma attacked Paige was the very same night Thomas Faust had

informed her she had less than a month to vacate the premises.

The prosecution would go on to argue that this was the straw

that broke the camel's back. This is what motivated Emma's

"heinous retaliation." Mr. and Mrs. Faust threatened to re-

move the roof over her head, so she lashed out. And when the
weight of her actions bore down on her, Emma crafted a sprawling and bizarre tale about alternate realities, endless laby-
rinths, ancient evils, and doppelgängers. As far as insanity
goes, this was the play. But how the chips would fall in court
was still very much up in the air.

(NOTE: Devin suggested that maybe we can add a joke here about how
the most unbelievable part of Emma's story is the fact that she
claimed two millennials could afford property? Dev thinks that type
of stuff does well with the younger generations. I'm not so sure. I
don't think it feels right, tonally speaking.)

Now, Officer Kieran opts to up the pressure, if only a small amount.
He waits for Emma to collect herself, then strikes with:

                            KIERAN

Look, I understand where you're coming from. Thomas was gonna
kick you to the curb. He took you in and then just tossed you
                         away like—

                            EMMA

He never took me in. I— I already told you, me, my partner,
          we bought that house, barely two months ago, she—

                            KIERAN
                     (glancing at papers)

Charlotte Bastion, right? We finally got ahold of her yesterday.
She says the two of you haven't spoken in at least a few years—

                          EMMA
                   (increasingly manic)
    No, that's not her. That's not *my* Charlie, I-I . . .

                         KIERAN
                        Charlie?

                          EMMA
My Charlie has a tattoo. A black triangle on her index finger
knuckle. M-my parents, Richard and Lannette Palmer, they live
            in New York. Have you gotten ahold of them?

                        NARRATOR
                 (Over paused footage)
At this point in the interrogation, even the jaded Officer
Kieran seems thrown off by her sincerity. You can see the
self-doubt on his face, perhaps even sympathy for Emma. Despite this, he went on to recommend the prosecution press
                charges in the highest degree.

                         KIERAN
                 (glancing back at notes)
Richard and Lannette Palmer, Rochester. I had one of my de-
                 tectives reach out to them.
        (flips through papers, stops, reads, looks up)
  They don't have any children; they don't know who you are.

                              EMMA
                        (shaking her head)
        No, no, you got the wrong ones. Th-there's other people with
                        those names . . . there's—

                             KIERAN
                       (sifting through notes)
          Richard and Lanette Palmer, 382 Pinehurst Ave?

Footage: Kieran holds up a photo of an older couple. It's clear from
Emma's reaction that she recognizes them. Or, at the very least,
she's doing a very convincing job at pretending to.

                             KIERAN
                      (setting the photo down)
                        They don't know you.

                            NARRATOR
                      (Over paused footage)
        The childless Mr. and Mrs. Palmer would go on to suffer in-
        ordinate amounts of harassment from a fringe, but devoted,
        group known as [redacted], a community of online conspir-
        acy theorists who are convinced that Emma Faust's delusions
        were caused by real events. This loosely organized community
        gained some mainstream traction after the televised trial
                but have mostly fallen back into obscurity.

Footage: Emma is at a loss for words.

> KIERAN

Emma, can you tell me why Thomas and Paige wanted you out of
the house?

Footage: Emma's eyes flick back and forth, and then she locks her
gaze onto Kieran. For the remainder of the tape's near two-minute
runtime, she does not blink.

> EMMA

I don't know . . .

> NARRATOR
>
> (Over paused footage)

We are about to witness the normally levelheaded Officer Kieran
have an uncharacteristic outburst in which he divulges information the suspect should *not* be privy to. A mistake he was
reprimanded for after the interrogation.

> KIERAN
>
> (has had enough)

We have a dead mother. We have three children so traumatized
they can barely string a sentence together without breaking
into sobs. Do you want to tell me why you did this? Or do you
want to waste more of the state's time and resources? We have
a father of three in a coma: shattered trachea, face torn
open. His life is hanging by a *thread*. This, right now, right
here, is your *only* chance at redemption, do you understand?

Either you tell me the truth right *now*, or you live with this
for the rest of your life.

NARRATOR

(Over paused footage)

An observant viewer would have noticed that Eve stopped listening to everything Kieran said after "We have a father of
three in a coma." Her panic, previously boiling under the
surface, explodes to the forefront.

EMMA

T-Thomas is still alive?

KIERAN

Lord willing, but—

Footage: Before Kieran can finish his sentence, Eve tries to stand,
a flurry of illegible panic. Stumbling, she finally shoots up from
her chair, starts for the exit.

EMMA

No, no, I-I have to get, I have to, I have to get out of
here . . .

NARRATOR

(Over paused footage)

It's at this moment when the footage infuriatingly ends. A malfunction with the CCTV system. Sources close to the matter tell
us that two other officers burst into the room and subdued her.

Producer Feedback: It's a so-so start. Right off the bat, let's cut out most of the narration stuff. It feels way too clunky/over the top/tonally off etc. (Please tell me we haven't paid a voice actor yet.) Also, if Marvin can't clear the footage by tomorrow, tell him it's okay, we'll hire someone else to do his job. Looking forward to chatting.

-.. .. ..-. ..-. . .-. . -. -

OLD WOUNDS

Everyone keeps calling me Emma Faust.

But my name is Eve Palmer. My current residence is 3709 Heritage Lane. My partner, the love of my life, is Charlie Bastion. We've been together for the better part of the last decade. I don't care what my supposed birth certificate says, what my ID reads—my name is Eve Palmer, but everyone keeps calling me Emma Faust.

And somehow, according to more "official documents," Thomas owns the house. "Our" parents left it to him, and he's presumably lived there with his family for over a decade. All the neighbors vouch for him, Heather included. Of the few people I've been able to contact from my old life, none of them know who I am. Not even my own "parents." And Charlie? I'll get to that.

As far as I can tell, I look the way I always have, but everyone treats me like I'm a completely different person. It's like I've been forced into a different reality altogether. Or maybe everything around me changed. I'm still figuring it all out.

But whatever happened, now, beyond all logic, all justice, I'm locked away in Greenwood Asylum, a criminal psych ward in downstate Washington.

Cooped up in a room no bigger than a walk-in closet. Beige walls. Cold light. Rickety bed. My only solace is a barred window overlooking a pond of turtles. I've memorized their routines, their hierarchies, who gets the best spot on the toppled log (that would be Greg). I've been here almost three years now. Feels like ten.

And thanks to the televised trial and the never-ending parade of tabloids, that horrific night was transformed into a nationwide spectacle. The vultures with cameras and microphones tastefully coined it the Faust Family Bloodbath. I suppose there's a ring to it. But still, many of those headlines are forever burned into my brainstem:

> "AFTER GOOD SAMARITAN BROTHER THREATENS EVICTION, MANIAC SISTER BRU-
> TALIZES FAMILY"

> "RUMOR ALERT: AVOIDING RESPONSIBILITY? EMMA FAUST CLAIMS SHE WAS
> 'HAUNTED BY AN EVIL SPIRIT THAT BENT REALITY' AND . . . REARRANGED FUR-
> NITURE?! FIND OUT MORE IN OUR EXCLUSIVE INTERVIEW WITH A NEIGHBORING
> COUPLE AT 8 P.M. PST"

> "FROM YOUNG FAITHFUL PROTESTANT—TO VENGEFUL PSYCHO-KILLER. THE EMMA
> FAUST STORY. A FIVE-PART MINISERIES"

I will spare you the rest.

After that night, as I'm sure you've heard, I was charged with one count homicide and one count attempted, but the jury found me "not guilty by reason of insanity." Somehow that felt worse than a conviction.

Though, after the trial, a small but loyal group of supporters formed. Some of them even wrote me letters and sent gifts. (I'm pretty sure more than a few of them are suffering from actual delusions, but still, it's nice to have support, no matter where from. No matter how fleeting.)

And circling back to Greenwood Asylum, let's just say, it's not what I'd expected. Before all this, I'd half imagined these places to be sprawling Gothic compounds: gargoyles, pointed roofs, swirling bats—all of it stowed away at the top of a perpetually stormy mountain, but . . .

Greenwood is across the street from a dairy farm and a Dollar General. And aside from the "secure-cell wings," it looks more like a low-cost nursing home than a baroque prison. Sky-blue walls, nonslip flooring. There's even a small library and a room with puzzles and board games for "lower-risk" residents.

But don't let all that fool you: this place is hell. Overcrowded, underfunded hell. No pits of fire, but those secure-cell wings are a close substitution. I spent my first three months in one of those underground nightmares—screaming and . . . I can't even talk about it without snapping back into full-blown terror, so let's not.

Of course, everything here, no matter the wing, is carefully controlled. Obsessively curated. Cameras in every corner, guards in every hall. Door handles are slanted downward to prevent hangings, and all the cutlery is made of flimsy plastic to prevent . . . well, you can imagine.

Now, my daily routine consists of pills at 8:00 a.m., a supervised "nature" walk at 9:00 (ten minutes of standing in a gravel courtyard next to a dying tree), pills at noon, group "therapy" at 2:00, pills at 6:00. And, once a month, a fifteen-minute debrief with the lead doctor, Preston Karver.

A name that about matches the way he looks: a tall, graying wisp of a man with a severe way about him.

I learned pretty fast (once I'd broken out of my three-month mania) that if I ever wanted to see the light of day, I needed to be strategic about how I talked with Dr. Karver, how I acted in general. When I first came in, I was frantic, desperately trying to prove my side of the story. Rambling about my past life, Charlie, Shylo, the evidence back at the house, photographs and the like. Things that would prove I was Eve Palmer—prove my version of events.

Soon enough, it became clear none of this evidence existed anymore. And

even if it did, I'd need a lot more than a box of photographs to convince anyone with actual authority. So I learned to play along, to pretend my so-called
delusions were just that: fantasies. Nothing more than a complex narrative
I'd spun to "cope with my heinous crimes." I pretended I was getting better,
bit by bit. Saying anything I could to shorten my time locked up here. To
avoid those secure-cell wings.

But all the while, I knew what the truth was. You don't need a PhD to
know that actual psychotic delusions and hallucinations don't resemble what
I experienced—so sudden and impossibly intricate. These weren't hallucinations. These weren't delusions. Somehow Thomas, or something in that
house, twisted reality around me like a frayed wire. And maybe his "sister"
Alison was in on it too. As for the rest of his family—Paige, Newton, Jenny,
Kai—I'm not sure if they were mindless puppets, hostages, or something in
between. Who knows?

In the weeks following the . . . incident, I thought *everyone* was playing
some terrible trick on me. Even the doctors. But I soon dropped that conviction. For the most part, they were all just as confused as I was. Like I said,
neighbors, friends, my own "parents," almost no one recognizes me anymore.
And the few who do insist my name is Emma Faust.

Charlie included.

About half a year into my incarceration, after dozens of tries, I finally got
ahold of her, or rather, this "Charlotte" version of her. It was a Monday, or
maybe a Tuesday. I was sitting alone in the ward's windowless phone room.
Nothing but the sound of the creaky ventilation, the buzz of lights, the murmurs of the staff outside.

As I held the phone to my ear, the dial tone rang out three times, and then—
"Hello?"

Even knowing it wasn't *my* Charlie, simply hearing her voice filled me with
hope. Like I'd been lost in a desert, dying of thirst, and come across a stale puddle. "Charlie," I said. "It's Eve, er, Emma. I, I've been trying to get ahold of you."

"I know." Charlie (Charlotte) paused, the silence heavy. "I'm sorry, I just, it's been a lot with the news, reporters, and I've been— I . . ."

"Charlie, er, Charlotte." Several thoughts came out at once: "I'm, I— I didn't, what they're saying about me it's not, it's . . ."

I refocused, calmed myself. *Breathe in. Breathe out.* "I've been gathering evidence, and soon I'll be able to prove my side of the story. I— I've found articles online, documents—bread crumbs. There's even a doctor in Norway, he had this patient with a similar thing, and, and, I'm not the only person this has happened to, I—"

"Emma," she cut in, sounding on the verge of tears. "I love you, despite how things ended between us, despite all this, I always will, but I can't. I just—I can't. I only answered because . . . I hope you get the help you need and—" Her voice cracked. "I can't do this, I have, sorry, I have to go—"

"Wait, Charlie, please, please, don't hang up. I . . ."

No response. Charlotte's breathing. And then, a soft voice in the background, an unfamiliar woman. "Is . . . everything okay?"

"Yeah," Charlotte replied, her voice turning from the phone. "I'll just be a second. Go back to bed." More silence. Had the call dropped?

"Charlotte . . . ?"

". . . Yeah?"

Almost to myself, I said, "What— Why did we end things?"

". . . You really don't remember?"

I shook my head, "I don't . . ."

"It's . . ." Charlotte sighed. "I don't think it's a—"

"Just . . . tell me."

Another painfully long silence. The buzz of lights. A ticking clock. Charlotte relented. "I— I woke up one night; your side of the bed was empty. You were in the living room, packing up your things. You barely said a word, you just . . . you just left."

Dead air.

Voice hushed, I said, "Why . . . ?"

"Why?" Charlotte absentmindedly clicked her teeth, just like *Charlie* used to do when she was stressed out. "I . . ." Charlotte sighed again. "I've been wondering that for the last few years, Emma." A short pause. "Look, I need to get—"

"The locket," I suddenly remembered. "Paige, she was wearing your locket. She was—"

"Locket?"

"The brass one, the one with the photo of me, the—"

"Paige was . . . ? Emma, I don't have— You need to let this go. All of this. You need to listen to the doctors, focus on getting better. Okay? I'm sorry, but there's nothing more to—"

"No, wait, I—"

CLICK.

And with that, Charlotte ended the call. I didn't burst into tears. I didn't even slam the phone into the receiver. Instead, I gently set it down, took a deep breath, and exhaled. My resolve to get out of here only grew stronger.

◆

If Greenwood Asylum didn't have a library, there's a good chance I would've actually lost my mind. And for patients who showcase "exceptionally good behavior," there are computers with internet. Slow internet, ten minutes a day, but still. That's where I was doing my research, outlining the real version of events, putting together my case. Like I said to "Charlotte," I was gathering evidence, documents. Nothing big enough to convince skeptics, but . . .

Eventually I just stopped. I stopped because the more bread crumbs of "proof" I found, the worse I felt. Like something was toying with me, giving me rays of hope, only to send me plummeting into more panic spirals. Hell, after coming across a stupid forum post about the Mandela effect, I fell into a state of terror so profound, I nearly got thrown back into the secure-cell wing. There's no telling what will set me off these days. *Maybe Charlotte was right*, I had thought. *Maybe I should just listen to the doctors, focus on getting better.*

So I went back to simply playing along, pretending like I was just another patient. Taking my pills. Going on my "nature" walks. Staying away from those library computers. Waiting until I could finally get out on probation. So long as I could avoid the secure-cell wing—stay stable, say the right things to the doctors—if nothing set me off, then maybe I could, at the very least, escape Greenwood.

Despite everything, I was hopeful. At least, I was until a few days ago . . .

I was lying on my bed when my eyes caught something—up on the white stucco ceiling: a solitary ant wandering in aimless circles—

"Emma?" A voice snapped me out of my daze. I turned. Standing in the doorway was a nurse with two security guards behind her. "Someone's here to see you."

Cold fluorescent light flickered over the family visitation area. White brick walls. Checkered tile floors. Spaced-apart tables. In the far corner, a play mat covered in long-neglected toys. Duplo, Lincoln Logs, stuffed animals. Guards stood at attention in every doorway.

The main door buzzed open and in walked:

Thomas Faust.

My so-called brother. A cold chill ran down my back, and my heart spasmed with a nauseating lurch. He caught my eyes from across the room and gave a bleak smile. The side of his face was gashed with a familiar scar, but considering the injury, it was surprisingly well-healed. And all his teeth were back. *Dental implants?*

I looked down at my handcuffed wrists, avoiding eye contact. Thomas padded over, pulled up a chair, and sat across from me. A long silence passed. Those buzzing lights. Distant weeping, muffled and sorrowful, slowly turning into maniacal screams, then falling silent.

"Emma?" Thomas nudged, finally breaking the silence.

I didn't look up. My eyes traced back and forth along the handcuffs' chain—it was attached to a metal hook in the table's center.

He cleared his throat. "They didn't tell you I was coming?"

I remained silent.

"It . . ." Thomas spoke softly. "It's okay if you're still not ready to talk. I understand. I just, I needed to share a few things." Again, he waited for me to acknowledge him. But I kept my eyes down, kept quiet. After another long stretch of nothing, he continued. "This, I'm not good with this sort of . . ." He tapped a finger against the table. "This was kind of a while back, but . . . you remember Buckley, right?"

Nope.

Regardless, Thomas went on. "Buckley," he said, "the chocolate Lab we got from the neighbors . . . I told Mom and Dad I'd take care of him." He breathed out his nose. "For two years, he was so good and then he just, out of nowhere, attacked me, bit my arm. We tried to put him up for adoption, but . . . well, you know." He paused. "Everyone kept trying to make me feel better. Except Dad: he said I needed to get over it by the end of the week." Thomas chuckled bitterly. "Mom told me pets come and go all the time, it's part of life. Buckley's up in heaven now." Thomas sighed, shifting his weight. "You— You were so young back then, I don't know if you remember this, but . . . you're the only one who actually made me feel any better."

Leery, I looked up.

Thomas was gazing down at the table now. "You just sat beside me," he continued, "wrapped an arm around my shoulder, and let me cry. That's it. No lessons. No advice. No ultimatums. You just sat there quietly, and that reminded me it's okay to feel like shit sometimes." He sniffed a little, eyes starting to water. "Gosh, Emma. I don't know. I've been thinking a lot about what happened lately and . . ."

He looked right at me. I looked away, focusing on a pockmark in the wall.

"It's okay if you don't wanna talk," he repeated. "I get it. I just wanted to let you know that . . ." He fell silent, thinking over his next words carefully. "I've been working on myself a lot, and through all this . . . recovering after my injuries, Paige's passing, raising the kids. I've rejoined the church. Don't know if you even knew I'd lost my faith, but . . ." He paused, again expecting me to say something. And still, I remained silent. He cleared his throat. "I've been talking with the doctors here, and they said you've made a lot of progress . . . They said as long as you keep at it, keep improving, following their guidance—as long as nothing unexpected sets you off—you could be out on probation sooner than you think."

In the corner of my eye, he kept staring at me, a blurred visage. Again the sincerity in his voice sent a cold wash of doubt into my psyche. Was I truly insane after all? Maybe I was supposed to be here. No, that—

"Look," he said. "I've come to accept you weren't in control of your actions. You have a condition. A condition you're being treated for and—I just wanted to let you know that . . . Emma?" He leaned in slightly. "Emma, could you look at me?"

Slowly, I turned and stared blankly into his eyes.

He stared back and then, with a sad smile, said, "I forgive you."

The words lingered between us like a rotting stench, but my expression remained neutral. A few tense seconds went by until he nodded slowly and put up his hands in a little surrender. "I understand. We can talk when you're ready." He stood up, turned to leave, and froze. "Oh . . . I almost forgot." Stepping back, he reached into his coat pocket and pulled out a manila envelope. "The guards said I could leave this here." He placed it on the table. "I know it meant a lot to you and Charlie."

Charlie?

For the last time, I looked at him. His somber face twitched, a barely perceptible movement below his right eye. Then he knocked the table twice, turned around, and went for the exit. Footsteps punctuated the silence. The door buzzed shut as he left.

I just sat there, staring at the envelope. I already knew what was inside— but I couldn't bring myself to look. Once again, seconds dragged by like minutes until finally I reached forward, opened it, looked inside . . . Just as I expected, it was the locket. Charlie's locket.

I pulled it out, flicked it open, and . . .

There it was. The blurry photo of me. The one Charlie took when we first started dating. The one she put up in her gallery on that rain-soaked day in Rochester all those years ago. The one in which, at the last second, I'd turned away, held up a hand, and hid my face.

The only known photo of Eve Palmer.

◆ ◆ ◆

DOC_E25_HELP

DESCRIPTION: Transcript of post on high-strangeness-forums.net.

◆

Post Title: My partner went missing, but everyone is telling me she never existed to begin with.

Body: I never thought I'd be posting on a site like this, but right now I don't know where else to turn. I've exhausted all other avenues: family, police, the fucking FBI—everything.

On [date redacted] I returned home to [address redacted] and found our recently purchased property looking as though it had been abandoned for decades. Boarded up. Completely falling apart. My partner, [name redacted], was gone. Only our dog remained, wandering around the nearby woods. All other evidence of my life with [name redacted], including photos, text messages, emails, all of it—vanished overnight. The authorities, my friends and family, everyone in my life, insists that [name redacted] isn't a real person. I've nearly been institutionalized multiple times, but I'm not giving up. If anyone has any idea, any information, no matter how out-landish, please. Help.

For more details, contact me here: [email redacted].

-. .- -- . ...

ACKNOWLEDGMENTS

This book would not exist without the support of countless people over my lifetime. Acknowledging every single one of them would take a second novel. Instead, I will try my best to name all who directly contributed to this story and/or my Reddit series that preceded it.

Firstly, I would like to thank my incredible superstar editor, Emily Bestler. Her guidance and patience as we worked through this manuscript together have made my introduction to the publishing world a dream come true. I am beyond thrilled to be collaborating with her on future books.

The same goes for everyone at Atria Books, Emily Bestler Books, and Simon & Schuster. Hydia Riley and Lara Jones, your thorough support and care assured me this novel was in great hands. And thank you both for patiently answering all my clueless questions and concerns about the publishing world. Can't wait to continue working together on the next one.

To everyone else on the publishing, marketing, editing, and production teams: it was an honor to work with you on this story. Publisher Libby McGuire and associate publisher Dana Trocker have done so much indispensable work behind the scenes in the creation and promotion of this novel. Publicists Debbie Norflus and Alyssa Boyden championed this book from early on and were instrumental in getting it into as many hands as possible. And, of course, the outstanding marketing team who went above and beyond, taking the strange, cryptic nature of the book and integrating it directly into its promotion: Maudee Genao, Morgan Pager, Karlyn Hixson, and so many more.

And huge thank-yous are owed to the senior managing editor, Paige Lytle; managing editorial coordinator, Shelby Pumphrey; production editor, Liz Byer; and copyeditor, Andrea Monagle. Thank you for taking on this befuddling labyrinth of a story, catching so many (unintentional) inconsistencies that had slipped right past my radar. And thank you for allowing me to put in a few intentional document errors too, as well as so many last-minute, "just one more thing" changes.

The fantastic cover was designed by Claire Sullivan (check out @csullivandesign on Instagram for more awesome work) with art direction from Jimmy Iacobelli (@bookcoversbyoj on Instagram). Thank you to the masterful photographer Brian Van Wyk (@brianvanwyk on Instagram) for taking my portrait (one of the few photographs of me in existence). And my architect sister, Jessika MacDonald, who painstakingly handcrafted the re-creation of "Old House Map" that opens the entire novel. She made hand-drawn house layouts, found copies of historic maps, and used a real antique typewriter to write the notes. For the use of public domain maps, I would like to thank the "Historical Maps of Manitoba" collection, the National Trust of Queensland, and the British Library. I would also like to thank the no-longer-operational Museum of High Strangeness Artifacts in Langford, Utah, for allowing us to reference their records in the recreation of "Old House Map."

The life-changing Netflix movie deal, and subsequent book deal, were negotiated by my agency, Verve; my manager, Scott Glassgold; and my lawyer, Ashley Silver. I am so proud to be a client of all three. On the movie side, David Boxerbaum and Adam Levine at Verve are both absolute powerhouses, who advocated for the Reddit series and crushed out a deal I still can't quite believe is real. The same goes for Scott Glassgold, who upheld this work from the very start, and put in so many painstaking hours to ensure this story (and so many others) was the best it could be. On the literary side: Liz Parker at Verve—not only did she get a debut author a three book deal, but she has consistently been a calming and grounding presence during such a crazy time in my life.

Thank you to the moderators, members, and fellow authors of r/NoSleep on Reddit. I never would have been discovered without you. There's a reason r/NoSleep has over 14 million members—it is home to some of the strongest voices in horror.

To those who read and gave feedback on early versions of this story: Whether through a comment on the Reddit series or direct input on the book's manuscript—hundreds of people have shaped what this novel is today. Among those who helped, in no particular order:

My sibling Charlie Kliewer: Your feedback and suggestions were crucial in protecting me from (at least some level of) public embarrassment. You are a storytelling force to be reckoned with, and I can't wait to see what you create next.

Kat Pölkki: Between Reddit and the novel, you've probably combed over this story almost a hundred times. Whether it was reading the same sentence out loud again and again to ensure it sounded just right, or providing a silver bullet to get the plot out of a rut—your insight, research, and contribution to this work was absolutely irreplaceable.

Dan Kagan: The vast majority of your advice and invaluable input on the original Reddit series is alive and well in this novel. Could not have cracked this story without your feedback and support from day one.

M.R. Gross: Thank you so much for taking the time to provide notes on this. As always, every single one of your suggestions led to vast improvements. Your understanding and insight into the craft of writing never ceases to inspire me.

Jonathan Gravelle: You've been a judgment-free sounding board to my crazy stories since elementary school. It is an honor to continue that tradition to this day.

Mom: You are the earliest champion of my work—ever since I was scribbling away about flying cities and sentient dinosaurs.

Dad: I'll never forget you reading us *The Lord of the Rings* and *The Hobbit* as kids. It's a big reason I'm writing today.

And thank you to so many others who provided notes, championed the story, and/or gave support while I was writing. Including, but certainly not limited to: Cassandra Hildebrand, Donald Ibsen, Nick Bottyan, Drew Dannes, Shoshannah Greene, David Goertsen, Kristoff Duxbury, Victor Sweetser, Tristan Stewart, Jag Kaliray, Conrad Stel, Alex Svarez, Chris Dudley, Jordan Tansley, Emanuel Nisan, Sinéad Lynch, Lighthouse Horror, and Boldly to name a few (there are so many more). Thank you to the staff (present and past) of Browns Socialhouse in Upper Lonsdale, and both Denny's locations in Abbotsford (I wrote the vast majority of this story in those places, huddled in booths, running on endless refills of decaf coffee and words of encouragement).

Thank you to Marianne Christensen, Rebecca Gronn, Erik Horn, and Geir Øglend for taking the time to give thoughtful feedback on the Norwegian language sections. Hopefully I followed your detailed notes and suggestions correctly.

Last, but certainly not least, I am obligated to acknowledge [redacted] for sharing their knowledge of "Old House Lore" and even providing a guided tour of the [redacted] wing to my research associates.

—Marcus Kliewer